"YOU NEED A PILLOW?"

His eyebrows rose, and his eyes took on a familiar gleam that seemed to waver between humor and hunger. "You had something else in mind?"

"Go to hell," Brooke growled.

"I changed my mind. There *is* something else I need."

"You—"

Brooke's words were muffled by his mouth. By the time he released her, she had to grab the doorjamb for support. "You *have* to stop kissing me."

His gaze dropped to linger on her mouth for a long, thoughtful moment. When he spoke, there wasn't a trace of laughter left in his voice. "I will—when *you* stop wanting me to."

Other *Love Spell* books by Sheridon Smythe:
MR. HYDE'S ASSETS

A Perfect Fit

Sheridon Smythe

LOVE SPELL NEW YORK CITY

A LOVE SPELL BOOK®

November 2000

Published by

Dorchester Publishing Co., Inc.
276 Fifth Avenue
New York, NY 10001

ISBN 0-505-52402-3

Printed in the United States of America.

This one's for my baby brother, Randall Lee Brannum. Wasn't it just yesterday that you toddled from the porch just before your first photo session? As the youngest of six children, you were a joy to us all. Is it any wonder that we spoiled you rotten? Now you're grown, with a wonderful wife, Treva, and two beautiful little girls, Miranda and Samantha. God bless you and your family. I love you all very much!

—Sherrie Eddington

I would like to dedicate this book to my good friend Debbie Reeves. I have had the rare privilege of meeting someone who thinks and feels as I do about almost everything. Our friendship has seen me through some really rough times, but it's easier to recall the good times. Too many to count—like the times we had playing tricks on people with the yard statue and all our other 007 escapades. We've grown together as friends and I hope we grow old together as friends—someday. Thank you for always being there for me. I love you.

—Donna Smith

In loving memory of Ann Eubanks
Wife, Mother, Grandmother and Friend
5/23/38 to 1/23/00

A Perfect Fit

Chapter One

"Looks like you've got trouble in Quicksilver."

Alex Bradshaw glanced up at the sound of his secretary's voice, grateful for the interruption—any interruption, even if her grave announcement did prompt ludicrous images of an impending shoot-out at the OK Corral. His eyes had begun to blur, a sure sign he was on the verge of developing one of those mysterious, frustrating migraines that had been plaguing him for the past three months.

Stubbornly ignoring the pain, he drawled, "Now, you wouldn't be exaggerating, would ya, Miss Kitty?"

"Doubtful. And I always thought Miss Kitty was a damned fool, pining her life away, waiting for Matt Dillon to come around."

Alex managed a grin, focusing painfully on the items she held: a sheet of paper, a glass of water, and two tablets. How did she know? he wondered. How did she always seem to know even before *he* did? He popped the pills into his mouth and chased them down with the water, eyeing her frowning face over the rim of the glass. When he was done, he handed her the empty glass and reached for the fax.

She snatched it away. "Why don't I tell you what it says?" she suggested.

"I take it you've already read it?"

Gloria feigned a withering glance. "Of course. I *am* your secretary. Besides, you know what the doctor said. If you keep pushing yourself, the migraines will only get worse."

Massaging his temples, Alex leaned his head against the chair rest. If it had been anyone else but Gloria, he would have gritted his teeth and demanded the paper. "Go ahead," he muttered.

"Well, as far as I can tell, they fired Daisy because she found out."

"Who's Daisy?"

"She *was* the secretary at your factory in Quicksilver," Gloria said, sounding outraged on Daisy's behalf. "I talked to her a few times on the phone a few months ago and she seems like a real nice lady. Been workin' there for twenty years, so you can see why she's so upset."

"Yeah," Alex agreed dryly. "Maybe upset enough to stir up trouble?"

"I don't think so." Gloria tapped the paper for

emphasis. "No, I think Daisy's stumbled into a den of rats—the rats being the supervisors at the factory."

Alex was beginning to regret coming into the office today. He was leaving first thing in the morning for a mandatory three-week vacation, doctor's orders. His father, retired these past six months, had jumped at the opportunity to stand in for him. He'd sounded so desperate, Alex hadn't had the heart to turn him down.

Alex smiled faintly at the memory before focusing on his secretary, who he knew loved a good mystery almost as much as she loved her husband. "Just exactly what's she accusing them of?"

"Embezzling."

He straightened in his chair. The factory in Quicksilver made the Bradshaw Corporation a lot of money, supplying a safety-conscious country with top-quality condoms. It was the main reason he and his father had purchased the factory less than a year ago.

The only drawback had been the fact that the factory was located a few miles outside a small town in the northern corner of Oklahoma— hundreds of miles away from their home office in Amarillo, Texas. "Have we inspected yet?"

"No. It's on your schedule for next month."

"Get me the files on all of the supervisors, and the plant manager—what's his name?"

"Kyle Lotus, and I have the files ready for you." She grinned at his startled expression. "Don't look so surprised. After ten years, I can practically read your mind, young man."

Alex managed to move his eyebrows in a suggestive wiggle. "Let's hope your husband doesn't possess the same talent, Mrs. Coltrain."

"Oh, you!" Gloria blushed to the roots of her graying red hair. Down home and kindhearted, she was a happily married woman with six grown children, but she could blush like a teenager when Alex teased her. Alex had decided a long time ago she was the last of her kind. It was a downright shame, too, and Alex didn't hesitate to remind her husband of his good fortune at every opportunity.

With a sigh, Alex closed his eyes and waited for the medicine to ease the pain, wondering if Quicksilver possessed a decent hotel. The way things were looking, he'd be making a small detour on his way to Hot Springs, Arkansas, a vacation spot recommended by his doctor. Alex grinned, remembering that his doctor had also suggested he find himself a willing woman and get down and dirty. *Relieve some of that pressure, Alex, my boy. It isn't healthy to go without sex.*

"Alex?"

Alex opened one eye at Gloria's hesitant query, surprised to find her hovering anxiously in the doorway. He'd thought she had left.

"You aren't thinkin' of going up there, are you?"

Shrewd woman, Alex thought. "Yes, I am. Why?"

"Rats can get dangerous when cornered. Just remember that."

She was dead serious, he saw. With an effort, he kept a straight face. "You watch too many movies."

"Maybe. Maybe not. Promise you'll be careful, and check in often?"

"I'll make you a deal: if you promise not to mention my little detour to the family, I promise to call you every day."

"It's a deal." Satisfied, Gloria scurried around and closed the shades before returning to her desk outside his office.

Little did Gloria know that his father, mother, grandfather, aunt Joyce, and his doctor had already extracted the same promise. Somewhere between the CAT scan and EEG they'd forgotten he was a grown man.

Heaven forbid if he found himself without access to a phone! Alex almost chuckled at the thought. They'd probably call out the National Guard, hire search helicopters, and put his picture on the back of milk cartons. Since the doctor had diagnosed him with migraines, the entire family—and staff—had treated him as if he were made of glass. Their suffocating concern had succeeded in increasing the frequency of his headaches.

Thank God he was leaving tomorrow.

Gloria's voice crackled over the intercom, reactivating the pain in his head. He jabbed a finger at the volume button.

"And don't forget my souvenir," she added sternly.

Alex couldn't resist teasing her. He'd suffered his share of ribbing since buying the condom factory; here was his chance to retaliate. "A souvenir? Sure, I'll bring you back a whole case of condoms."

"You are *not* funny, mister. I meant from Hot Springs."

He started to laugh, but groaned instead.

"You're pregnant."

Brooke Welch stared at her teary-eyed baby sister as if she had announced she'd slept with Charles Manson. "You're pregnant," she said again in a croak, because croaking seemed to be the most she could muster by way of sound. "And I didn't even know you were seeing anyone."

As Brooke continued to stand frozen in the middle of the room, Dee put her face into the mattress and mumbled, "Nobody knew because he's . . . engaged to someone else. . . ." The rest of her words trailed away into an almost indistinguishable whisper.

Unfortunately, Brooke understood her. *Very* unfortunately. Her fingers closed around the base of the lamp on the nightstand beside the bed. *Don't do it,* her mind commanded. *Don't throw the lamp.* Brooke took a deep breath and closed her eyes, envisioning the stack of chipped, cracked plates in the cabinet above the microwave; she'd bought them at a garage sale for the single purpose of breaking them. But first she would try to *imagine* breaking them.

Sometimes it was enough.

Sometimes it wasn't.

In her mind, she closed her fingers around the top plate, pulled it free, and sent it sailing across the room. And in her mind, it landed with a satisfying crash against the wall, shattering into a hundred pieces. In fact, the sound was so satisfying, she pulled another from the shelf, then another—

"Brooke? Are you throwing plates again?"

Dee's interruption helped thaw her frozen brain. She reluctantly pried her fingers from the lamp and opened her eyes.

"Why is he seeing *you* if he's engaged to someone else?" It was a reasonable question, and one she hoped to high heaven Dee Dee had thought to ask the two-timing son of a—

"She's got money." Dee lifted her face and shoved a thick, heavy swath of honey blond hair from her baby blues. Her nose was red and her mascara looked like chocolate melting in the sun, but she was still beautiful.

And pregnant! Brooke inhaled sharply as the realization took full effect. Her brothers would kill the bastard—*if* they got to him first. Thank God they lived out of town! "What did he say when you told him?"

"I . . . I couldn't get in touch with him, so I left a message. He's not answering my calls."

Dee sniffed, silent tears rolling down her

cheeks as she continued in a dreamy voice that made Brooke want to gag.

"You should see him, Brooke. He's the handsomest man I've ever met. Just hearing his voice over the phone makes my knees weak. When I'm with him, he makes me feel special, like I'm the only woman in the world."

The scum, the bastard. Any man who could inspire her sister to babble soap-opera nonsense inspired Brooke's instant dislike. And the dreamy, dazed look in Dee's eyes made her shudder. Dee had it bad—real bad. Worse than *she* had had it for that cheating bum, Kyle.

"Where did you meet him?" Brooke demanded, her fingers itching to grab the lamp again. She took a series of deep, supposedly calming breaths instead. It didn't work; she still wanted to break something. A lot of somethings, and not just in her mind. Maybe the whole stack of plates, which she could ill afford—even as cheap as they were. She had just recently replaced the last stack after finding out she didn't get the promotion from Level C supervisor to Level B.

"I met Cliff at school. He came to do an interview for the paper—"

"He's a *reporter?*" Brooke squeaked in horror. Dee knew how she felt about reporters, and had often claimed she felt the same. The day their parents died, she and Dee had received the devastating news not from a sympathetic policeman, but from an overzealous reporter. From that moment on, Brooke couldn't think about a reporter without getting queasy.

And now she had even more reason to avoid them.

"Well, you're not dropping out of school, so don't even think about it. Lots of girls go to college while they're pregnant, and for God's sake, Dee Dee, why didn't you use a condom? I *work* at a condom factory, so it's not like we can't afford them! In fact . . ." Brooke yanked open her nightstand drawer, reached inside, and withdrew a handful of square packages. She held them in the air. "Name your color! And we even have the ones with the little ticklers on the end."

Dee flushed. "I'm not stupid, Brooke! We *did* use a condom. It . . . malfunctioned."

"Malfunctioned?" Brooke gave a disbelieving snort as she tossed the packages into the open drawer and slammed it shut. The lamp she'd been coveting for the past fifteen minutes wobbled and began to tip over. Snarling, Brooke grabbed it and slammed it down. If the lamp was going to get broken, then she'd be doing the breaking! "Safe and Secure condoms are the most dependable—"

"You sound like a commercial," Dee cut in. "I'm not lying, Brooke. The damned thing broke!"

I give up, Brooke thought, marching into the kitchen. She snatched a plate from the cupboard and sent it sailing into the sink. With the stress-relieving sound of breaking china ringing in her ears, she returned to the bedroom and said, "You won't be raising this baby alone. He's going to pay, and he's going to pay dearly."

Dee sat up, looking very much like a lost little girl. Only she wasn't a girl, Brooke reminded herself. Dee was a twenty-year-old woman who should know better than to get mixed up with a playboy like Cliff. Brooke's brothers had been urging Brooke to get a life for years. Maybe they were right. Maybe *she* was slowing Dee's growth by mothering her, but at the time of her parents' deaths, Dee had been a very fragile teenager of fourteen.

Mothering Dee had become a habit over the years.

"What are you going to do?" Dee asked.

"I'm going to call him."

"I don't think he'll talk to you."

"Oh, I think he will," Brooke said in a soft snarl as an idea began to form. "I think he'll come running, and when he does, I'm going to grab him."

This time there was not only doubt, but fear in Dee's voice. "Brooke, what are you planning? Please don't hurt him. He's . . . he's the father of this baby."

Offended, Brooke glanced at her. "Dee Dee, I don't break *people*, just things. I've never struck another soul in my life." She raked her gaze down the length of her own petite frame and grimaced. "Besides, it's not like I could hurt anyone if I tried."

"You might be small, but I've heard people

from the factory talk about you. They're afraid of you."

"I'm their supervisor," Brooke scoffed, not believing her for a moment. "They're not afraid of me; they just respect me because I can get them fired." Afraid of her! Ha! The suggestion itself was ludicrous—almost as ludicrous as the thought of her getting someone fired. "Get packed. We're going to be spending the weekend at the cabin." When Dee looked bewildered, she added grimly, "Cliff will be joining us."

"He won't come." Dee sounded weepy again.

"He will." Brooke pivoted toward the kitchen and the mess she'd made. She flung over her shoulder, "Because I'm going to make him an offer he can't refuse."

Four hours later Brooke pulled into the parking lot of Treva's Diner and shoved the gearshift into park. She'd left a message for Cliff to meet her at five o'clock.

It was time to see if Mr. Sure Shot had taken the bait.

Brooke was fairly confident he would. After all, what reporter could resist a hot story like the one she'd concocted on the spur of a desperate moment? She was fairly certain a very happily married Mayor Zimmerman would never think of having an affair with the high school principal, especially a high school principal who'd had a sex change at the age of sixteen, but with any luck, no one would ever have to know about her little white lie.

She winced. Okay, it was a *big* fat lie. A horrendous, ridiculous lie that made her squirm with shame.

But if it worked . . .

The door to the diner opened. Brooke straightened, her gaze glued to the man emerging into the sunshine. He paused as if to study his surroundings—and turned in her direction. Her breath caught, then rushed out in a whoosh of disbelief.

He wasn't young, as she'd expected.

He wasn't scruffy, as she'd imagined.

And he wasn't handsome, as Dee had described.

No, he wasn't any of those things.

The man made every fantasy every woman had ever had about a man pale in comparison.

And he acted as if he knew it.

A square, stubborn jaw shadowed by a day's growth of beard thrust upward as he squinted at the sun. Even from a distance of twenty yards or so, Brooke could see the black fringe of his lashes. His dark, wavy hair, cut in a careless style that screamed *sexy,* brushed the collar of his hunter green shirt. His rolled sleeves revealed more dark hair along his arms, and Brooke knew with certainty his chest would be a temptation of soft, matching curls that would dwindle in a provocative line to his . . .

Her gaze dipped, focusing on muscled thighs and a prominent crotch outlined by his jeans, before returning hastily to the relative safety of his face.

22

He was big, tall, and drop-dead gorgeous.

Her heart sank. This man would probably consider Dee a snack between meals, for it was clear by his arrogant, self-assured stance that here was a man used to getting what he wanted, when he wanted it, how he wanted it—and, without even trying, making the woman love it.

Good grief, even *her* heart was beating like a wild thing's, and she didn't like the man! She had no reason at all to admire his fantastic looks, or to note the confident way he moved.

"Oh, Dee," Brooke whispered, surprised at the dry, croaky sound of her voice even as her anger toward this careless heartbreaker rose, "you've gone and done it this time. It would take a dedicated nun or a blind woman to resist a man like this one, and you're neither."

She wasn't either, but righteous anger was her weapon, and she felt confident it would be more than enough to keep her head clear and her libido in cold storage.

Ignoring her pounding heart, Brooke took a deep breath and reached for Hugo on the seat beside her. She curled her fingers around the smooth, hard plastic base of the test model. Disguised by her jacket pocket, she hoped it would make a convincing weapon.

It was time Cliff learned that no matter how sweet the song, there was always a piper to pay.

Chapter Two

Quicksilver turned out to be a friendly little town, and the food wasn't bad either, Alex decided as he stepped from the cool air of the diner into the warm June sunshine. If nothing else good happened as a result of his stop, he'd walk away with the memory of the best peach cobbler he'd ever tasted—and a copy of the recipe.

Alex smiled faintly, giving his shirt pocket a satisfying pat where the recipe lay neatly folded. The owner of the diner, a forthright, earthy woman who had reminded him of Gloria, had assured him the recipe was as simple as one, two, three. In return, Alex had left her a twenty-dollar tip.

Yes . . . Quicksilver was a warm, friendly—

"See that blue Pinto over there? I want you to walk very slowly to the driver's door and get inside."

The low, menacing voice that came from behind him startled Alex. Something hard probed his spine, halting his impulsive turn before he could get a glimpse of her face.

"Don't try anything funny. This isn't a screwdriver in my pocket, lover boy."

After his initial surprise, Alex realized it had to be a joke. He was standing in full daylight outside a busy diner, a highly unlikely time and place for a robbery.

Of course it was a joke.

Then he remembered his father didn't have much of a sense of humor, and that his grandfather didn't either. They would never pull a stunt of this magnitude. It was a waste of time and money—two of the things they valued most.

On the heels of that uneasy realization was the memory of Gloria's warning: *Rats can get dangerous when cornered. Just remember that.* Had someone from the factory discovered he was in town? Had he been too hasty in dismissing the possibility of danger?

"You thought you were going to hear a hot story, didn't you?" the voice continued to rasp as they inched across the parking lot of the diner toward a dented, rusted old Pinto. She continued to hold the point of her weapon firmly against his spine. "Well, I've got a hot story for you, but I don't think you're going to like it, and I've got a hunch the only person you're going to be telling it to is a judge."

Alex got his first glimpse of his kidnapper as she reached around him to open the car door. The word *danger* suddenly seemed ludicrous.

She was small—incredibly small. Her head barely reached his shoulder.

She didn't look big enough to harm a flea.

"Don't be fooled by my size," she snapped as if she'd read his mind, tossing her short, strawberry blond hair aside to reveal glittering, whiskey-colored eyes. "I know how to use this." She wiggled the pocket of her jacket up and down, drawing his gaze to the outline of the weapon.

It looked like the barrel of a gun, all right.

Alex felt an eyebrow climb, and quickly put a halt to the motion. Until he found out what she wanted, he figured it might be safer to keep his amusement to himself. Instead he said, "If you plan to rob me, I think it might interest you to know that my credit cards are in my briefcase, and my briefcase is in my hotel room."

"I'm not interested in robbing you, lover boy." Her contemptuous gaze crawled slowly along his body, pausing on his boots. Her lip curled. "You've got nothing *I* want, but apparently some poor family of lizards had something *you* wanted. Get in."

"Rattlesnake."

She blinked up at him. "What?"

"Rattlesnake. The boots are rattlesnake skin."

"Oh, well, in that case . . . it's a shame some poor rattlesnake had to die so that you could wear his skin," she amended sarcastically. "Now get in the car."

Alex sat on the seat, swiveled around, and drew his legs up. His left knee barely fit between the steering wheel and the door panel . . . if there had *been* a door panel. It was gone, revealing the rusty inner workings of the door. In fact, he didn't see a door release either, which meant escaping while she scurried around to the passenger's seat wasn't an option. So he settled his hands on his knees and waited as she climbed into the passenger seat.

Her knees had plenty of room, Alex noticed.

Gloria would probably call him crazy, but he was more intrigued than frightened. The woman had an agenda, and he couldn't help wondering what it was. She wasn't altogether as cool as she'd like him to think, either, because he could see her free hand trembling as she pulled the creaky car door closed.

"Start the car and get going," she ordered.

Alex turned the key and started the engine. He pressed his foot hard on the accelerator, figuring he'd have to give it a goose to get the old thing going. Gravel spun beneath the wheels; the car backfired with a loud pop. She shrieked and glanced at her jacket pocket.

Alex prudently turned his face away to hide an involuntary smile. Whoever she was, it was becoming clearer with each passing moment that kidnapping wasn't her forte. He just hoped she didn't accidentally shoot herself or him before they reached their destination.

Speaking of which . . . "May I ask where we're going?"

"You can ask, but that doesn't mean I'll answer." She shot him a glowering look that completely mystified Alex before adding, "You'll find out soon enough. Just keep driving."

A black pickup pulled onto the road in front of them, forcing Alex to slam on the brakes and quickly swerve around it, narrowly avoiding a very nasty rear-end crash. The accident wasn't nearly as shocking as the sound of her furious voice.

"Moron!" she shouted at the vehicle, leaning over and slamming the heel of her hand against the wheel. The warbling sound the horn made resembled a groan more than a honk, which didn't surprise Alex. If anything, he was amazed the horn worked at all after suffering that type of abuse.

This time he didn't hide his smile in time.

"You think this is funny?" she demanded, pressing her foot on top of his and pushing hard.

They accelerated at the speed of light, and Alex was surprised by the old car's performance. When she finally removed her foot, he said, "What amuses me is your aggressive driving. Did you know they have classes you can take?"

The glance she cut his way should have sheared him in two. She carried a lot of heat in those whiskey-colored eyes, he decided, his gaze dropping to move along her body. A thrill of desire tightened his groin.

"Take my word for it: The only thing you get from those classes is a serious case of heartburn—Stop looking at my legs!" She yanked ineffectively at her short denim jumper, aiming her jacket pocket at him again.

Her tanned legs were shapely and interesting to look at, but they weren't to *die* for, he decided hastily, glancing away. "Sorry, I couldn't help myself."

He could clearly hear the sound of her teeth grinding as she said, "I should stop the car and shoot you right here and now. It's scum like you who give other men a bad name, you know."

No, he didn't know. In fact, he didn't have a clue as to what she meant by that low-voiced, contemptuous remark. He didn't get the opportunity to ask, however.

"You want a hot story? Well, I'll give you one. You, Mr. Hotshot, are not going to get away with it. No, sirree. You are going to own up to your part in this little adventure. You are going to pay, and you are going to pay for a long, long time. Eighteen years, in fact. Maybe longer if the kid decides to go on to college."

Okay, so this was not a simple robbery. The woman was obviously delusional—quite possibly insane—therefore more dangerous than he'd first thought. Alex was embarrassed he hadn't realized it sooner. Those whiskey-colored eyes had distracted him, along with her bare legs.

He cleared his throat and, careful to keep his voice neutral, asked, "Would you mind telling me what this is all about?"

She ignored his question, glancing instead at the speedometer. Alex followed her gaze; the needle hovered around seventy. Where were the cops when you needed them? he wondered. And what in the hell did she have beneath the dented hood? A racing engine?

Her next statement wiped his mind clean of all thoughts with the exception of one, and that one thought was clear and precise.

"We've got condoms lying all over the house, and you just had to pick the one with a hole in it."

The vote was in; the woman wasn't just delusional; she was *certifiable*.

He didn't even have the decency to be embarrassed by her bald statement, Brooke fumed. Just as he hadn't been afraid when she pressed Hugo into his back and demanded he get into the car.

He thought it was amusing—that *she* was amusing. He probably thought getting Dee pregnant was a joke, as well. And then to have the utter gall to stare at her legs as if he were eyeing a juicy leg of lamb! He was scum, all right. Engaged to one woman, impregnating another, and ogling her.

She almost wished she *had* a loaded gun.

Brooke took a slow, measured breath and forced her anger just below the exploding point. There was nothing handy to break, so she would just have to ride this one out.

Eventually rational thought returned.

Thank God she *didn't* have a loaded gun. Kidnapping was serious enough without adding homicide to her list of crimes.

She shuddered to think what would happen if her plan backfired and the couple didn't work things out. He could—and probably would—press charges against her. She would go to prison, and Dee would have to raise the baby alone. Maybe she could convince Logan and Dean Jr. to move back to town and keep an eye on their baby sister.

"I think you've got me confused with someone else."

His calm announcement made her jaw drop. In all of the scenarios she'd pictured in her mind about what might occur when she came face-to-face with Mr. Sure Shot, she hadn't once considered that he might deny knowing Dee at all.

She squeezed Hugo so tightly, she imagined she heard the plastic crack. If it had been a gun, and her finger had been on the trigger, she would have put this . . . this womanizer out of his misery.

Despite several attempts, she couldn't will the shaking from her voice. "Do you have any idea how many children are raised without fathers these days? Do you have the slightest inkling how difficult it is to raise a child single-handedly? Well, let me tell you, Mr. Sure Shot, it's damned hard. I'm a supervisor at a factory, as you probably know from Dee, and there are about two dozen women who work under me. Out of those two dozen, at least half are single mothers."

"You—"

"I'm not finished." Brooke struggled for control. "Those women will do anything for their children. They grab all of the overtime they can get to buy those special gym shoes or to pay for those dance classes—and those are just a few examples—while at the same time suffering enormous guilt for the hours they're not spending with their children. I've seen women come to work and stumble around all day after being up all night with a sick child. They don't even come close to making production. Exhausted, sick with worry, they end up taking sick leave for themselves."

"Why don't they just take it when their child is sick?"

Brooke took a deep breath. He'd sounded almost human, and genuinely concerned. Maybe she was getting through to him. Personal dislikes aside, she had to remember he was the father of Dee's baby. "Because the company doesn't pay for sick days unless the *employee* has a doctor's excuse."

"I see."

He was silent for a moment. When she glanced at him, she was surprised to find him frowning.

33

He was rugged, tanned, and far too handsome for comfort, she couldn't help noticing.

Dee had noticed, too, and look at the mess she was in!

"Has anyone attempted to talk to someone in charge about this?" he finally asked.

As if he cared. Brooke shot him a suspicious, narrow-eyed look. Was he trying to distract her from the subject at hand? Well, it wasn't going to work. But for Dee's sake, she answered, "Yes. Kyle Lotus, the plant manager." *Another two-timer—no, make that four-timer—just like you,* she wanted to add, but didn't. "He says the new boss isn't interested in losing money, only in making it."

"And this Lotus person, he says he talked to the owner directly?"

"Yes." Impatiently Brooke added, "Look, I know what you're trying to do, so drop the concerned act, okay? Let's get back to the baby and Dee."

"Dee."

"My sister," she snapped, hearing the question in his voice but not believing it. He knew damned well who Dee was! She wondered viciously if he'd captured the rattlesnake while fighting over the same hole. It wouldn't surprise her one little bit.

"And you would be . . . ?"

"Oh, for cryin' out loud! I'm Brooke Welch—same last name, and don't say that Dee hasn't told you about me. I know that she has, although I can't say the same for you. I didn't find out about you until this morning, and believe me when I say that after meeting you, I wish I hadn't. The only thing worse than a reporter is a two-timing reporter."

"Let me see if I've got this straight. You believe that I'm the father-to-be of your sister's baby, and you've kidnapped me in the hopes of convincing me to accept responsibility."

"I don't just believe it—I know it. Dee has no reason to lie."

"I'm not saying she lied," came his surprising answer.

"Then you admit it?" He was silent long enough to elicit a loud, aggravated sigh from Brooke. "Well?"

"I'm saying . . . that you don't know the whole story."

"Then please enlighten me, by all means," Brooke drawled sarcastically. "And while you're getting your lie straight, make a left at this next road." She pointed to a dirt road branching off from the blacktop. He slowed the Pinto and made the turn, frowning as he eyed the road.

Grass grew tall in the middle, brushing the underside of the car. Brooke prayed the coat hanger holding the muffler to the carriage would hold. For some odd reason, the possibility of it falling off with him in the car embarrassed her. She'd never cared before, and certainly couldn't fathom why she would now. If this gold digger didn't realize her car was a classic, then it was his loss.

"Why don't we make a deal? We'll take turns asking questions. The first one to refuse a question loses a turn."

Brooke was so stunned by his absurd suggestion, she shifted her foot over and slammed it onto the brake pedal. The Pinto ground to a stop. There was a familiar clatter that made Brooke groan inwardly. She'd been so worried about the muffler that she'd forgotten that damned ornery hubcap!

She pointed Hugo right at his black heart. "In case you've missed it, you're not in a bargaining position, lover boy. Now get out and put the hubcap back on the wheel."

His grayish green eyes never wavered from her face; the challenge was clear. "Well, if you're too chicken . . ."

"I'm not chicken." And she wasn't falling for his childish attempt to dare her into playing his game. Dee's future and that of her unborn baby was not a game.

But damn it, she was curious. She watched him as he rolled the window down and opened the door from the outside. He was back in the car in a flash, muscles rippling beneath his shirt as he folded himself behind the wheel.

"Why do I get the feeling that's happened before?"

"Because it has?"

"Ever thought about getting new hubcaps?"

"They're the originals." Against her better judgment, Brooke reverted to their earlier discussion. "What questions could you possibly be interested in asking me?" If they were personal, she vowed she wouldn't be responsible for her actions. With Hugo's help, she might produce a decent-size knot on his conceited head.

"Questions about the running of the factory. I might be able to help bring about some of those changes you mentioned."

"How?" She didn't bother hiding her skepticism, and she was highly suspicious of his motives. He was slick . . . and handsome—a deadly combination, as Dee could attest.

Brooke stiffened her spine at the reminder.

"It's my experience that companies avoid publicity, especially the bad kind."

He had a point, Brooke grudgingly conceded. They didn't like bad publicity, but there was one major point he was overlooking. "And you think I'd risk my own job to help put the company in a bad light?"

"I don't have to reveal my sources."

He was quick, and he was also right. Although why she should consider trusting him . . . "Can I get that in writing?"

"You have my word."

Brooke snorted, then laughed outright. "I don't trust you any farther than I could throw you." Not that she could pick him up to throw him. Just the thought of putting her hands on him made her mouth go dry, and to her mortification, she realized it wasn't because the idea repulsed her.

"You could always hunt me down." His gaze

dropped to the outline of her weapon, then returned to her face.

He was serious, Brooke thought. Shaking her head, she said, "Okay, but I go first." His quick smile told her that he'd expected her capitulation. She caught herself on the brink of smiling back, changing it to a fierce scowl in the nick of time. He *was* drop-dead gorgeous, but that didn't change the fact that he wasn't worth spitting on. "My first question is . . . do you intend to break up with your fiancée?"

"It's a possibility. Now it's my turn. How well do you know the other supervisors at the factory?"

"*Very* well. I—" Brooke caught herself before she turned her answer into two. He had made the rules. No sense in volunteering information he didn't ask for. "Do you intend to marry Dee?"

"I'd have to say that would be up to Dee, don't you think?"

"Is that a question?" Brooke countered.

He shook his head. "Have you noticed anything unusual at the factory?"

Brooke tucked her tongue in her cheek. "Well, the rate of pregnancies hasn't decreased even though Kyle has been giving free condoms as a reward for exceptional production."

"That's cheating."

"Is not. You asked, and I answered." She shifted in the seat, refusing to feel guilty. He had probably invented the word *cheating!* She wondered if he and Kyle Lotus could possibly be kin. "My turn. Are you really marrying this other woman for her money?"

Without hesitation, he shook his head. "Do any of the supervisors feel they're being underpaid?"

But Brooke was still thinking about his answer. If he wasn't marrying the other woman for her money . . . then that must mean he loved her. She didn't like the answer, not at all, and it canceled her next question.

"Brooke?"

"Hm?"

"Are you forfeiting your next turn?"

"No!" She scrambled to remember his question. "We haven't gotten a raise since Bradshaw bought the company, so I'd have to say that everyone feels underpaid, including me. Pay increases are on hold until Mr. Greed comes to inspect the place. I don't think he's in any hurry." She clamped her lips shut, scowling at his triumphant look. *Four answers!* "Last one. Are you willing to talk to Dee?"

"I'll talk to her, but I think you're forgetting something."

Brooke gestured for him to drive on. She might have been willing to talk because she wanted answers to her questions, but she still didn't trust him. When they began to move again, she asked, "What did I forget?"

"You went first. I get the last question."

She sighed and rolled her eyes. The man had apparently forgotten the weapon in her pocket. "Go ahead."

"Do you think Lotus would be willing to answer a few questions if I approached him?"

Frowning at the road, Brooke took a moment to think. Finally she shook her head. "Kyle's funny about those things. He likes to run the factory his way, and he doesn't like anyone to question his authority. Sometimes I think he believes he owns the place."

"Hm."

"What's that supposed to mean?"

"Sounds like he takes his job very seriously."

"He does," Brooke agreed. "We all do." Kyle took his women seriously, too, at least until he grew bored and began to look for greener pastures. Not something she planned to share with Mr. Sure Shot. "By the way, we're almost there."

"Which tells me absolutely nothing," he said dryly.

Brooke shrugged. "I guess it won't hurt, since you can't do anything about it now, unless you want to risk heatstroke walking back to town. We're going to my father's fishing cabin. It's very primitive—and isolated, so we'll have all the privacy we need to get this thing settled."

"We?"

"You, me, and Dee. She's waiting for us." Brooke glanced at him to gauge his reaction, catching his faint frown. Her earlier anger returned. "What's wrong, lover boy, won't you be glad to see your old flame?"

"Of course." He paused before adding enigmatically, "But don't count on her being glad to see me."

Chapter Three

Brooke Welch.

Alex couldn't believe his luck.

Not only was his gutsy kidnapper one of the most intriguing women he'd ever met, she was one of his supervisors.

Luck . . . or design? Alex frowned. What were the odds of his stepping into an employee's path an hour after arriving in Quicksilver? True, Safe & Secure employed roughly three hundred out of the town's five thousand inhabitants.

Still, he wasn't comfortable with the odds. Perhaps she didn't have a sister waiting at the cabin. Maybe it was just a ruse to keep him calm until they arrived.

The logical side of his brain scoffed at the

idea of a kidnapping conspiracy in this small town, headed by a petite firecracker of a woman. What could they possibly do? Hold him until he agreed to keep his mouth shut? *Yeah, right.*

Ludicrous, Alex decided, dismissing the possibility. Running into Brooke Welch was just a wild coincidence, as he'd first thought. Life was full of those, and only imaginative people like his secretary read more into them than was warranted.

Besides, nobody but his imaginative secretary knew he was going to make a quick stop in Quicksilver.

Using his excellent recall—something he'd inherited from his grandfather—he reviewed the information he'd read about Brooke Welch from the file in his briefcase; twenty-six years old, high school graduate with two years of college, no children . . . and single.

Her file had not, of course, mentioned her sexy cap of strawberry blond hair, her hot, whiskey-colored eyes, or her eye-catching legs. The entire package had knocked the breath from his lungs, and stunned his brain longer than he cared to admit.

According to her file, Brooke had been employed at Safe & Secure for the past six years. Her intelligence, dedication, and leadership qualities had eventually landed her the job of Level C supervisor. Alex slanted a quick glance at the indignant tilt of her chin, wondering if her petite size had anything to do with her aggressive attitude.

Maybe she just hated men in general.

Alex was very curious—and very eager, he noted with mild surprise—to find out. Since his divorce from April, he'd deliberately distanced himself from any woman who sparked more than his libido. In fact, his libido hadn't been sparked in quite a while, either.

Casting her covert glances as he navigated the Pinto along the rutted road, Alex was tempted to reveal his true identity before they reached the cabin. Once her sister saw him, his cover would be blown anyway.

Brooke wouldn't be happy about his silence, he mused, his lips twitching as he imagined her reaction. She also wouldn't appreciate the way he'd manipulated her into answering his questions about the factory.

"We're here."

Alex looked through the dusty windshield, immediately impressed with the rustic scenery. The cabin sat on top of a hill surrounded by pine, oak, and hickory trees. The building itself was small, perhaps three rooms, with a wraparound porch made of rough-hewn logs. It looked like something out of a travel brochure, Alex thought.

"My father built it," Brooke said, staring moodily at the cabin. "There's a pier out back where he used to fish." She blinked rapidly and thrust her chin out, as if she realized she'd let her guard down. Alex suspected it didn't happen often. "Maybe you'll stay long enough to see the view."

He doubted it. The moment she found out who she'd really kidnapped, she'd take him back to town. Truthfully, he said, "I guess that will be up to you."

The look she cast him sizzled and burned. "No, it will be up to *you*, lover boy." She hiked the pocket of her jacket up and at him. "Now get out of the car."

Alex rolled down the window, lifted the outside latch, and stepped out of the car. He was more than glad to stretch after the cramped drive.

"Wait here," she commanded.

He watched the sassy swing of her hips as she strode to the cabin and let herself in. Seconds later she was back, and she looked murderous. This was it, Alex thought. Her sister had been watching from the window, and Brooke now knew he wasn't "lover boy."

"She's not here. I can't believe she's not here. I don't think she's even been here!"

It took a moment to sink in. When it did, Alex smiled. A reprieve. He'd gotten a reprieve, and he was going to take advantage of it. Not only did he want to know more about Brooke Welch personally, but he wanted to know everything she knew about his factory. Small compensation for being kidnapped, he decided.

"What the hell are you smiling about?" she demanded suspiciously. Her eyes widened, as if an idea suddenly occurred to her. An unpleasant idea. "If you think you're going to get lucky, buster, you'd better think—"

"Get lucky?"

"With *me*, like you did with my sister. I'm not so gullible."

"Oh." Alex swallowed a laugh. They were back to "scum like you." And he thought they'd gotten past that point. He hooked his thumbs in his jeans pockets, leaned against the dusty Pinto, and crossed his ankles. He was aiming for a safe look.

It didn't work, because his eyes wouldn't obey the commands from his brain. They slid over her slowly and with great appreciation.

She moved before he could bring them under control, stomping back to the cabin. The door slammed shut with a bang. Seconds later, Alex heard the sound of shattering glass. Adrenaline flooded his bloodstream with a powerful rush of fear.

He loped to the porch.

Something shook the walls.

He opened the door and rushed inside. The cabin was isolated, and a beautiful woman like Brooke would be a perfect target for someone lying in wait.

The sound of her enraged voice stopped him cold. He turned, realizing it was coming from the closed door to his right.

"I can't believe she isn't here! After the risk I took, and riding in the car with Mr. Testosterone . . ."

Alex listened, stunned, as another object hit

the wall and disintegrated. He couldn't believe his ears.

"I could go to jail for what I did!"

True, but he was having too much fun to think about pressing charges. Of course, she didn't know that. He inched closer and placed his hand on the doorknob.

It was suddenly wrenched from his grasp, startling him.

She stood in the doorway, panting from her exertion, her hair a wild, sexy tangle around her face.

Alex inhaled sharply, resisting the urge to snatch a handful of that glorious hair and pull her forward, bring his mouth down on hers, and taste her fire. God, until now he'd never been tempted to take what he wanted and ask permission later.

Maybe he *was* a scumbag.

"What do you want?" she asked, panting.

Her innocent question, breathless as it was, conjured devilish images of him baldly announcing his wants and her huskily agreeing.

Forcing himself to step back before he did something he might regret, Alex said, "Are you OK?"

"Do I look OK?"

He wondered if she growled in bed, then decided that if he wanted to live to see the dawn, he'd better switch his line of thinking.

The woman was in the grip of a tantrum, and they were alone.

And she had a gun, not that he believed she

would use it. But better safe than sorry . . .

"You look . . . fine." The *fine* part stuck in his throat, because what he really wanted to say was, *You look good enough to eat.*

Somehow he knew she wouldn't appreciate his compliment.

"Don't bother lying," she said, using that growling voice that drained the moisture from his mouth. "I know exactly what I look like after I . . . after I get mad."

Obviously their opinions differed greatly. "Do you get mad often?" He hadn't meant to sound so hopeful, but luckily she wasn't paying attention.

"Unfortunately, I do." She grimaced and thrust her fingers through her tangled hair. "It's one of my biggest flaws."

One of? Alex couldn't find a single one, including her penchant for throwing things, not when it brought results like hot, flashing eyes, a heaving chest, wildly mussed hair, and a growling voice that made him want to sink his teeth into something—namely her.

He managed to say evenly, "Nothing wrong with losing your temper now and then. They say it's healthy."

She gave a derisive snort. "Now and then might be okay. I lose mine at least twice a day, sometimes more."

Alex saw heaven looming on the horizon. "You do? I mean, you don't say?"

* * *

Dee wasn't coming.

Brooke might have gone back to town, but she didn't want to leave him alone, and she couldn't risk taking him with her. She wasn't giving him up until the couple had a chance to talk. Call her stubborn—and she wouldn't deny it—but she'd gone to too much trouble bringing him out here to just give up.

Swallowing a frustrated oath, Brooke fished the Tums out of her purse and viciously chewed two of the fruit-flavored tablets. Since her tantrum, she'd retreated to the small bedroom, angry with herself for revealing even the smallest amount of personal information.

And to a reporter, of all people! What had gotten into her? No doubt he found her penchant for throwing things as amusing as he found Dee's pregnancy.

When she found Dee, she was going to deliver a tongue-lashing such as that girl hadn't heard since their parents died. Not only had she mucked their plans by not showing, she'd forced Brooke to keep company with Mr. Cocksure.

Alone, in an isolated cabin, with nothing more than a plastic model of a penis! Hugo would be no help if her captive decided to get feisty on her.

The realization made Brooke break into a sweat. Oh, she didn't think he was dangerous . . . at least not physically dangerous.

But the man definitely had a talent for creating tension. He was a flirt, a womanizer. Only this time he'd messed with the wrong sister. This time he'd pay for his crimes, if not with a ring and an "I do," then with a sizable child-support check for the next eighteen years.

Brooke hadn't decided if she'd rather have him for a brother-in-law, or just a distant father-of-her-nephew or -niece. Men like him couldn't be trusted, and if he did decide to marry Dee, he'd probably wind up breaking her heart all over again.

Fortified with renewed determination—and a liberal dose of heartburn medication—Brooke went in search of her prisoner.

She found him lounging against her car, surveying his rustic surroundings as if he'd just discovered the perfect vacation spot. He'd been kidnapped, accused, and verbally assaulted, yet there was an odd serenity to his expression that made Brooke hesitate to interrupt. Ridiculous! she scoffed silently. The man was a user. His entire attitude was likely a scheme to get her to relax her guard.

"See anything of interest?" she asked tautly, her fingers closing around the comfort of Hugo in her pocket. At the sound of her voice, he swung his gaze in her direction.

some mouth curved into a smile that held a hint of mischief—and a hell of a lot of healthy male appreciation. "Yes, I do." And then his gaze grew heated and moved down slowly, leisurely, leaving her in no doubt of his meaning.

Brooke knew his game. Of course she did. But

she felt as if she'd been sucker punched, none-theless. The man possessed more than his fair share of charisma, she admitted. A remarkable talent, but nothing she couldn't handle. She knew him for the blackguard he was, thank God.

"Have you given up on your sister?"

Given up? Never. Not while she lived and breathed. "No, I haven't. She'll be here." And why didn't he address Dee by her name? Brooke felt her stomach clench with disgust. Was Dee so insignificant that he hardly recalled their af-fair?

"Am I spoiling your evening plans?" she jeered.

He shrugged and transferred his gaze to the sinking sun as it slid behind the trees. "I might be missed, but no, I don't have any concrete plans this evening."

The fact that he seemed unaffected by her scorn goaded Brooke into snapping recklessly, "Good, because we're not leaving until she shows, even if it takes all night."

His gaze swiveled back to hers, pinning her with heated interest. The toe-curling smile was gone, but humor still lurked. "You're the boss."

"Damned right I am," Brooke muttered to herself as she headed back to the cabin. He was mocking her, of course, but this time she wasn't going after the bait. Out loud, she said, "I'll see what we have in the way of food. Don't wander off."

His soft, drawling voice stopped her in her

tracks. "Oh, I've no intentions of letting you out of my sight."

And suddenly, with that single statement, Brooke felt a terrifying shift of control from captor to captive. Her heart began to thud heavily as she realized that she just might have misjudged him.

Slowly, she turned around.

Chapter Four

If he thought to scare her, he was in for a disappointment.

Brooke looked him straight in the eye—she could because she was standing slightly uphill—and demanded, "What did you mean by that?" Just for good measure, she aimed Hugo at him.

He shrugged his broad shoulders. "Oh, nothing."

Oh, nothing. Brooke clenched her teeth. He wouldn't know how badly she hated for someone to say those frustrating words instead of what they really meant. He wasn't getting away with it, either. "Look, Mr.—what is your last name, anyway?" She seasoned her question with just the right amount of disgust to let him

53

know that she really didn't give a damn.

Those bedroom eyes gleamed with something she couldn't fathom. She thought it might be amusement.

"Whatever you want it to be."

"You think this is just all a cute little game, don't you?"

"Not at all. I think you're totally serious."

And with that he began to unbutton his shirt.

Brooke stared at his fingers, her throat constricting with shock. "What . . . what are you doing?" Did she want to know? Did she really, really want to know?

"I'm removing my shirt."

Smart-ass, she thought. "Well, stop."

His gaze clashed with hers. Heat flashed through her system like high-octane fuel through a carburetor.

"Why?"

Because it's bothering me hovered on her lips and died a quick death. She was fast learning that she had to watch her words around this man. He was likely to tangle them up before she could get them out. "Because any moment now, Dee could drive up, and—"

"If you believe I'm the father of her baby, then I'm sure she won't go into shock to see me without my shirt," he remarked dryly.

Brooke tried again, swallowing in search of moisture. He'd reached the third button. "But you still haven't explained why you're taking it off."

He glanced at the sun sinking behind a grove

of trees. "I thought I might catch a few rays while I'm waiting. You don't mind, do you? It's been a while since I've had time."

Mind? Did she mind? Of course she minded! She didn't know him—he was a stranger—and her sister's boyfriend to boot! There were other disturbing factors she didn't care to think about just at the moment. "Yes, I mind." His eyes narrowed, but Brooke couldn't tell if it was because of the sun, or because of what she'd said.

"Why?"

There was that damned word again. "Because."

"Does it bother you?"

He was goading her, she realized, kicking herself for taking so long to notice. Maybe it took so long because he was now working on the last button. "Don't flatter yourself. You forget—I know who and what you really are."

"Ah, yes. Mr. Sure Shot, scumbag, lover boy, and a few others I can't recall at the moment." He pulled his shirt from the waistband of his jeans and shrugged it off, hanging it on her car antenna before turning to look at her. "Well, some other time I might assure you that you're right about all of the above, but right now I'm just going to take a break and catch a little sun."

Brooke stared at his chest, a marvelous map of muscle and sinew. A dusting of dark hair began at his nipples and continued down, narrowing to a point that disappeared into his jeans, confirming her earlier prediction. His stomach was slightly rippled, his waist trim, and the prominent bulge in his crotch wasn't her imagination.

She swallowed very, very slowly, so that he wouldn't notice.

He noticed.

A dark brow rose to taunt her. "Like what you see?"

"I . . . I wasn't looking." Mortified at the husky note in her voice, Brooke cleared her throat. This was getting out of hand. "I'm sure Dee did, but you're not my type."

"The chemistry's there. You can't deny it."

Now *his* voice sounded husky. Brooke's heart gave a panicked flutter. "I'll deny any damned thing I please," she said in a growl, then blew her tough answer by taking an involuntary step backward.

His chuckle was like a jolt of electricity.

Before she did or said something she'd regret, Brooke turned and headed for the cabin. Once inside, she resisted the urge to look out the window and see what Mr. Sure Shot was doing now. But she wanted to, and that galled her.

Where in the world was Dee?

Chirping birds. Serenity. A light, warm breeze. Sunshine against his bare skin.

The company of a little fireball of a woman with intoxicating eyes and an earthy quality that fired his lust. The tantalizing possibility of making love to her.

Alex couldn't have been happier.

He linked his hands behind his neck and

threw back his head, closing his eyes against the pure pleasure of being away from the daily grind of the business world.

For just a short while, he wanted to savor the moment.

Maybe his doctor was right. Maybe this was what he needed. He couldn't deny that he already felt better, less tense, and the lurking, almost constant ache behind his eyes seemed to have waned. Good thing, too, he thought, because he'd left his meds in his briefcase back at the hotel room.

Brooke had said they'd stay all night if they had to. Alex hoped they did. In fact, he felt as if he could stay in this one spot for at least a few days, leaning against a dented Pinto with the sun warming his skin.

After that he could move to the charming, quaint front porch and relax in the rocking chair another few days. Then there was the beautiful, inviting lake he'd glimpsed through the trees, not to mention the sexy woman inside the cabin.

Gloria would worry.

The thought jarred his peaceful doze and intensified the ache behind his eyes. Alex sighed. He supposed he should use his cell phone and call his secretary as he'd promised. Otherwise she'd send out a posse. Bending over casually, he slipped his hand into his boot and removed the slim phone from a Velcro strap inside. He'd had to do something after losing his fifth phone, and he refused to carry a purse.

He palmed it and straightened.

If she happened to be looking out the window at him, she would have a side view. Alex was fairly certain that if he were careful, she wouldn't see the phone against his left ear, and if he kept his voice low, she wouldn't hear him talking. Dialing the number without looking would be tricky, but if he took his time, he thought he could manage it.

He missed on the first try, realizing afterward that he must have pushed *end* instead of *send*. Turning as if he were viewing the forest to his left, Alex held the phone against his leg and looked down as he punched in Gloria's home phone number.

This time he pushed the right buttons.

Resuming his original position, he brought the phone to his ear. Finally, after what seemed like an eternity in which Alex imagined Brooke emerging from the cabin a dozen times, Gloria answered.

"Gloria, this is Alex. Listen, I can't explain now, but I've been delayed in Quicksilver. I'm just calling to—"

"Alex? Something's wrong, isn't it? You're talking funny. I knew you shouldn't have gone up there alone!"

Damn Gloria and her overactive imagination, Alex thought, mastering his frustration. It was the woman's single flaw. He had just opened his mouth to tell her that he'd found a little slice of heaven and had decided to stay a few days, when Brooke shouted from the porch.

Alex nearly dropped the phone.

"I've decided I want you back in the cabin so that I can keep an eye on you! I didn't go to all that trouble to kidnap you just to have you hot-wire my car and hightail it out of here."

"Who's that?" Gloria demanded sharply. "What's she saying? Alex, are you in trouble?"

Brooke hadn't seen the phone—he was sure of it.

He had no choice; he found what he hoped was the right button and pushed it, cursing beneath his breath. Stealthily he lowered his arm and dropped the phone to the ground. With a casual sweep of his booted foot, he kicked it out of sight—and hopefully out of earshot—beneath the Pinto.

But as luck would have it, he could still hear Gloria's high, squeaky voice coming from the phone. With a casual swagger, he pushed himself away from the Pinto and began to walk in Brooke's direction.

"Get your shirt."

Alex paused, reached behind him, and grabbed his shirt from the antenna. He put it on, but left it unbuttoned. The sight of his bare chest seemed to unsettle his little kidnapper, and he liked her unsettled. In fact, he'd like to unsettle her right out of her clothes. Suddenly the rocking chair behind her sparked a new interest—and with it a sharp, erotic image of Brooke sitting astride him, naked and eager.

"What makes you think I know how to hot-wire a car?" he asked, reaching the porch and propping a booted foot on the bottom step. She lifted a contemptuous blond brow, but her gaze dipped involuntarily to his chest. Alex prudently swallowed a grunt of satisfaction. He'd never considered himself anything out of the ordinary, but Brooke had a way of looking at him that made him feel like *People* magazine's Sexiest Man of the Year.

There was definitely chemistry zinging between them and around them, whether she'd admit it or not.

"I thought reporters knew how to do everything."

"This one doesn't." Alex drew his gaze along her tense, petite body, deliberately provoking her. "But I'm not averse to a few lessons, if you're interested." By now she'd know that he wasn't talking about hot-wiring a car. He was, however, most definitely interested in hot-wiring *her*.

"Find yourself another teacher." She whirled toward the cabin door, mumbling beneath her breath, "Sex maniac."

Alex heard her old-fashioned description, just as he suspected she meant for him to. There was nothing subtle about Brooke Welch, he was fast discovering. Or predictable. He liked that about her. Hell, he not only liked it, he amended, it turned him on!

"You have something against sex?" he asked, his lips curling as she froze in the doorway. Her shoulders twitched, warning him ahead of time.

He wiped the smile from his face before she could make a full turn.

Whiskey-bright eyes regarded him with open disgust. Slowly she brought the point of her jacket pocket level with his chest, her meaning unmistakable. Color him stupid, but he'd lost his apprehension a long time ago.

"Did you ask Dee that question? Did you come on to her like you're coming on to me?" Her voice was soft, with an underlying pain that made Alex wince—and reminded him of who she believed he was. "Is that how you seduced my baby sister? By feeding her this bull? Because if you did"—she advanced until she was even with the top step, glaring down at him— "I can forgive Dee for believing you. But I can't forgive you for taking advantage of her innocence."

Alex searched for a suitable answer, and came up empty-handed. Without revealing his true identity, what could he say? The man she thought him to be was probably everything she claimed he was. He could hardly disagree. In her place, he would be every bit as angry and disgusted.

"It's my fault, you know," she continued in that same, level voice. Alex thought he might drown in her eyes, they were so liquid and intense. "I taught her to believe the best of everyone, to overlook the bad. I never dreamed she'd meet someone like you. Someone without a conscience, someone who makes a game out of seducing women."

The heated gaze that crawled over him now had nothing and everything to do with sex. Alex felt its searing fire right down to his very soul. Instinctively he knew that even while she wanted him, she hated him just as much. She was a tigress defending her young, and outraged because she believed she'd failed.

He considered telling her the truth again—and again and again until he saw doubt flare in her gut-punching eyes. But in this instance, Alex didn't think the truth would set him free.

Brooke Welch wasn't going to be a happy camper to discover she'd not only missed her target, but had kidnapped her new boss instead.

Chapter Five

Forcing him to come inside was a bad idea, Brooke decided, slapping peanut butter on a stale cracker. She was standing at the sink, and Mr. Testosterone was standing right beside her, watching. In fact he was so close, a mere inch to the right would send her elbow crashing into his.

She clamped her lips shut. Telling him to move would undoubtably make him think he was getting to her. And he was, of course, but she would walk across hot coals before she'd give him an inkling.

"Excuse me," she muttered.

He moved just enough to allow her to stretch in front of him and pitch the dirty knife into the kitchen sink. Brooke took her time moving back into position, as if she weren't the least bit aware of his slightly sweaty, sun-scented skin bared by the open shirt.

"Are you always this tense?" he asked, his gaze following her every move.

Brooke popped a cracker into her mouth and chewed. Nothing like a stale cracker and dry peanut butter, she thought with a grimace. Okay, she wasn't that hungry. She shoved the rest of the crackers aside and leaned her arm along the counter. When she finally managed to swallow, she said, "What if it were *your* sister pregnant? Are you saying you wouldn't be upset? A little tense? Kinda concerned?"

His lips twitched. "You do sarcasm well."

"Thanks." Brooke folded her arms, wishing she could ditch the jacket. It was growing warm in the cabin, and he wasn't helping any by crowding her space. There really wasn't any reason not to remove her jacket, she thought dryly. She'd already figured out the "gun" in her pocket was about as effective as a piece of wood. Or a piece of plastic. Alone as they were, he could have overpowered her any number of times.

But she kept the jacket on because it made her feel safer, and gave the ogler less to ogle.

"So . . . wouldn't you?"

"I don't have a sister, but yes, I would be concerned if she were to get pregnant before she wanted a child. I'd also be mature enough to realize it takes two to tango."

Brooke thought about ignoring his last comment—and the way his shirt gaped open when he shifted—but on second thought, she nodded. "You're one hundred percent right. It does take two. But unlike the male party, the female doesn't have a choice about taking her share of the responsibility."

"There are choices."

She tightened her arms at his implication, but when his gaze dipped and she realized the motion caused her breasts to swell above her arms, she immediately relaxed. *Good grief!* No matter what she said or did, he managed to turn it into something sexual. "Are you suggesting that Dee get an abortion?"

"I was speaking of adoption."

"That would make things easy for you!"

"And for your sister."

"Dee," Brooke snapped. "Her name is Dee! I'm sure you said it often enough when you were . . . when you were . . ." She faltered, cursing the heat that crept into her face. "Too bad you didn't think about Dee before."

"You said something earlier about a faulty condom. Wouldn't that make this a no-fault accident?"

Brooke worked in a condom factory, where the joke of the day was anything that had the word *condom* in it. There was absolutely no excuse for the blush that heated her cheeks. But it was there nonetheless. "Maybe, but there's still the baby, and the fact that you refused to answer Dee's calls. You're lucky I didn't call my brothers."

"Why didn't you?"

"Because I didn't want them to go to jail." She didn't think she needed to elaborate. In fact, her threat should have left him shaking in his rattlesnake-skin boots, if Dee had told him anything at all about Logan and Dean Jr. and their infamous tempers. Brooke couldn't imagine Dee not telling him, if she loved him half as much as she professed to love him.

But of course it didn't scare Mr. Cool. He didn't so much as twitch an eyebrow, and that flicker she kept seeing in his eyes when he looked at her bore no resemblance to fear. *Dee, where are you?*

She sucked her bottom lip between her teeth, remembering and regretting her earlier promise that they'd stay all night if they had to. Pride was a funny thing, and sometimes not a good thing. Instead of getting in her car and getting the hell away from him, she said, "It's getting dark. I'd better turn the power on." Anxious to put some space between them, Brooke found a flashlight in one of the kitchen drawers and sped past him. The breaker was outside—away from him—and she couldn't get to it fast enough.

"I'll come with you."

"I don't need protection," Brooke flung over her shoulder as she opened the front door and stepped onto the porch. "Besides, I've got Hu— Um . . . this, if I need it." She indicated the shape in her pocket. "You should know there's nothing dangerous around here anyway." *Except you.*

"I'm from Texas. How would I know?"

Dee had mentioned nothing about Texas, but Brooke sensed he spoke the truth. She should have figured it out the moment she saw him. Instead she'd been too busy trying to keep her eyes from popping out. She was a sick individual, she decided, for even noticing how handsome he was.

He was her sister's boyfriend.

The father of her sister's baby. Make that the *reluctant* father.

But what if he isn't? a very unwelcome voice whispered inside her head. What if he didn't even know Dee? Would she be running into his arms instead of away from him?

"He is, so the question is moot," Brooke mumbled.

"Did you say something?"

Brooke jumped, then cursed. He was right behind her. "I thought I told you I didn't need your protection!" she said in a growl, swinging the flashlight around and into his face.

He winced and shielded his face with his hand.

Surprised by his reaction, Brooke quickly lowered the flashlight. "Sorry. I wouldn't have guessed you'd be light sensitive after the way you were soaking up the sun earlier." An image of his bare chest flashed in her mind.

"I'm not light sensitive."

"Then what's the problem?" His hesitation sparked her curiosity.

"I have occasional headaches."

"Oh." Brooke navigated the steps and trod through the grass, mulling over his reluctant confession. To her consternation, she found herself wondering if Dee's baby would inherit the ailment. She shook the silly thought from her head.

Twilight had fallen, and Dee knew total blackness was soon to follow. In the woods, it wasn't just *kind of* dark; it got black dark, the kind where you couldn't see your hand in front of your face. She wasn't afraid, but she wasn't crazy about bumping around in the dark with him. Why, his chest looked hard enough to crack a walnut. She could imagine what it would do to her head if she should run into him.

A slow, forbidden shiver danced along her spine at the thought. Shame quickly followed. She was sick indeed, lusting after—

She drew in a sharp breath and stopped in her tracks.

Mr. Hard Chest slammed right into her from behind, proving her earlier suspicions about just how hard his chest was.

And not just his chest!

His arms came around her to prevent her forward tumble. For an alarming moment, they touched from head to toe, and Brooke could feel every hard, shocking inch of him against her.

Just as she gathered her breath to demand he

let her go, his hand moved up, covering her mouth and effectively silencing her.

"Be quiet!"

His harsh, urgent whisper chilled her blood. She grew still as her predicament became very clear.

The shifting of power was complete.

If Alex had kept his eyes where they belonged as he walked behind her, he might have spotted the man sooner. But her tight little buttocks had distracted him, and now they stood, locked from stern to helm, directly in the path of a mean-looking rifle.

And the man who held it looked alarmingly at ease.

Alex had never faced the end of a barrel—had never come close, that he could recall. To experience the same uncomfortable feeling twice in a day stunned him for a moment.

Coincidence? He didn't think so.

Early on he had dismissed the possibility that Brooke might be the decoy in a more sinister plot to keep him from the factory. He'd scoffed, deciding he would never have considered the possibility if his wildly imaginative secretary hadn't planted the idea in his head.

Now he wasn't so certain.

She had brought him here, and she had lured him outside just as Grizzly Adams happened along with his rifle. The amazing coincidences were adding up, and Alex didn't like the total.

Keeping a wary eye on the man with the rifle,

Alex slowly moved his hand to Brooke's jacket pocket. He wasn't certain what he would do when he found the gun, but one thing he was sure about: He wasn't going to calmly go along with the man as he had with Brooke. It was time to put an end to their small-town games before someone got seriously hurt—namely him.

The moment she realized his intent, she began to struggle wildly, trying to scream beneath his hand. Alex grunted as her sharp elbow jabbed him in the ribs.

"Let her go, mister," the stranger ordered.

Instead of answering, Alex tightened his hold and slipped his hand into her pocket, keeping his other hand firmly over her mouth to keep her from communicating with her partner. He didn't think the man would make a move with Brooke in the way. In fact, he was counting on it.

His hand finally found the weapon. Adrenaline surged through his veins as he pulled it from her pocket. At the same instant, she bit down hard on his hand. With a curse, he let her go, instinctively aiming the weapon at the man.

Only it wasn't a gun, he saw. Not even close. He blinked, his brain slow to believe what his eyes were seeing. It looked like . . .

He fastened his incredulous gaze on Brooke, who actually had the gall to snicker. "You kidnapped me with your *vibrator?*"

Another snicker joined the first. When he remained stone-faced, she sobered. "I don't like guns, and that's not a vibrator."

Alex looked at the object again, then back at Brooke. It was like saying a cat didn't look like a cat. "Then do you mind," he drawled sarcastically, "telling me what it is?"

She had the grace to blush and duck her head. "It's . . . it's a test model of a . . . penis. We use it to test condoms at the factory."

"So you stole it to use for your little scheme?"

"I didn't *steal* it," she began defensively. "I—"

"Are you all right, Brooklyn?" the stranger interrupted, reminding Alex of his ominous presence. " 'Cause if you are, I got a pot of beans boiling on the stove. . . ."

"Yes, I'm fine, Elijah. Thanks."

"I'll be gettin' along, then."

Alex glanced at the stranger, relieved to note that he'd lowered his rifle. Brooke had called him Elijah, and she spoke as if she knew him well, and he'd called her Brooklyn—obviously a pet name. Considering his suspicions, the knowledge didn't ease his mind.

"Brooklyn? I take it you know him?" He turned back to Elijah just in time to see him blend into the grove of trees as he disappeared as silently as he had appeared.

"Elijah's called me that since I was a toddler. My middle name is Lynn, so he kind of strung it together. He's an old friend of my father's."

Because of the encroaching darkness, her features were blurred and indistinct, but Alex heard the sorrow in her voice, and felt it in his bones. He immediately hardened his heart. Until he found out what was really going on, he'd keep his sympathy to himself.

"A few years ago, a group of teenagers decided they'd throw a party here. They pretty much trashed the house. Since then, Elijah's been keeping an eye on the place for us."

"He lives nearby?"

"Yes, but he doesn't have a phone," she said quickly. "And he's hard of hearing—just in case you're thinking of calling for his help."

Alex made sure his smile came about slowly and leisurely. He wanted to make doubly certain she understood his meaning when he said, "Good. Then he won't hear *you*, either."

"What . . . what do you mean?" she asked with an admirable thrust of her chin. She spoiled the effect by taking a step backward.

His smile broadened.

"Meaning you and I are going to have a heart-to-heart. Meanwhile"—he pitched the test model at her—"why don't you give me the flashlight so that we can finish what we came out here to do? That way if we stumble upon another Elijah, I won't be so surprised."

Her eyes narrowed. "Elijah wouldn't harm a flea, unless someone were harming me or my sister."

Alex ignored her dig. "Forgive me if I have a little problem with people pointing guns at my head."

"Maybe if you didn't have such a guilty conscience, you wouldn't be so paranoid."

"Still sticking with your story?" He thought

he heard grinding teeth. The flashlight was a blur as it made an arc through the air. He caught it before it fell to the ground.

"Still disappointed because I didn't give you something worth printing?" she countered. "Don't you want all your newspaper buddies to know what a big, virile man you are?"

Playing the part of Playboy Cliff did have its moments, Alex decided, because he had the perfect comeback to her saccharin-sweet taunt. "Almost as much as you want to know!"

She gasped. "I do not!"

"Liar." Playing Cliff the womanizer also had its advantages, because it gave him an excuse to do what he did next without feeling the least bit guilty. After all, it wasn't his fault she didn't believe he wasn't Cliff. He had tried to tell her.

With wicked intent, he started toward her.

Chapter Six

Of course it was fear that made her heart race and her blood pound heavily in her ears as he approached her with that swagger he called walking. It certainly wasn't anticipation, because Brooke would never be tempted by scum, especially scum like Cliff.

So what was it, then, that made her lips part expectantly when he placed his finger there?

Not anticipation. Never anticipation.

Dee, where are you?

They stood nose-to-nose in the darkness, the flashlight's beam pointed toward the ground. He challenged her, and she accepted the challenge by not running for her life. She wouldn't run. She wouldn't cower. She would show him that she was immune to his brand of cheap charm. For Dee's sake, she would pierce his ego with the sharp edge of her anger. Nothing in the world would make her happier than to show him he wasn't God's gift to every woman.

His finger dipped inside her mouth for moisture, then returned to slide erotically along her bottom lip. Brooke kept her gaze wide and still on his, fighting the urge to flick out her tongue.

She trembled because it was growing chilly now that the sun had set.

She quivered inside because she was only now realizing how foolhardy her plan had been. But then, she'd never dreamed she'd wind up alone here with him.

And when that same finger dropped abruptly to explore her hardened nipple, and his warm mouth closed in on hers, she responded because . . . because . . . Brooke jerked her eyes open, and her mouth from his. With a strength she hadn't expected to possess, she knocked his hand away. She was breathing hard, but that could be construed as anger, when in reality it was self-disgust. A big heap of self-disgust.

"I lied about Elijah not hearing well," she rasped. "He can hear very well, and if you touch me again, I'll scream."

He responded by taking her hand and placing it on his hard length outlined through his jeans. His bold, unexpected move nearly buckled her knees. Heat burned her palm, and she could feel him pulsing against her. For an insane moment, she drew her hand along the thick bulge. His sharp intake of breath shot a thrill right down to her toes and caused a flood between her legs.

"So *you* touch *me*," he commanded huskily. "I promise *I* won't scream. At least not yet."

His voice jarred Brooke back to reality.

The heat spread from him to her, rising swiftly to her face. Brooke took her hand away— not quickly, but slowly. She looked at him, forcing herself to ignore the droop of his eyelids and its meaning. "Okay, you've proved that you're big and virile and excellent at seducing women." She didn't bother hiding her self-contempt. "But you didn't have to go to all that trouble. I already knew you were, from Dee."

As she let her words sink into his conceited head, she plucked the flashlight from his fingers and turned her back on him.

She was shaking—and aching in places that made her feel more ashamed. How could she, even for one insane moment, respond to her sister's boyfriend that way? For six months she had fought Kyle's hands and resisted his pleas. The timing had just never felt right. Now she was glad she hadn't slept with Kyle.

But one moment with *him* and she was stroking his . . . his Hugo!

The breaker box was jammed. Brooke gladly beat the flashlight against it until it gave way. With trembling fingers, she flipped the power switch and slammed the rusted metal door shut, trying to remember how many plates she'd seen in the cupboard. She could always replace them later.

He grabbed her arm before she could stomp by, forcing her to acknowledge his presence when all she really wanted to do was pretend he didn't exist, that this day had never happened.

"I'm sorry."

Damn him for sounding sincere. She didn't want to forgive him! Or herself, for that matter. With a bitter twist of her lips, Brooke said, "It's a little too late for that, don't you think?"

"It's not as bad as you think."

Her laugh was as bitter as her smile. "Oh, yeah? Maybe not for you, but it is for me."

"Because we turn each other on?"

A hot denial hovered on her lips. Brooke finally shook her head. Lying at this point would be silly, but she didn't have to acknowledge his bald statement. "Because Dee loves you."

"What if I told you she doesn't?"

For a second hope leaped in Brooke's heart. Then the sharp image of Dee's dreamy face squashed it flat. "You'd be lying. Believe me, she loves you. She also wants this baby—*your* baby—and I'm not taking you back to town until you two get a chance to talk."

"I could walk."

Brooke considered his threat. It was true; he could. But somehow she didn't think he would, at least not tonight. His jumpy reaction to Elijah reinforced her belief. "Like you said before, I could always hunt you down." She paused before adding softly, "And don't think I wouldn't.

I didn't make it to supervisor because of my amazon build."

"I admire tenacity."

"In my case, you should fear it."

"Okay, I believe you."

"You do?" She slanted him a look full of suspicion. "Is this another trick?"

"No tricks." He made an *X* across his heart. "Let's go inside and talk."

"About you and Dee and the baby?"

"Hm." He nodded. "And about the factory. I'm still interested in doing an article. . . ."

Alex knelt before the small grate and held a match to the pile of dried kindling. The flame quickly became a blaze as it devoured the pile of sticks. He added a few larger pieces of wood to the pile and sat back on his heels, watching it grow.

The hungry fire reminded him of his own reaction to Brooke Welch. He had to admit he'd gone overboard playing the part of Playboy Cliff, but damned if he could help it. She brought out a side of him he hadn't known existed—a reckless, wild side that would have made his family clamor for another CAT scan.

No other woman pushed his buttons the way Brooke did. Even now, he was intensely conscious of her moving around in the adjoining kitchen area of the two-room cabin.

Alex turned to watch her.

She was pounding the heel of her hand

against a small white packet on the counter. His brow rose. That was another thing about Brooke Welch: She was always doing something unusual.

As if she sensed his gaze, she looked up. A blush crept into her cheeks as she answered his unspoken question. "Hot chocolate. I guess it's a little out of date."

"You don't come here very often?"

She shook her head, bending her gaze to the hard packet on the counter. A silken swath of her hair fell forward, concealing her features. "It's not the same . . . since Mom and Dad died. I think it's even harder for Dee. She was only fourteen."

Suddenly she looked up, pinning him with her molten gaze. In the depths of her honey-colored eyes, Alex fancied he saw flames every bit as hot as the ones that warmed his back. Not for the first time, he was very glad he wasn't Cliff.

"But you know all of this, don't you? Feeling the way she does about you, she would have told you."

"She didn't." At least it wasn't a lie, Alex thought.

She grabbed a pan from the counter and slammed it onto the small two-burner stove. While the water heated, she leaned against the counter and folded her arms.

For a long moment, Alex held her angry gaze. Finally she said, "Maybe you just weren't listening. Tell me, do you care about Dee at all? Or was she just another piece of ass to you?"

Alex winced at her crudeness, not because of what she said, but because of the bitterness her remark contained.

He said the only thing he could think of to say, and there wasn't a nice way to put it. "Maybe you should mind your own business for a change."

Wrong answer.

"We've tried that, remember? And Dee *is* my business. I've been taking care of her since Mom and Dad died."

"She's old enough to make her own decisions now." It was guesswork, because Alex didn't have a clue how old Dee was, or how long Brooke's parents had been dead. He figured by the way her eyes narrowed that he might have gotten lucky, though. Like a blind man stumbling through the forest, Alex made it up as he went along, relying on instinct and sheer guesswork. "Maybe it's also time you let her make her own mistakes—and live with them."

She stiffened. "It's not just *her* mistake, Mr. Sure Shot."

So they were back to name-calling again. Alex supressed a sigh. She was right, too, although she didn't know that she was talking to the wrong man.

And he was sick of defending the creep when what he really wanted to do was find him and strangle him.

He tried changing the subject. "How long have you worked at the factory?" He knew, of course, from her file, but he was hoping she might drop some clues.

She took her time answering, filling their cups with hot water and stirring the mixture vigorously. Alex felt himself getting hard just watching her, wondering again if she put that much energy into making love. He accepted the cup she offered, pretending he didn't notice the hard brown lumps of petrified cocoa floating on top—and hoping she wouldn't notice his uncomfortable condition.

After she had settled onto the floor beside him, she stared into the fire as she said, "Six years."

"Did you go to college?"

"For a couple of years. I dropped out when Mom and Dad died."

"To take care of Dee?"

The look she slanted him held a glint of suspicion. "Is this leading to another lecture about how I should let Dee live her own life?"

Her full lips curled with disdain, tempting Alex to blurt out his true identity so that she'd stop hating him and start loving him.

With the hostility out of the way, the possibilities could be endless, he thought, frustrated. But then he remembered who she was, and how it probably wouldn't make much difference if she did know he wasn't Cliff. He'd stop being Hotshot and start being Boss Man, which he didn't like much better. And knowing Brooke, she'd make the switch without losing her fantastic talent for sarcasm.

He smiled into her wary eyes. "No lectures, I promise."

"Okay. I did drop out to take care of Dee. My brothers were already married and living their own lives."

"So that left you." He said it softly, and didn't bother hiding his admiration. She took a sip of her chocolate and made a face. Alex chuckled. "Glad you tasted it first."

Her lips twitched. "It does taste bitter."

Simultaneously, they set the cups on the brick fronting the fireplace. With his hands empty, Alex had a difficult time keeping them to himself. Lust aside, he ached to hold her.

"Dee took their deaths pretty hard," she said with a shrug that didn't fool Alex. "She was the baby, and we all spoiled her rotten."

He gave in to the urge to touch her, reaching out to hook her short hair behind her ear, letting his fingers linger against her heat-flushed skin for just a moment. "And you?"

She focused on the flames, dislodging his hand. With another shrug as bogus as the first, she said, "The last thing Dee needed was for me to fall apart."

Alex let her words sink in. It didn't take him long to come to several interesting conclusions: Since her parents' deaths, he suspected Brooke had gallantly ignored her own grief. If he was right, it would explain her fierce protectiveness toward her sister. Not that he blamed her for trying to protect Dee. Quite the contrary, he admired her.

But it didn't excuse or explain the outrageous risks she'd taken today, kidnapping him and dragging him to an isolated cabin. Alex clenched his jaw. What if he hadn't walked out of that restaurant at that exact moment and she'd brought the real Cliff here—or some other dangerous character? As fierce and as clever as she was, she was no physical match for a man.

He felt unaccountably angry at her foolish actions. And to think—her only protection had been a plastic penis, for crying out loud. Grasping her chin in a rough grip, he forced her to look at him. "I admire your loyalty," he told her gruffly. "Hell, I admire everything about you, but bringing me here wasn't exactly a smart thing to do."

Looking startled, she licked her lips. "Why is that?"

"Because you're a beautiful, sexy woman." *And I'm a horny beast,* Alex wanted to add, but wisely didn't. He figured that by now it would be old news to her anyway. "And you think I'm a sex maniac. We're alone in an isolated cabin. Aren't you concerned that I might decide to take advantage of the situation?" He watched her throat move as she swallowed, but he detected no fear in her eyes.

"Dee was supposed to be here," she defended

herself, trying to pull from his hold. He held tight. "And I doubt you're planning to rape me."

Alex leaned close, his gaze locked on her glistening lips. "Who said anything about rape?" he asked softly, just before his mouth covered hers.

Chapter Seven

She'd made him angry, Brooke thought as his lips touched hers, and now he was trying to frighten her.

Nothing was going as she'd planned.

Deliberately—or was that desperately?—she closed her mind to the feel and texture of his mouth as it moved persuasively over hers. She knew from his earlier kiss what he could do with those lips, and she wasn't taking any chances.

Her lips were sealed tighter than the vault at Quicksilver Bank.

It was really embarrassing, though, to feel her nipples harden and that now-familiar dampness pool between her legs.

Just from the touch of his mouth on hers.

Lord, she hated to imagine what her turncoat body would do if he really put his talents to work! It was more than embarrassing: it was humiliating.

A tiny sigh of relief escaped her when he lifted his mouth from hers. She managed a lip-curl—one of her most disdainful. "Ooooh. I'm so scared."

His eyes narrowed.

Okay, maybe it wasn't a good idea to taunt him, she thought, just seconds before he funneled his hand through her hair and brought her lips against his again.

This time he caught her with her mouth open. He thrust his tongue inside and staked his claim, giving a whole new meaning to the saying, Possession is nine-tenths of the law. He knew how to possess, and he knew how to kiss.

It was the sound of someone moaning—and the jarring, mortifying realization that it was her own voice that gave Brooke the strength she needed.

Bracing her hands on his chest, she shoved him away.

They were both breathing hard. His eyes glittered, and she dared not think about what she looked like. "Okay," she said in a shaky voice that had to belong to someone else. "You've proven your point. Maybe I should have given this plan more thought before I acted. But just because I made a mistake doesn't give you the right to . . . to . . . molest me."

His eyebrow winged upward at her choice of words. "Molest you? Where I come from, they call it kissing."

Brooke felt her anger rise. It was a comforting feeling, and far more welcome than desire for her sister's boyfriend! "Call it whatever you want, just don't do it again."

He sat back on his heels, hands planted on his knees as he regarded her through sultry, hooded eyes. "I can't make any promises," he said. "How long do you plan to wait for your sister?"

"She's probably working through an attack of nerves. If she doesn't show tonight, she'll be here in the morning." Brooke wished she felt as confident as she sounded. Truth was, she was worried. What if Dee had had an accident? What if one of their brothers had shown up at the house? The latter would explain her delay, because Dee would not want Dean Jr. or Logan getting his hands on Cliff.

"I guess you expect me to sleep on that lump you call a sofa?" he asked, nodding to the couch behind her.

Brooke bit her lip. It *was* uncomfortable—not that she particularly cared about his comfort, she reminded herself. And where in the heck did he think he'd sleep? In her bed? *Not a chance. Not ever.* "Dee and I always bunked down in front of the fire. There are plenty of blankets, if you'd rather go that route."

His gaze strayed to the lumpy couch. Finally he sighed. "I'll take the floor."

"Fine. I'll just get the blankets, then."

Five minutes later, she returned to the living room with a pile of musty-smelling blankets and found him once again removing his shirt.

She quickly averted her gaze from the sight of his spectacular chest. "Um, here you go." Dumping the pile on the sofa, she turned to leave with every intention of locking herself in the bedroom—away from Mr. Temptation.

"Stay and talk."

He hadn't asked, Brooke noted; he'd demanded. Who in the hell did he think he was? "I'm not in a talkative mood." She could have bitten her tongue off when she realized what she'd said and how it could be misconstrued.

Fully expecting a mocking, sexually explicit comment about what she might be in the mood for, he surprised her by saying, "If I promise to behave, will you stay?"

Hmm. Depended on his definition of *talk.* Slowly she turned, keeping her gaze averted. "What do you want to talk about?" she asked, not bothering to hide her skepticism. Several times during their six-month relationship, Kyle had claimed he wanted to "talk" about the factory and her job, when in fact he really meant he wanted to lure her into his bed. She'd later overheard him complaining to one of his friends that he'd wasted six months on her. Only instead of saying her name, he'd called her a cold bitch.

Two weeks after that, he'd promoted someone else to Level B supervisor, when Brooke had been waiting for the promotion for the past two years.

"About the factory."

Startled by his uncanny words, Brooke forgot she wasn't supposed to look at him. She blinked, reminding herself that this man wasn't Kyle, and couldn't possibly know what she'd been thinking. He was, however, just as devious. And dangerous. Maybe more so, because he definitely had Kyle beat in the looks department.

Squaring her shoulders, she kept her eyes on his face as she demanded, "Why are you so interested in the factory?"

He looked surprised by her vehemence. "I told you, I might be interested in doing a story."

Gingerly, she perched herself on the edge of the sofa. If he made a single move, she was going to clobber him, she decided. "What can I say that I haven't already said?"

"Pretend I'm the owner. . . ."

"Alex Bradshaw," Brooke supplied.

"Yes. Him. Pretend I'm him. What would you say to him if you had the opportunity?"

"And he was prepared to listen?"

"Right."

"Off the record?"

"Off the record."

"If you print a single word, I'll sue you."

"Fair enough."

The temptation to ease her frustrations proved too great. And as a supervisor at the factory, she had many frustrations. Brooke carefully leaned back on the sofa, sticking her hands in her jacket pockets. "First I would tell him what a jackass I think he is."

"Why?"

"For neglecting his company. He wanted it badly enough to kick old man Donaldson when he was down, yet he hasn't visited one single time since he bought the factory."

"So it was a hostile takeover?"

"No, not exactly. Rumor had it that Donaldson needed cash to cover a few bad investments, and was looking to sell anyway. Bradshaw found out about it and made him an offer way below the asking price."

"And Donaldson couldn't refuse?"

"He wasn't in a position to refuse."

"So you think Bradshaw took advantage of Donaldson?"

"After what I just told you, don't you?" Brooke countered defensively.

He shrugged. "Sounds like business as usual to me." He added a rueful chuckle. "But then, what do I know? I'm just a reporter. So after you scolded him for neglecting his business, then what?"

"I'd tell him what I thought about his mandatory once-a-month Saturday."

"I'm not following you."

"It's mandatory for every worker to put in at least six hours one Saturday a month."

"You said earlier that most of your employees jump at the chance for overtime," he reminded her.

"They do, but this isn't overtime." When he frowned, Brooke nodded. "Some employees don't make production, so everyone is required to work those extra six hours—at regular pay—to make up for it."

"You're kidding. How long has this been going on?"

"Since the takeover." Brooke smiled bitterly. "We're not unionized, so what can we do? If we make a fuss, then we get canned, and nobody can afford that luxury. I'm telling you, this guy's a ruthless thief. A throwback from the Dark Ages. No wonder his wife left him. At least, that's the rumor."

"Hmm. Any other complaints?"

"Oh, yeah. I was just getting warmed up. I would also tell him what I think about his policy of demanding a doctor's excuse for the employee."

"I remember you mentioning it earlier. This is Bradshaw's work, too?"

Brooke shook her head. "No, it's always been that way, and it's always been the *wrong* way. Employees should have sick days—period. Not sick days just for themselves, but for family members as well. Most day-care centers won't take children if they're sick, and I don't blame them. The mothers have to stay home, and because of this stupid company policy, they don't get paid. It isn't fair."

"I agree," he murmured.

"Then there's the leaky roof in the break

room, and the old equipment, and the sexual harassment—"

"Whoa, back up! Sexual harassment?"

Brooke felt a slow burn creep into her face. Why did she have to go and mention sex? *Stupid, stupid, stupid!* "Scratch that."

"No."

Her gaze widened on his stony features. "Look, I didn't mean to say—"

"Yes, you did."

By the look of his stubborn jaw, he wouldn't let the subject go. With a sigh, Brooke said, "Being a man, you'll probably disagree with me, or think I'm silly."

"Try me."

"It's the jokes."

"Jokes?"

"Yes, the jokes. Each week the Bradshaw Corporation faxes a memo to the supervisors with a new condom joke. Some of them are pretty raunchy, and a few are illustrated rather graphically."

"As in offensive?" he queried, his tone oddly soft.

She should have known Mr. Sex Machine would think she was overreacting. Her chin angled. "Yes, offensive. There are a couple of the supervisors who have threatened to quit."

"I see."

"Do you?" she snapped. "I don't think you do. It's not only the jokes themselves—which are usually demeaning to women—but the fact that he believes we actually enjoy them. He's a sick son of a bitch."

"And you'd tell him so?"

"In a heartbeat!" Brooke nearly shouted.

The silence that fell was sudden and deafening. Guilt stabbed Brooke. The problems at the factory weren't Cliff's fault. "I'm sorry. I wasn't yelling at you, but at—"

"That perverted son of a bitch, Bradshaw," he concluded.

Brooke almost smiled at his overexaggerated Texas drawl, until she remembered that she shouldn't like *him* any more than she liked that bonehead, Bradshaw. She must be a lot more tired than she realized, to be thinking of finding anything about him amusing.

"Well, I think I'll go to bed," she announced, rising from the sofa. She'd already shared more with him than she shared with most people she'd known all of her life. The knowledge not only disgusted her, but frightened her.

"Good night," he said.

She glanced at him, then looked quickly away as he stretched. "You won't slip out on me, will you?"

"Hmm. You could always chain me to your bed."

Brooke felt a strange relief at his suggestive comment. *This* man she recognized and disliked. For a few moments while they were discussing the factory, he'd seemed almost human. Nearly likable.

She shivered, then stiffened as the rough pads

of his fingers trailed along her exposed neck. He'd come up soundlessly behind her, the rat.

His breath tickled her ear. "If you get lonely, you know where I am."

"Not in this lifetime, lover boy," she whispered back.

Husky laughter followed her mad flight to the bedroom. Once inside, she quickly shut the door and locked it. She sank onto the bed and covered her face with her hands.

Her anger at Dee dissolved completely. She forced herself to admit that to remain mad would make her the biggest hypocrite in history.

A knock at the door made her jump.

"I forgot something," a deep, muffled voice said.

What now? she wondered, staring at the door. Maybe if she kept quiet, he would give up and go away. She didn't want to look at him, his chest, or any other part of his glorious anatomy another single instant.

"Hello? Are you all right?"

Half growling, half laughing at her own ridiculous reaction, Brooke rose from the bed and stomped to the door. She jerked it open. "What do you want?"

He stood in the doorway, bare-chested and sexy and every bit as glorious as she remembered, right down to his long, narrow feet. He smelled of wood smoke and sunshine.

"You keep looking at me like that, and I'm going to need more than a pillow."

Mortified to be caught ogling him, Brooke jerked her gaze up. "You need a pillow?"

His eyebrows rose, and his eyes took on a familiar gleam that seemed to waver between humor and hunger. "You had something else in mind?"

"Go to hell," Brooke said in a growl, stomping to the bed and snatching up one of the pillows. She brought it to him and stuffed it into his arms.

"I changed my mind. There *is* something else I need."

"You—"

Brooke's words were muffled by his mouth. By the time he released her, she had to grab the doorjamb for support; her bones had turned to jelly. "You have to stop kissing me." She had meant to shout, but her voice emerged as a whisper.

His gaze dropped to linger on her mouth for a long, thoughtful moment. When he spoke, there wasn't a trace of laughter left in his voice. "I will—when *you* stop wanting me to."

Chapter Eight

Brooke awoke with the dim light of dawn filtering through the single cabin window, and Hugo poking into her ribs; she'd fallen asleep with her jacket on.

With a grimace, she sat up and struggled out of the wrinkled jacket, casting it onto the bed beside her. Her eyes ached and itched, and her throat felt dry and scratchy.

Coffee. She needed coffee in the worst way.

Much more than she needed to remember the dream she'd been having—the one that generated all the sweat that was now drying to a sticky film on her body. The one where Mr. Broad Chest climbed into bed with her, stripped her naked, and ravished her until she screamed.

From pleasure, that is. Lots of raw, piercing screams of pleasure as he did things to her she'd only read about. Down-and-dirty things, sexy, mind-blowing things that made her writhe and beg for more.

And she did things to him, things that made *him* moan and gasp, which in turn made her hot all over again.

It was a dream, of course, because in reality no couple could have that many orgasms in one wild session of raw, no-holds-barred sex.

Brooke moaned and rubbed her throbbing temples. *Could they? No, of course not.* But then, how would she know?

Elijah. Elijah would have coffee. Strong, black, and probably bitter, but beggars couldn't be choosers. Maybe by the time she had had coffee and walked the distance to Elijah's house and back, she would be better prepared to face the half-naked man in the living room.

As for Dee, Brooke wasn't certain she'd *ever* be able to face her again. The enormous guilt she felt for allowing him to kiss her—not once, not twice, but *four* times—would surely kill her. Granted, he'd caught her by surprise all of those times, but she hadn't exactly fought him.

The first time pride had kept her still.

Okay, so it had been her infernal pride the second time as well.

Brooke frowned and pinched the bridge of

her nose. The third time she had recklessly goaded him, and the fourth time she should have anticipated. She never should have opened the door.

How would she explain it to her sister? Dee loved the man, worthless lump of muscle that he was. If he had forced Brooke, if she had hated it, then she might have a wobbly leg to stand on.

But neither of those excuses applied, and she wouldn't allow herself to believe they did. It galled her to admit it, but she was no better than he was.

Heart aching, Brooke tiptoed to the door and eased it open. She held her breath and listened, moving forward only when she identified his gentle snores.

Five breathless minutes later, she was trotting through the woods down the overgrown path to Elijah's house. When she emerged into the clearing where his cabin stood, she stopped to catch her breath.

"Been expecting you," Elijah said.

Startled, Brooke glanced up. In his customary blue-jeans overalls, Elijah sat in an old, weathered rocking chair on his front porch, a mug of coffee balanced on his crossed knee. He'd trimmed and combed his beard, and his long, gray-streaked hair looked newly washed. Beneath the overalls, he wore a white T-shirt that looked as if it had just emerged from the package.

He'd cleaned up just for her, Brooke thought, her heart softening as she looked at him. A few more wrinkles had joined the lines on his face, and his faded blue eyes had lightened another shade, but all in all he hadn't changed much in the past year since she'd last seen him. She felt ashamed for not visiting him sooner.

"Your coffee's gettin' cold, and I'm waitin' to hear about your new boyfriend."

"He's not *my* boyfriend," Brooke said, grabbing the mug of coffee from the porch railing. She cursed the guilty flush that heated her skin and took the chair beside him on the porch, sinking onto the worn cushion with a sigh.

All around them, the woodland creatures began to stir. There were several squirrel feeders nailed to the trees in the yard, and as she watched, the squirrels converged on the dried ears of corn impaled on the spikes. They chattered and nibbled, ignoring Brooke and the generous man who kept them supplied with food.

"Well?" Elijah demanded in his gruff way. "If he ain't your boyfriend, what's he doing at the cabin?"

Brooke took a fortifying sip of the coffee. It was hot, strong, and delicious—not bitter, as she had expected it to be. Apparently Elijah had taken her advice about not *boiling* the coffee. "He's Dee's boyfriend." She paused to clear the hoarseness from her voice. "His name is Cliff, and he's the father of her baby."

Nothing, it seemed, shocked Elijah. "Hmm."

He took his time, watching the squirrels fighting over the corn with obvious enjoyment. "So Dee's at the cabin with you?"

This, Brooke thought, was what one called an awkward moment. "She's not there yet, but she's coming." She hoped. "I sort of . . . um . . . forced him to come with me so that he and Dee could talk." She felt Elijah's shrewd eyes on her reddened face.

"I reckon I'm wondering how you managed to force him, seeing how big he looked. Course, my eyesight ain't what it used to be. . . ."

"He thought I had a gun in my pocket," Brooke blurted out. But of course Elijah knew, because he'd been there when Cliff realized it wasn't a gun. Her face heated several more degrees. What had been funny then wasn't funny now. Elijah was old-fashioned; she'd probably offended his sensibilities with the plastic—

"Yep, that was pretty funny," Elijah surprised her by saying. "The look on his face . . ." He chuckled and slapped his knee, jostling his coffee. "Bet he didn't take too kindly to your foolin' him."

Mildly put, Brooke mused, her lips twitching. "You're right, he didn't find it too funny." And his brand of revenge was something she didn't care to remember.

Her lips stopped twitching at the reminder.

"So after he found out you didn't have a real gun, he didn't hightail it back to town?"

"I don't think those rattlesnake-skin boots were made for walking," Brooke said dryly.

"We talked, and he agreed to stay until Dee arrived."

"What do you reckon happened to little Dee Dee?"

Brooke shrugged. "I can't imagine, unless she chickened out. Her excuse had better be a good one, after leaving me alone with Mr. Sure . . . er, Cliff all night," she amended hastily.

The chair creaked as Elijah leaned forward and propped his elbows on his knees. He cradled his coffee mug in his hands and began to roll it back and forth between his palms. "You ain't afraid he'll press charges?"

"I didn't have a real weapon."

"But he thought you did," Elijah retorted. "The fact is, kidnapping is a felony." He glanced at her, his faded blue eyes widening as if an alarming thought had just occurred to him. "You could go to jail!"

Brooke tried to laugh at his concerns, but the sound came out a little shaky—and none too confident. "What would he tell them? That he was kidnapped by a hundred-pound woman carrying a plastic . . . plastic—"

"It ain't like I've never heard the word 'penis,'" Elijah said mildly, shocking Brooke into silence.

After a stunned moment, she burst out laughing. Elijah joined her. The startled squirrels ran for cover, and the rickety old floorboards beneath their chairs shook from the force of Elijah's pounding feet.

Gasping for breath, Elijah finally managed,

"It's time for the home town news. You want more coffee while I fetch the radio?"

Nodding and chuckling, Brooke handed him her empty mug. "Thanks, I'd love another cup." When he'd gone inside the small cabin, she let out a long sigh and leaned back in the rocker. This was just what she needed to regroup and refresh her mind, she decided. Good company, strong black coffee, and the peaceful serenity of the surrounding woods.

Elijah returned toting a fancy boom box and fresh coffee. He handed her the mug and set the metallic silver stereo on the worn boards of the porch beside his chair. He pulled out the antenna as far as it would go and flipped the power switch. When he caught sight of Brooke's grin, he flashed her a toothy, sheepish smile.

"Damned thing takes a fortune in batteries, but it gets good reception, and the sound rocks."

Impressed with his modern slang, Brooke lifted a brow as she said, "Hey, whatever works. What happened to your old transistor?"

"Kicked the bucket. Tried to find a replacement, but they don't make them anymore." He bent over and fiddled with the knobs. Snatches of conversations zipped by at an amazing speed. Finally, with one ear cocked, he let out a satisfied "ah" and settled into his rocking chair. "Nobody tells the hometown news like Benny."

She had to agree. Benny, whom she vaguely remembered from high school, possessed the deep, disc-jockey voice common among radio announcers. Right now he was informing his listening audience that it was going to be another warm day in Quicksilver, Oklahoma, with a slight possibility of scattered thunderstorms.

"And this urgent report just arrived on my desk," Benny said as Brooke took a cautious sip of her coffee. It was hot. Eyes burning, she held it in her mouth to let it cool, and set the mug down on the railing. She'd been listening with only half an ear, but Benny's sudden, urgent tone snagged her attention.

"Business tycoon Alex Bradshaw is reported missing this morning. Unrevealed sources claim foul play is suspected, and an investigation is under way."

Brooke bolted forward in her chair with a mouthful of cooling coffee. Her throat had closed tight. Alex Bradshaw—her new boss—was missing! She tried to swallow and couldn't, not knowing whether to rejoice or cry. If something happened to Bradshaw, what would happen to the factory? Benny's next words wiped those thoughts from her mind.

"En route to his vacation in Hot Springs, Arkansas, Bradshaw was last seen wearing a hunter green shirt, jeans, and rattlesnake-skin boots." As Benny chuckled, Brooke's heart did a triple somersault. "Snakeskin boots . . . he sounds like a Texan, all right."

No! It couldn't be!

"But here's the real kicker, folks! Bradshaw was last seen right here in our hometown by the owner of Treva's Diner, Treva Brannum. She claims she gave him a recipe for peach cobbler. Kinda hurts my feelings, because I've been after that recipe for—"

Brooke spewed lukewarm coffee onto the porch, choking on the small amount that had managed to trickle down her throat. Concerned, Elijah reached over and pounded her on the back hard enough to knock her lungs loose.

"You okay, gal?" he asked, pounding the flat of his hand steadily onto her back.

Gasping, Brooke drew in a gurgling breath and managed to say in a croak, "Yes! I'm . . . fine." She wasn't fine. She was beyond shock, beyond stunned.

She was . . . she was . . . she wished she were dead! *Please God, let it be a joke. All of it. Dee's pregnancy—everything leading up to this moment. I swear I won't be mad. I won't break a single dish. I won't yank a single hair from Dee's head, and I'll stab Alex Bradshaw only in places that won't cause too much damage.*

But Benny didn't end his all-important bulletin with a laughing confession and a squeaky "Surprise!"

"A ten thousand-dollar reward is being offered by the Bradshaw corporation for any information pertaining to the whereabouts of Alex Bradshaw. Ooh, baby, what a pile of dough! I'd turn in my own mother for that kind of money!"

Elijah finally stopped pounding her back. He

sank back in his rocker and muttered in a wounded voice, "I guess the coffee's too strong for ya."

Brooke held her hands to her shaking knees and tried to hold them still.

They knocked her hands loose.

She firmly clamped them back down, watching her hands jitter along with her knees. Her teeth picked up the beat. Standing was out of the question.

Throwing up was a definite possibility.

Clenching her teeth to keep them still, she squeezed her eyes shut and threw back her head, forcing herself to face the awful, mortifying truth.

She'd kidnapped Alex Bradshaw.

Her new boss.

And then, to make matters worse—as if those facts weren't bad enough—she recalled every derogatory, hateful, mean thing she'd told him about Alex Bradshaw. *Pretend I'm him. What would you say to him if you had the opportunity?*

Oh, God!

Fate wouldn't be so cruel, so inhumane, so terrible.

Oh, God!

She'd kidnapped, humiliated, and thoroughly reamed Alex Bradshaw, the new owner of the factory where she was supervisor.

She was dead meat, or at the very least, soon to be unemployed. Possibly convicted of kidnapping. No—*probably* convicted of kidnapping. A ruthless man like Alex Bradshaw wouldn't let someone of her caliber go unpunished for such a crime.

"Brooke? You okay? You're looking pretty green around the gills. Want me to get you a shot of whiskey?"

In a fit of hysteria, Brooke grabbed the straps of Elijah's overalls and nearly toppled him out of his chair as she pulled him close. He grabbed the arm of his chair for balance, his faded blue gaze alarmed as he looked into her wild eyes.

"I have made the biggest mistake of my life," she said in a hoarse croak. "I have kidnapped . . . my . . . boss! Alex Bradshaw . . . is my . . . boss!"

Elijah licked his lips and tried to pry her fingers loose. When she wouldn't let go, he tried to reason with her. "Now, Brooke, you just settle down, ya hear? Tell ol' Elijah what's wrong."

"I . . . just . . . *told* you!" Brooke gritted out, squeezing his straps so hard the buckles bit into her fingers. She felt sanity slipping away at an alarming rate.

To give him credit, Elijah attempted to make sense of her disjointed words and ease her mind. "You kidnapped your boss? You mean instead of Dee's boyfriend, you kidnapped your boss? Well, seems to me you made an honest mistake."

Feeling as if her lungs would burst, Brooke let go of Elijah and lurched to her feet. The world spun. She grabbed the porch post for support, clutching it like a lifeline. When the trees stopped moving, she tried to focus on Elijah's alarmed face. "You don't understand," was all she could manage to articulate.

"You kidnapped your boss by mistake," Elijah repeated.

She flinched at his words. "Yes, I did." The mistake part hardly mattered at this point.

Elijah straightened his overall straps and thrust out his chin. "Well, why didn't he tell you he wasn't who you thought he was?"

Brooke slowly closed her eyes. "He tried," she whispered, remembering the clues he'd dropped. "I didn't believe him." *What if I told you she doesn't?* he'd said when she'd reminded him that Dee loved him.

Of course Dee didn't love him! She didn't even *know* him.

And even earlier he'd said, *I think you've got me confused with someone else.*

"He could have shown you his ID, couldn't he?" Elijah demanded, rising from his chair with a groan and a grunt. "Seems to me this young feller's been having fun at your expense."

Elijah was right, Brooke thought. He could have told her outright, and she also *should* have demanded to see his driver's license. But in a small town like Quicksilver, drop-dead-gorgeous men like Cliff—*Alex*—weren't exactly a dime a dozen. Going by Dee's eloquent description, she had automatically assumed the man exiting Treva's Diner was Cliff.

A stupid, stupid assumption.

Alex Bradshaw lay sleeping half-naked in her cabin.

Brooke gripped the post more firmly, her knuckles turning white as she remembered every kiss, every erotic, mind-blowing comment he'd made since she had forced him into her car, as if he were having the time of his life instead of *fearing* for his life.

What she had only suspected suddenly became an embarrassing reality: Alex Bradshaw not only didn't fear her, he'd probably known who she was the moment she told him her name. He'd played along, deliberately deceiving her. Why? Hoping she'd talk about the factory?

Brooke normally welcomed the familiarity of anger, but this time it frightened her. She now realized that the crushing guilt she'd felt since that very first kiss was needless. A big, not-so-funny joke.

He wasn't Dee's boyfriend.

In fact, according to the factory gossip, he wasn't anyone's boyfriend. His wife—*ex*-wife—had left him two years ago. And no wonder. The man possessed a very cruel sense of humor.

Launching herself away from the post, Brooke navigated the porch steps and made her way purposefully onto the path through the woods—to that black-hearted, half-naked devil sleeping on the floor in her cabin.

Elijah appeared at her elbow, his tone anxious. "Brooke, you're not fixin' to do something you might regret, are you, gal?"

"I don't know. Ask me *after* I kill him. Right now I can't imagine regretting it." Brooke was surprised to hear how calm her voice sounded. She almost frightened herself.

"Maybe you should stay awhile, let your temper cool down," Elijah suggested, breathing hard as he tried to keep up with her furious strides. "Your daddy would have given this some thought."

"It won't work," Brooke said in a hiss. "And you know damned well Daddy would be just as furious as I am."

Giving up, Elijah stopped on the trail and cupped his bony knees with his hands, gasping for breath. "At least give yourself time to think!" he called after her.

Brooke shoved a branch aside, wondering if the rising sun had anything to do with the reddish haze that clouded her eyesight.

She didn't think it did.

Chapter Nine

Alex awoke to the sound of pounding. He groaned, thinking the sound was the steady beat of an impending migraine knocking at his brain. Lying very still, he waited for the sharp, darting pain he knew would soon follow.

Five tense seconds ticked by. Above the muffled, distant pounding, he could hear birds chirping outside; inside the cabin it was blissfully quiet. No ringing phones, no radio, no television, not even the background hum of a refrigerator. He inhaled the lingering scent of wood smoke from the fire of last night, and the slightly musty smell of the unused cabin.

Primitive and wonderful.

Finally Alex allowed himself to believe the

pounding wasn't inside his head. In fact, his head didn't hurt at all—a reason for celebration in itself, he thought, gingerly sitting up. And a good thing, too, since he'd left his medicine at the hotel.

He glanced around at his rustic surroundings, his curiosity aroused by the erratic *thack-thack*ing sound.

Brooke . . . Brooke would know what it was, he thought, her name conjuring a heated image in his mind. Throwing the covers aside, he got to his feet. He stretched and thought about putting on his shirt, but with a wicked grin, decided not to. On bare feet, he padded to the bedroom and eased open the door.

The bed was empty, the covers bunched as if the sleeper had suffered a restless night, and he spotted Brooke's jacket on top of the blanket. So she'd finally taken it off. Somewhere—close, he hoped—Brooke was walking around with her shoulders finally bared for his view. Buoyant at the thought of seeing her again, Alex returned to his makeshift bed and pulled on his boots. He grabbed his shirt and headed for the front door.

It was just as he suspected, a gorgeous day without a rain cloud in sight. Not that he would have minded the rain. Hell, he didn't care if it snowed, as long as he wasn't in the city. This was an ideal vacation spot, surrounded by nature, and with the prospect of seeing Brooke again, Alex couldn't think of anywhere he'd rather be right now.

And for the first time in months, he hadn't awakened with a headache.

Filled with this amazing revelation, he loped off the steps, following the strange *thunk-thunk*ing sound to the backyard.

What he saw when he rounded the corner of the cabin stopped him in his tracks.

It was Brooke, and she was chopping wood with an angry desperation that he could almost feel. Slowly he approached her, but wisely kept clear of the swing of the ax. Beyond her, a small, private lake sparkled beneath the morning sun. A family of ducks swam close to shore, four quacking ducklings swimming frantically to keep up with their mother. A silver flash caught the sunlight as a fish leaped over the surface.

Thunk! The blade sheared the piece of wood in two before lodging into the tree stump. Brooke yanked it loose with impressive strength, swept the split wood from the stump, and quickly reached for another log.

Alex waited until the blade was once again safely lodged in the stump before he asked, "What are you doing?"

She froze with her back to him, her shoulders rigid. "I'm baking chocolate-chip cookies," she said in a nasty growl that definitely alerted him to her current mood.

As if he hadn't guessed by the maniacal way she swung the ax! From the look of her sweat-soaked body, she'd been at it awhile, too. "Looks like you're chopping wood. Mind if I ask why? There's a good supply piled beside the cabin." He wished she'd look at him. Maybe if he could see her expression, he could glean a clue or two about what was bugging her. Could she possibly still be upset about last night? Granted, maybe he'd gone over the line with that last kiss, but could he help it if she was irresistible?

She lifted the ax, and just as she brought it crashing down onto the hapless piece of wood, she ground out viciously, "I'm chopping wood because I don't want to break Daddy's dishes. They aren't much, but it just didn't seem right."

Ah, that explained . . . absolutely nothing. Before she could reach for another log from the pile, Alex handed her one. Without looking at him she snatched it from his fingers and slammed it onto the stump.

"Something tells me you're angry."

Alex had no difficulty identifying the snarl that emerged from her very kissable mouth.

"How astute of you," she said in a hiss, still swinging and chopping, swinging and chopping.

Perplexed, Alex propped his hands on his hips, wishing she'd pause long enough to talk to him face-to-face. But then again, maybe it wouldn't be such a good idea for her to get a good look at him at the moment. He seemed to have little control over his libido where she was concerned—especially when she made those sexy growling noises in her throat. "Look, if you're angry about last night, I'll apologize."

"*If* I'm angry?" And finally she did look at

him, eyes blazing, lips quivering with fury. Tendrils of damp, sweat-soaked hair clung to her flushed cheeks. She wore a white T-shirt beneath her denim jumper, and it, too, was sweat-soaked and plastered to the curvy mounds of her heaving breasts.

Alex shifted uncomfortably. It was a dangerous time to get aroused, but this little spitfire could do it to him in no time flat.

"You"—she jabbed a very sharp ax in his direction—"let me believe *all night* that you were my sister's worthless, womanizing boyfriend!"

So the cat was out of the bag, Alex mused, thinking fast. "You've talked to your sister?"

Eyes that reminded him of hot caramel narrowed, but Alex knew it had nothing to do with the bright morning sun. This little warrior was on the warpath, so to speak.

She ignored his question. "Why? Why would you let me suffer like that? What kind of . . . of beast are you? I've been flogging myself since you first . . . first—"

"Kissed you?" Alex supplied helpfully.

"Yes! Then I felt so guilty I wanted to just die because . . . because—"

"You wanted me?"

"Yes!" she cried, then snapped her teeth together so hard he heard the sound. She sucked in a sharp, horrified breath, causing her breasts, outlined by the wet T-shirt, to swell above the V neck of the jumper. "You jerk!" she spat accusingly. "You cruel . . . insufferable . . . insane maniac!"

"Insane?" Alex asked, offended. Insane for wanting her? Was that what she meant? Surely she was aware of her considerable appeal.

Brooke embedded the ax in the stump with one swift, agitated move. She stood with her hands on her hips, glaring at him. "Yes, insane! I think you actually enjoyed being kidnapped, so you have to be crazy."

With the ax safely out of her hands, Alex took a chance on stepping closer. Softly he asked, "What man wouldn't enjoy being kidnapped by a beautiful woman?"

"You were never frightened," she stated almost wearily.

Alex decided a little white lie wouldn't hurt—to protect her pride. "Of course I was, um, *cautious* when I thought you had a gun. But the attraction that has been growing between us soon made me forget about being afraid."

"There *is* no attraction between us!"

He smiled at her hot denial and dropped his gaze to the telltale points clearly outlined by her jumper. "I think the lady protests too much," he murmured. "Maybe a little reminder . . ."

"No, don't!" She put up a hand to ward him off. "Don't you take another step. I'm . . . I'm hot and sweaty and . . ."

"Keep going," he murmured.

". . . still furious with you! So back off! I'll . . . I'll just go inside and take a shower, then take you back to town." Her mouth firmed and her chin came up in a now-familiar way. "You go your way and I'll go mine, and we'll just forget this ever happened."

Alex let her take a few steps in the direction of the cabin before he stopped her with a softly drawled, "Oh, I don't think so."

She paused, her back rigid. "Why not?"

"Because I think I deserve a little compensation. After all, I've been kidnapped, threatened, and verbally abused." All of which he'd thoroughly enjoyed, and most of which she knew. Still, kidnapping was kidnapping.

With an audible hiss, she whirled around to face him again. "You plan to press charges?"

"That depends." He paused, drawing his gaze along her tense form, then back to her taut face and glittering eyes. Her breath had quickened, he noted with inward satisfaction. "On your cooperation," he added.

Thirty minutes later, Brooke emerged from a cold shower, furious to realize the frigid water had not cooled anything but her skin, and then only for a brief time.

She still wanted to jump his bones.

With a tiny moan, she buried her face in the damp towel. How could she still want to have sex with him? He was her boss, a man she had good reason to dislike, and he had just moments ago issued an ultimatum that was nothing short of blackmail.

Her bluff hadn't worked. She was fairly certain that he didn't know that she knew who he really was, but his not knowing hadn't helped her get out of this ridiculous situation. Her plan had been to get him back to town and to part ways as quickly as possible. Then, later, when he came to inspect the factory, she would act totally surprised—and mortified—to discover he was the very man she'd kidnapped.

If he were any kind of gentleman, he would have gone along with her plan.

But no, he wasn't a gentleman, and she was the crazy one for thinking that her weak, pathetic little plan would work. He was a man, and he'd made it extremely clear that he wanted compensation.

A hot thrill set fire to her belly. Brooke pressed one hand over it, hoping to put out the flames before they spread.

It didn't work. Every time she thought about Alex, she got an itch between her legs. It was a new and frightening—and appalling—experience for her. It was bad enough she'd felt this way thinking he was Dee's boyfriend, but just as bad when she knew he was her boss!

The really awful part was that since she'd found out he wasn't Cliff, it had gotten worse. For the first time in her life she wanted to jump into bed with a man to have hot, raw, unbridled sex.

Brooke let out a long, shaky sigh and released her death grip on the towel. *Okay.* So she wanted to get hot and wild with Alex just as much as he seemed to want to get hot and wild with her.

So why didn't she just do it? She was a con-

senting adult with a normal, healthy sex drive—
or at least she had one now—so why not just
get it over with? Get it out of her system?
Scratch the itch? That it would be the most
memorable experience of her life, she had no
doubt. Any man who could reduce her to a cowardly, trembling heap hiding in the bathroom
would undoubtedly rock her world.

Afterward—if she didn't die from pleasure—
they could put this silly thing about kidnapping
and mistaken identity behind them. They could
go their separate ways, and when they did meet
again, perhaps they'd share a smile, maybe a
laugh or two, then forget about it. It would be
their little secret, one she could dwell on from
time to time in the privacy of her own bedroom.

Thoughtfully, Brooke rose, reaching for the
denim shorts she'd found in the bedroom
drawer. They were Dee Dee's left from long ago,
but since Dee then was the size Brooke was
now, they fit. The faded, oversize T-shirt that
had belonged to her dad nearly touched the
hem of the shorts, but at least the clothes were
clean.

Since she wasn't wearing panties, the rough
denim material brushed against an area that
had become embarrassingly sensitive in the
past fourteen hours. She tugged at the hem of
her shorts, ran her fingers through her short,
wet hair, and took a deep breath.

It was time to face the music. With any luck
they could have a hot, very satisfying tumble on
the bed and be back in town by noon. After that

she planned to find Dee and force her to listen to the longest lecture in history about responsibilities and leaving older sisters in very sticky situations.

Brooke's hand trembled as she grasped the doorknob. Doubts assailed her. What was she doing? What was she thinking? Was she seriously considering having a meaningless, one-night—*one-hour*—stand with Alex Bradshaw, the hotshot, selfish boss who cared about no one but himself? The fact that he would blackmail her proved that the rumors about him were true! He was ten times worse than Kyle, who was fast making his rounds with the female employees at the factory.

But to compare Alex to Kyle was like comparing Mel Gibson to Pee-Wee Herman, Brooke mused. Besides, no one would have to know. In fact, she would die if they found out she had consorted with the enemy. The workers under her supervision—mostly women—would never trust her again. They'd regard her with disgust and suspicion, and with good reason.

But this wasn't business. This was personal.

Brooke placed her hand over her quivering middle and opened the door.

Chapter Ten

Alex stared after Elijah long after he'd disappeared down the trail, pondering the enlightening conversation that had just taken place. Absently he retrieved his cell phone from beneath the Pinto and strapped it into his boot.

The elderly man had come to plead Brooke's case, unwittingly revealing several interesting facts: Brooke not only knew he wasn't Cliff, she knew he was Alex Bradshaw, and according to Elijah, she feared he was going to haul her before the sheriff on kidnapping charges. Almost as an afterthought—and quite contrarily—Elijah had warned Alex to watch his back, that Brooke hadn't been herself since her folks died. *Brooklyn's keepin' it bottled up inside, and one of these days I'm afraid she's going to blow!*

Interesting. Very interesting.

Why didn't she tell him? he wondered. What possible motive could she have for keeping silent about knowing who he was? Embarrassment? Likely, and understandable. Fear? Alex frowned, then shook his head. No, despite what Elijah had said, he couldn't imagine the little fireball fearing anything. Oh, he believed she feared what he made her feel, but not him physically.

She could fear losing her job, something he could well understand. And she should fear it, he thought. Why, most men in his position would probably declare her a lunatic and fire her on the spot. They would believe her unstable, and he should as well.

But he didn't. This wasn't an ordinary, well-thought-out kidnapping, and Alex knew it. Brooke had been trying to protect her kid sister—a sister she'd taken care of since her parents' deaths. He might very well have done the same in her shoes. No, Brooke wasn't dangerous—as Elijah had subtly implied. *Fiercely protective* better described Brooke. Passionately loyal, too. As a businessman, Alex could admire those traits in his employees.

But then, there were a lot of things he admired about Brooke Welch. Alex jerked his mind from the gutter and concentrated on the big question.

Why didn't she tell him she knew? Could it have anything to do with what was supposedly going on at the factory? Alex hated to return to his earlier suspicions, but he knew that he couldn't discount them just because he was in lust with Brooke. He was here on a rat hunt, and if Brooke turned out to be one of those rats . . . then he would deal with it. He'd be disappointed, true, but he was a practical man.

And if it turned out that she had nothing to hide . . . well, then, she might be useful in helping him find out who did. Meanwhile he could relax right here at the cabin for as long as it took. Combining business with pleasure had never sounded better.

Now that Alex had a plan, he was ready for action. He headed into the cabin in search of Brooke. A quick glance into the small bathroom where she'd been taking a shower proved it empty, but a slight rustling noise to the right drew him to the open doorway of the bedroom.

She was making the bed, and the enticing sight of her denim-clad bottom was enough to erase every logical thought in his brain. If my doctor could see me now, he mused, catching himself just before he drooled on his shirt.

With a bemused shake of his head, he knocked lightly on the open door. She jumped and swung around, a hand to her heart.

"Oh, it's you," she said with a shaky, sexy little laugh.

Alex lifted an eyebrow, fighting a wicked urge to tumble her onto the bed and destroy her hard work. "You were expecting someone else?"

"N-no. Just you."

Intrigued by the genuine blush that crept slowly into her cheeks, Alex advanced into the room and grabbed the edge of the quilt. With a nervous glance in his direction, she allowed him to help her spread the quilt.

"Thanks," she said softly, casting him another one of those shy, mysterious glances.

"No problem." Something had changed, Alex thought, wishing he knew what the hell it was. She wasn't acting like . . . Brooke. Instead she was being nice and almost . . . coy?

They both reached for the pillows on the floor. Their heads collided with a solid *thunk*. With a rueful laugh, she held her hand to her head, brushing his concerns aside.

"I'm fine, really. You've got a hard, um, head."

When her gaze dropped slowly and deliberately to another part of his anatomy that was definitely hard, that elusive something became crystal clear.

Brooke was coming on to him. Brooke of the sarcastic wit and the volatile temper . . . was flirting with him, and as with everything else she did, she did it with an energy that stole his breath.

As the realization reached his groin and knocked another inch into his arousal, Alex held his breath and waited for her wandering gaze to come back to his face.

It took a breathtakingly long time. So long, in fact, that Alex feared his jeans would bust wide open. And when she did finally look at him again, her eyes fairly shimmered with heat. An invitation had never been so honest, so open.

The bed was there, ready and waiting, and if he read the signs right, so was Brooke Welch. Alex was struck dumb for a moment. Granted, it was a long moment, one in which he considered staying silent until he'd slaked his thirst on the sexiest woman he'd ever had the pleasure of bumping into.

Afterward he could think about why she'd changed her mind.

But there was one tiny working brain cell left, and that brain cell popped the intrusive question before he wanted it to—before he eagerly shucked his clothes and hers, too.

Why had she changed her mind? He'd love to think it had nothing to do with her finding out who he was, but Alex hadn't become the success he was by wearing rose-colored glasses and thinking with a hard-on.

So it was with deep regret that he stated hoarsely, "You know who I am."

Her eyes changed in a heartbeat. The words *flash freeze* came to Alex's mind. He'd always wondered how it was done; now he knew. For a split second, he wondered if she *hadn't* known his identity.

"You had to go and do it," she said softly. The delectable mounds of her breasts rose as she gathered another mouthful of scorching words. "You just *had* to go and screw things up!"

Alex was completely baffled at her reaction. "All I said was—"

"Don't say it! Do *not* say it again. You've already ruined everything."

"What in the hell are you talking about?" Alex demanded, growing angry himself. He hated being in the dark, and it was pitch-black right now inside his brain. The woman made absolutely no sense at all. Ruined *what?* Ruined her plans to file a sexual harassment suit against him? Ruined her plans to cry rape? Was this what her come-on was all about?

The possibility made Alex's blood heat. Her next statement sent him into a tailspin again.

"It doesn't matter now."

"*What* doesn't matter?" He ran a frustrated hand through his hair. She sounded as if *he'd* done something wrong. In fact, she sounded downright disappointed.

"I can't sleep with you now that it's been said," she announced gloomily, folding her arms across her chest and glaring at him.

"What—" Alex snapped his mouth shut. What good would it do to ask another question? Obviously she intended to drive him crazy, and obviously he wasn't about to get lucky!

Wonder of wonders, she enlightened him.

"I know that you're Alex Bradshaw, my new boss. I was trying to forget that long enough to . . . to . . ."

This time Alex remained unhelpful.

"Well, to get you out of my system," she finished, trailing away to a whisper.

It was the self-disgust he recognized in her voice that made Alex mad. She wanted him—

apparently enough to postpone the moment of reckoning—but now that they both knew that she knew who he was, she couldn't go through with it.

He had a feeling he knew why.

"I didn't send those condom jokes to the factory," Alex said. "And I didn't know about the leaky roof, or the bad equipment."

She lifted a skeptical eyebrow. "And the sick pay?"

"I planned to visit the factory next month. Chances are I would have noticed the outdated policies and made plans to change them."

"Then why are you here now?" she asked sharply.

Alex glanced at the bed, then shifted his gaze to Brooke. Despite the gravity of the conversation, he found it hard to concentrate while standing in the bedroom with her. Incredibly painfully hard. "Let's go into the living room, shall we?"

"Of course." Keeping her arms folded, she marched into the living room.

He followed, taking a stand by the cold fireplace as she perched stiffly on the couch.

"I guess you're going to fire me," she said, sounding so certain of it that Alex almost smiled.

"That depends."

"Here we go again. Look, I'm not going to compensate you by sleeping—"

"And I wouldn't ask," Alex interrupted in a hard voice. "When I mentioned compensation,

I wasn't thinking about sex." *Liar.* He cleared his throat. "I need your help with something that concerns the factory."

Still suspicious, she peered at him through a wisp of strawberry blond hair. "What kind of help?"

"I need some information."

"What makes you think I'd help you?"

"Because until you agree," Alex countered softly, "I remain kidnapped."

Her eyes rounded, then narrowed to glittering amber slits. "You were never actually kidnapped." She flushed and looked away. "Well, maybe at first in the car when you thought I had a gun, but after that you could have left anytime you wanted to."

"I know that and you know that, but it's something the local authorities don't know—until I inform them otherwise."

"Elijah has a big mouth," she muttered.

Sensing victory, Alex relaxed against the mantel. "Meanwhile I'll stay here. I was on my way to vacation in Hot Springs, but this will do nicely."

"You'll get bored," Brooke stated rather smugly. "No TV, no radio, no phones . . . no one to harass."

Alex leisurely drew the victory sign in the dust on the mantel. She'd regained her sarcasm, which he thought was a good sign. Brooke without sarcasm was like a good party punch without the liquor.

Calmly and with more excitement than he'd

felt about anything in a long time, he lit the fuse. "Oh, I don't think I'll get bored. As a matter of fact, I find your company very stimulating."

"But I won't be here," she cried.

He looked at her, watching the light of comprehension dawn in her eyes. "Yes, you will."

Chapter Eleven

He was bluffing. He had to be. Brooke couldn't possibly continue to spend time around Alex Bradshaw without . . . without going stark, raving mad. Look what he'd reduced her to already! Only moments ago she'd been on the verge of undermining her own self-imposed morals by jumping into the sack with him.

No, it just wouldn't work.

"I can't do what you asked," she said in a panicky voice she couldn't control. "You . . . the . . . we . . ." His wolfish smile made her heart seize up like a locked engine.

"Don't worry," he drawled. "I'm not in the habit of forcing myself on an *unwilling* woman."

Brooke leaped to her feet, her fists clenched. She chose to ignore his emphasis on *unwilling*. She knew the description didn't apply to her, and after her mortifying come-on in the bedroom, Alex knew it, too. "That's a laugh! You're forcing me to spy on my own people. Isn't that what you're making me do?"

"I think you owe me."

"Owe you?" Brooke nearly bit her tongue as she spat the words at him, words he'd delivered in a hard-edged, businesslike tone she'd never heard him use until now. "Kidnapping you was an honest mistake." She curled her lip. "Believe me, if I had known who you really were, I wouldn't have come within a hundred feet of you!"

"That's another thing," he said with a casualness that made her want to shove him up the chimney. "Before yesterday you'd never met me, yet you believe everything you've heard about me. I think it's only fair for you to give me the opportunity to change your mind."

Brooke's laugh was filled with scorn. "Oh, you're getting off to a great start by blackmailing me into doing your dirty work. What's this all about, anyway? Did you discover a case of missing paper clips or something equally bogus? Starting out with a new crew would save you millions, wouldn't it? There are a lot of workers close to retirement." When he frowned, she added smugly, "Ha! You didn't think we'd find out? We've heard the rumors about your plan to clean house."

"I own the factory. If I wanted to 'clean house,' I wouldn't have to have an excuse."

"But if you *had* an excuse, it would be just peachy, wouldn't it? Think what a relief that would be for your conscience!"

"You're blowing this all out of proportion. I'm here on a tip from a former employee."

Brooke lifted a taunting brow. "About the missing paper clips?"

"No, it's not about missing paper clips," he snapped impatiently. "It's about someone stealing millions of dollars from the factory." His eyes, now as frosty as her own, locked with hers. "Did you know Daisy Pelinsky?"

"Daisy? The secretary who recently retired?" Brooke gasped at his grim nod. "That sweet little old lady wouldn't steal a pencil, much less millions of dollars!"

"So you trust her implicitly?" he persisted.

Brooke nodded so hard her hair fell forward. She shoved it away. "Yes, I do. She's worked there for years. Surely you can't honestly believe she's the—"

"*She's* the source of the tip, and she didn't retire; she was fired. If we can find out who fired her, then we've probably got our first clue."

Dazed by his news, Brooke sank back down onto the lumpy sofa. If Alex was right and someone was embezzling from the factory, then whoever it was should be caught and punished. "We all just assumed she'd taken an early retirement," she mused out loud.

"Who has the power to fire her?"

She blinked and focused on Alex. "The plant manager, and I suppose any of the supervisors could file a complaint against her." A chill shimmered down her spine. "Didn't Daisy tell you who was responsible?"

Alex shook his head. "I tried to get in touch with her, but her phone had been disconnected. The fax said only that I should check it out."

"Don't you monitor the financial records from your end?"

"Whoever it is has covered their tracks well." His slight hesitation had her tensing for more bad news. "If we can't find anything on our own, I'll have to bring in an auditor."

She gave a shaky sigh of relief. "Oh, I thought you were about to say you'd have to shut the factory down."

"That's a possibility."

Brooke froze, thinking of the hundreds of people who depended on their jobs. People with families. Single mothers with kids. Husbands and wives who both worked at the factory. Even a week without pay could mean the difference between eating and starving. And last but not least, her own job. She paid for Dee's college tuition, the mortgage on the house, and basically all of the household expenses with her salary.

Dry-mouthed, she asked, "What kind of time frame are you talking about?"

He shrugged. "Anywhere from a few days to a month."

Slowly she closed her eyes. No wonder he

looked so grim, she thought. Shutting down the factory would cost him more millions aside from the millions he might have already lost. But while his bank account might suffer a blow, Brooke doubted he would have to worry about starving, or losing his home as so many others would—including herself. She'd mortgaged her home to help offset the cost of Dee's college education.

She was what old-timers called "stuck between a rock and a hard place." If she agreed to spy on her own people and they found out, they'd never forgive her. Plus, there was always the possibility her efforts would be in vain.

But if she refused even to try . . . Brooke shuddered to think of the consequences. Not only would she be a criminal if Alex forged ahead with his threat to press charges against her, she would be jobless, and possibly responsible for hundreds of others losing their jobs.

"What do you want me to do?" she heard herself asking without her usual sarcasm. His smile almost warmed her heart—until she remembered his threat.

"Would your presence at the factory today generate any suspicion?"

Brooke shook her head. "Sometimes I drop in on Saturdays for a quick check." She didn't add that she often filled in for women who couldn't get weekend care for their children.

"See if you can get Daisy's file. There should be a copy of her termination letter."

"Yeah, right. If someone fired her, but wants

everyone to think she retired, do you honestly believe they'd leave that kind of evidence?"

"Good point, but pick it up anyway. She might have left a forwarding address or a clue or something."

She flushed at his admiring look. "I'll pick up some food while I'm out. Do you want me to go by and pick up your things from the hotel?"

"I'm not sure that would be a good idea," Alex mused dryly. "If they're looking for me, they might have someone watching my room."

He *would* have to remind her of the threat hanging over her head, Brooke thought, scowling as she retrieved her jacket and Hugo from the bedroom. She'd "borrowed" the model from the test lab and needed to return it before Monday. There would be hell to pay if Brandy, who tested the condoms at random, discovered it gone.

When she emerged from the bedroom, she glared at him. "Anything else, Your Highness?"

He grinned at her sarcasm. "I wouldn't mind a change of clothing, if you can manage it without looking too suspicious." As he spoke, he pulled out his wallet and extracted a couple of bills.

Brooke's eyes widened at the amount he placed into her hand. "Alex, if I start brandishing hundred-dollar bills around town, they'll not only arrest me, they'll think I robbed the . . . bank. . . ." Her words trailed away when she noticed he'd gone still.

"Say it again," he commanded softly.

"Um, what?" Brooke's mind was suddenly blank. What had she been saying? And what had she said to make him look at her as if . . . as if he'd like to smear her on a Ritz cracker and swallow her whole?

"My name. Say my name again."

Oh, God. She had called him by his first name, Brooke realized with an inward groan. Quickly she tried to undo the damage. "It was a slip of the tongue. You're my boss—"

"I don't care," he interrupted roughly. "Right now I'm on vacation, and you're not at work. Let's forget the boss/employee thing, okay?"

"Not okay." Brooke's chin shot up. "Because I'm not likely to forget who you are, and there's that little matter of my job hanging in the balance if I don't do what you say."

"I'm not the reason your job's in jeopardy."

With a rolling of her eyes, Brooke drawled, "Oh, right. How could I be so stupid? You wouldn't have to fire me. I just wouldn't be able to come to work because I'd be in jail. And of course, that wouldn't be *your* fault, now, would it?"

She should have remembered that she was within snatching distance, and snatch her he did—smack against his chest and nose-to-nose. Her body reacted like a nymphomaniac's after a long abstinence—she had instantly hard nipples and a dampness between her legs.

"I have the damnedest reaction to your temper," he said in a husky growl.

She tried to squirm free, but succeeded only

139

in rubbing her supersensitive nipples against his shirt, and the rough denim of her shorts against that other sensitive area of her body.

Swallowing, Brooke stared into his heated gaze and made a valiant attempt to tone down the sarcasm. "I'll have to remember that."

His hot gaze dropped to her lips. "That would be a shame."

"Why—" Brooke prudently bit her tongue. Instead she reminded him in a raspy voice that betrayed her own arousal, "The factory closes at noon on Saturdays. I should get going."

He brought his mouth temptingly close to hers. "Hurry back . . . I'm hungry."

"Then I'll bring plenty of . . . *food*," Brooke emphasized, praying her jelly legs would hold her when he finally let her go. His deep, rumbling chuckle told her he hadn't missed her hint.

Finally she was free. She wasted no time getting to the door and away from her hunky new boss.

"Oh, and grab a box of condoms while you're at the factory."

A box of condoms? Sliding to a wobbly halt in the doorway, Brooke stumbled around and gaped at him. The nerve of the man! Though she didn't deny he . . . tempted her, that didn't mean that she was willing to compromise her integrity to—

"I might as well inspect the merchandise while I'm here," he added, his expression far too innocent to be real.

"Oh." Red-faced, Brooke slammed out the door, mumbling names beneath her breath that probably would have made him blush to hear.

Still chuckling over the expression on her face, Alex watched from the window as she climbed into the Pinto and started the engine. She peeled the tires and kicked grass and gravel from the wheels as she pulled onto the road.

She'd gone only a few yards when he saw the red glare of her brake lights. Even from this distance, Alex could see her lips moving when she emerged from the Pinto and stomped a few feet behind the car. She leaned over and picked something up, then marched back to the car.

His chuckles turned to belly-rolling laughter when he realized she was putting the errant hubcap back onto the wheel of her car.

Brooke Welch. Sexy, feisty, and single, she was the most exciting thing to happen to him in a long time.

He turned from the window, feeling on top of the world. And why wouldn't he be? He was on vacation, and he hadn't suffered a headache in over twelve hours. True, his factory could be in trouble, but he felt confident he would discover the culprit before too long—with Brooke's help. So he had exaggerated about a few things, like the audit and the factory closing, and the amount of money he believed to be involved. He seriously doubted someone could embezzle millions without arousing a single suspicion.

But what harm could it do to add a little motivation?

This way Brooke could feel like a true heroine and soothe her guilty conscience for spying on her people. *Her people.* Alex smiled. Brooke was loyal and fierce, and not just about her family, he mused. It appeared her loyalty extended to her job as well, which pleased him immensely.

Maybe . . . just maybe Gloria wasn't the last of her kind. Alex grinned and shook his head. No, Brooke and Gloria were *not* alike. Gloria was slow to anger and possessed a vivid imagination that drove Alex to distraction. She was loyal like Brooke, true, but she lacked Brooke's fierce energy and adventurous spirit.

The gravity of his thoughts surprised Alex, as did the pang of longing he felt. Was it more than just a raging lust he felt for Brooke? He shook his head, reminding himself that he hardly knew her.

But if he wasn't feeling more than lust, then why was he already missing her?

Bemused, Alex pushed his chaotic thoughts about Brooke aside for the moment and reached into his boot for his cell phone. It was time to call his overimaginative secretary and straighten out this nonsense. He'd leave it to her to contact the authorities, and ask her to stress the fact that he wanted to remain incognito in Quicksilver. Maybe having to explain her embarrassing mistake would teach her not to jump to conclusions next time.

Of course, he had no intention of letting

Brooke know about the call, or that the police would no longer be looking for him. At least, he wouldn't tell her right away.

For as long as he could, he would use whatever underhanded means necessary to keep her coming back to the cabin.

Alex flipped the cell phone open and pushed the power button. He swore when it began to beep and flash LOW BATTERY across the tiny screen.

The charger was in his briefcase. At the hotel. In Quicksilver. In a room that might be under surveillance.

Damn. He had intended to let Gloria and his family know that he was all right and having the time of his life. Now they would be worried sick, and as a supervisor at his factory, Brooke might be under surveillance.

And she wouldn't have a clue.

Chapter Twelve

Normally Brooke wouldn't panic to see flashing lights in her rearview mirror. She'd gone to high school with both city cops, and her father had been good friends with the sheriff. Any of the three had been known to stop her just to ask her how she was getting along.

But this wasn't an ordinary day, and she didn't feel exactly innocent; she'd kidnapped an important man. To be stopped today of all days seemed far too coincidental for her peace of mind.

"This is it," she mumbled, pulling onto the graveled shoulder. The cop car pulled in right behind her, crushing her faint hope that he'd merely been signaling her to move out of his way. *No such luck.*

Filled with dread, Brooke gripped the wheel and waited. She silently rehearsed her speech. They would believe her. They had to. They'd known her since kindergarten.

They knew she was harmless.

Okay, maybe not exactly harmless when it came to protecting Dee, but mostly harmless. Not your usual, run-of-the-mill kidnapper. They wouldn't even have to use handcuffs, and she already knew her rights. In fact, she knew where Sheriff Snider kept the keys to the jail cells.

A tap at the window made her jump and stifle a shriek. She slowly turned her head.

It was Duncan Gregory, wearing dark shades and a blue uniform that looked fresh from the cleaners. Happily married with four kids, he was tall and slim, with beautiful straight white teeth and a penchant for wearing too much cologne.

He flashed those teeth now in a smile, but with his expression hidden behind the shades, Brooke couldn't relax. Duncan was a small-town cop, but she knew that beneath that casual, laid-back manner there pulsed a sharp brain.

"Hey, Brooke."

Quickly rolling down the window, Brooke took a deep breath, inhaling a lungful of Stetson cologne. "Hey, Duncan." *What's up? Why did you stop me? Do you know what I've done?*

"Guess you have a lot on your mind," Duncan said, bracing his arm across the top of her car and bending down until he was at eye level.

The smile was gone. He looked so stern that Brooke's heart stuttered to a stop. "Wh-what do you mean?"

Duncan's brows rose above his shades at her squeaky question. "Well, I figure you must have, or you would have noticed this falling off." He held up her battered hubcap, his earlier smile returning at her shocked expression. "I've seen you stop and pick this up a dozen times, but today you just kept on going. Don't know why you just don't get another set."

It wasn't the first time someone had made the suggestion, but it was the first time Brooke actually considered listening. She mustered a shaky smile and pulled the hubcap through her open window, pitching it carelessly into the backseat. She didn't care if she ever saw it again. "You know, Duncan, I just might do that. And thanks for going to all the trouble of stopping to pick it up."

Blushing, Duncan tipped his hat. "No trouble, Brooke. None at all. You take care now, you hear?"

"You, too," Brooke said, feeling as if her smiling lips would crack from the strain. He'd stopped her—nearly giving her a heart attack—because of that damned . . . ornery . . . *hubcap!*

"Give Dee Dee my best, will ya?"

"I will." Dee would get a lot more than that, Brooke determined.

When he turned and headed back to his vehicle, Brooke melted against the seat, letting out a long, shaky sigh of pure relief and calling herself a fool. She jerked upright again as Duncan suddenly popped his head into her window.

"Say, did you hear about Alex Bradshaw?"

"Wh-who?" she said in a croak.

"Alex Bradshaw. He's your new boss, remember? I heard you tellin' Sheriff Snider the other day that if you had the chance, you'd tell him what a jackass he was."

Brooke felt hysterical laughter bubble to the surface. She firmly swallowed it. Oh, she'd told him all right.

Right after she had kidnapped him.

She could well imagine Duncan's surprise if she blurted out *that* confession! "Oh, yeah. *That* Alex Bradshaw. What about him?" It wouldn't hurt to get an update. God knew she needed all the help she could get. . . .

"Seems he's missing," Duncan informed her importantly. "Treva Brannum over at the diner was the last person who saw him."

Old news, Brooke mused. She opened her eyes wide and hoped she looked surprised. "You mean he was here in Quicksilver?" she asked in an awed voice.

"Yep. Nobody's seen him since yesterday morning, and he never arrived in Hot Springs like he was supposed to."

"Is that right?"

"Yep, that's right."

"Hmm." Brooke tapped her nails on the steering wheel, hoping Duncan would take the hint. She had about fifteen minutes to get to the factory and think of an excuse to get into the office for Daisy's file.

But Duncan, it seemed, was in the mood for conversation. "Sheriff Snider says the FBI might be called in on this one."

Brooke stiffened. "Isn't that a little extreme? I mean, it's not like they know he's been kidnapped, right? He's just missing."

Duncan shook his head. "I can't tell you anything else. In fact, I shouldn't have said that much."

"Top secret?" Brooke's sarcasm sailed right over his handsome hat.

"You might say that."

A speeding car saved her from further frustration. With a muffled curse, Duncan hurriedly tipped his hat again and jogged back to his patrol car. In a flurry of squalling tires and ear-splitting sirens he tore out after the speeder.

Brooke was left alone to mull over the tiny bit of new information Duncan had let slip. *FBI?* A small shudder swept over her at the possibility. Fooling Duncan and Sheriff Snider, and even Gerald—the other Quicksilver officer—was one thing; fooling the FBI was quite another.

She had a very bad feeling she would rue the day she had kidnapped Alex Bradshaw!

An hour later, with Daisy's file tucked safely beneath the front seat of her car, Brooke let herself into her house. She couldn't wait to hear

Dee's excuse for leaving her caged up all night with the Man of Steel.

The house was empty, but there was a note on the kitchen table that more than explained everything. In fact, it explained things so well that Brooke had to sit down before her knees gave way.

Dee had a good excuse, all right. While Brooke had been kidnapping Alex Bradshaw, Dee had been with Cliff on their way to Vegas to get married. *Cliff called right after you left to go meet him. I'm sorry, Brooke, but you can be scary sometimes. I told him to pick me up here so you wouldn't have the chance to ruin things.*

Brooke knuckled moisture from her eyes, lowering the note to the table. Was she really that scary? Dee's words forced her to stop and consider that maybe she *was* a little . . . excitable? So excitable that she'd pushed her baby sister into possibly making the mistake of a lifetime.

Another tear fell. Brooke gamely got rid of it and forced her chin up. Dee was a grown woman, she reminded herself. If she was big enough to get pregnant, well, then, she was big enough to get married without her sister's help. Worrying would do absolutely no good. She couldn't very well follow Dee to Vegas and make sure everything turned out all right. Besides, wasn't this what she wanted? For Cliff to accept his share of the responsibility?

But she hadn't really believed that he would, hadn't really believed that Dee had picked a suitable mate without her help and guidance.

Hadn't *wanted* to believe it.

The truth was painful, but Brooke forced herself to face it: She didn't want to let go of Dee, because with Dee gone, the nest would be empty. She'd not only be alone, but restless and lost. Since her parents' deaths, she had focused her energies on Dee and on her job, to the exclusion of everything else. Even though she loved her job, she didn't think it would be enough to fill the void with Dee gone.

What would she do without Dee to look after and worry over?

Slowly Brooke looked around at the large kitchen. Her father had owned his own construction business, and he'd designed and built the house when Dee was just a baby. With four bedrooms and two baths, it was too much house for one person.

She should sell it, buy something smaller or rent an apartment. Maybe a two-bedroom for when Dee came to visit. Keeping something this big would be a waste of money.

Brooke picked up the note, her vision blurring on the hastily scrawled postscript at the bottom of the paper. *Get a life, Brooke. You deserve it.*

Get a life, as if she were an aging, pesky maiden aunt or something, living with a relative who didn't have the heart to throw her out. Well, she had a life. She had a wonderful job, and as of yesterday morning, her life had been anything but boring. She'd kidnapped Alex

Bradshaw, head of the Bradshaw Corporation, and had just a few moments earlier added theft to her growing list of crimes by stealing Daisy's file from the new secretary's filing cabinet.

Why, just this morning she'd come a hair-breath away from throwing her ethics out the window and having hot, wild sex with her hunky new boss! Brooke sniffed and straightened her spine. In fact, she could consider this an adventure, and obviously a timely one. If she were busy running around breaking into offices and fighting her own surprisingly strong sexual urges, then she wouldn't have time to snivel about Dee running off to get married, or worry herself sick that Dee was making a mistake.

With determination in her heart, Brooke threw the note aside and stood. She'd let Dee handle her own life for a change. Meanwhile she had a job to do, one that could possibly save hundreds of jobs, not to mention keep her out of jail.

She had a rat to help catch.

Chapter Thirteen

Secrets were hard to keep in a small town like Quicksilver, and normally Brooke didn't mind; before yesterday, she really didn't have much to hide.

But today she did. She felt exposed, as if she wore a T-shirt emblazoned with the words, I KIDNAPPED ALEX BRADSHAW.

It didn't help when Kayla Banes, who worked part-time at the downtown clothing store, pounced on her the moment she came through the door. Kayla's mother and three of her cousins worked at the Safe & Secure condom factory.

"Brooke! Have you heard the news? They think someone kidnapped Alex Bradshaw!"

Around Dee's age, Kayla was dark-haired and plump, with brown eyes that sparkled with energy. She skittered around the counter and began straightening garments on a rack. "Can you imagine anything like that happening in Quicksilver? Are you worried? I mean, what if they find him dead somewhere? What will happen to the factory? Mama's about to have a fit!"

Brooke finally managed to get a word in. "Duncan says he's missing. They haven't verified that it's a kidnapping yet."

Kayla yanked a dress from the hanger and held it to her plump body; it was about two sizes too small. With a grimace, she shoved it back on the hanger. "If he hasn't been kidnapped, why would they offer a reward?"

"Well—"

"I say he's been kidnapped. He's a rich man, and rich people get kidnapped all the time." Hands on hips, Kayla finally gave Brooke her full attention. "So what are you looking for today? Something to wear to Dee's wedding?"

Brooke shouldn't have been surprised, but she was. "How did you know about Dee?"

Kayla grinned. "She and that hunk of hers stopped by here on their way out of town. He bought her that white linen traveling suit we had in the window, and a black negligee."

So while Brooke had been committing a felony, Dee had been buying sexy negligees with Cliff. The irony was just too much.

Shaking her head, Brooke said, "Actually, I'm here to buy . . . Dean Junior something for his birthday." Confident that Kayla wouldn't know Dean's birthday was another three months away, Brooke blithely continued, "I thought I'd get him a couple pairs of jeans and a shirt or two."

"Practical gifts are always good," Kayla agreed brightly. "Let me see. Dean's about a size thirty-six in the waist, and about . . . a thirty-two in length? Does that sound about right?"

"Um, no. I think he's lost some weight. I'd say about a thirty-four in the waist, and make the length a thirty-four." When Kayla's eyebrows shot upward, Brooke swallowed an exasperated curse. "He can always exchange them later."

Finally, after another thirty minutes of blood-boiling argument over shirt sizes, Kayla totaled Brooke's purchases. She must have sensed Brooke's simmering anger, for she didn't blink an eye as Brooke handed her two one-hundred-dollar bills.

Relaxing, Brooke grabbed her change and the bags and made it to the door before Kayla stopped her. She sounded like her usual perky self, but Brooke thought she heard an underlying suspicion that hadn't been there earlier.

"I think it's a good idea to buy presents early, while you've got the money. November will be here before you know it, won't it?"

Kayla was Dee's age, a full fifteen years younger than Dean, who was about to turn thirty-five. Brooke couldn't think of one single reason the girl would know Dean's birth date. None. Zilch.

But she did.

With her hand on the door, Brooke said as calmly as she could manage, "Yes, it *is* a good idea." And because she couldn't resist, she added, "The money came from my savings account, in case you were curious."

"I was. Thanks."

Brooke exited the store before she exploded, and ran smack into her fellow supervisor and friend, Dixie Comford. A few years older than Brooke, Dixie was married with two children. Her husband worked for the local telephone company.

"Brooke! Have you—"

"Yes, I heard about Alex Bradshaw," Brook said in a snarl. When Dixie looked startled, Brook sighed and shook her head. "Sorry. I've been in town only a couple of hours and already I'm sick of hearing about it."

"In town? You mean you've been gone?"

Belatedly realizing her slip, Brooke groaned to herself. "I meant in town as opposed to my house, which is not on Main Street." If she didn't get out of town fast, she was going to blow her own cover!

"Oh." Dixie hooked her long, permed hair behind her ear and grabbed Brooke's arm, drawing her close. "Have they questioned you yet?" she asked in a whisper.

A tremor shot through Brooke; she hoped Dixie hadn't noticed. "Um, no, they haven't. Did they question you?"

Dixie nodded. "Asked me if I'd ever met Alex

Bradshaw, and how I felt about him in general. They've talked to Kyle and a couple of other supervisors, too."

"Who's *they?*" Brooke asked, casting a longing glance at her Pinto parked a few feet away. She wanted to hop in and get the hell out of Dodge!

"Sheriff and some slick-looking guy I've never seen before."

FBI? Brooke's throat went dry at the thought. Alex had been missing less than twenty-four hours. What would happen after a few days . . . a week? From the sound of things, the town would be under siege! She'd have to convince Alex to talk to the authorities and let them know he was not missing—or kidnapped—before this thing got completely out of hand and they arrested someone.

Like herself. The embarrassment alone made her cringe. Even if Alex didn't go through with his threat to press charges, she'd be teased and talked about for months, even years. She could hear it now: *Have you met Brooke Welch? She's the one who kidnapped Alex Bradshaw by mistake!*

Forty years from now she'd still be the one who had kidnapped her boss. There would also be speculation about what they'd done for recreation up in the cabin all alone, and people at the factory—people who trusted her—would wonder what they'd talked about.

A few minutes later, Brooke managed to get away from Dixie and into her car with a promise to call her later. It was an empty promise, but Brooke chalked it up to another necessary lie.

Armed with food, Daisy's file, Alex's new clothes, and the burning knowledge that Dee was probably now in Vegas having the time of her life while Brooke dodged FBI agents and told one lie after another, she headed back to the cabin and her sexy, blackmailing boss.

She watched her rearview mirror more than she watched the road, eating Tums and preparing her speech.

She and Alex Bradshaw had a few things to get straight between them. It was time he realized he couldn't push her around just because he was her employer. Sexual harrassment was only one of the charges she could bring against him, she decided righteously. She could also charge him with blackmail.

By four o'clock, Alex had begun to wonder if Brooke would return. He'd turned on the small, ancient refrigerator, tidied the counters, and caught half a dozen perch using the fishing tackle he'd discovered in the small utility shed behind the cabin.

The perch, cleaned and salted, lay sizzling in foil on the grill out back. A good, cold beer would go nicely with the fish, he thought, hoping Brooke remembered his request.

Alex inhaled, getting a good whiff of his shirt, which smelled of sweat and fish. Once Brooke arrived with his new clothes, he could shower and change into something a little less . . . fragrant. He smiled, imagining her reaction when she saw that he'd prepared dinner.

They'd have a nice, quiet evening. Talk, get to know one another better. He had a feeling Brooke was definitely worth knowing. She'd loosen up, realize he wasn't the monster she thought he was. When she was relaxed, he would pick her up and carry her to the bedroom and make slow, sweet love to her. Okay, so maybe the first time he'd make frantic love to her. Save the slow stuff for the second or third time around—

The sound of a car engine broke into Alex's arousing fantasies. He dried his hands on a towel and went out onto the porch, anticipation zinging through his bloodstream like tiny currents of electricity.

Brooke emerged from the car and eyed him over the top of the battered Pinto, her insolent gaze setting fire to his groin. "You gonna help, or just stand there gawking at me?"

With that stinging remark, she moved to the trunk and stuck her key in the lock. She had to give it a few sharp whacks with her fists before the lid creaked open, disturbing a layer of dust that had settled on the car.

Alex curbed his grin and went to help her, his hungry gaze skimming over her gut-punching figure outlined by snug jeans and a short white tank top. Caught off guard, he grunted as she pushed a bag of groceries into his chest and flicked him a hot, angry glance.

He shifted the sack to one arm and lifted a questioning brow. Five seconds in her company and he was hard as a rock. "Something on your mind?"

"Yes." Reaching inside for another sack, she turned around and caught him in the act of ogling her pert behind. Her eyes narrowed. "And I can see there's something on *your* mind, too."

Prudently, Alex pretended innocence. "Did you get Daisy's file?" She rose and shoved another sack into his other arm before disappearing into the trunk again.

"Yes, I got Daisy's file. I also found out the whole town is looking for you, and the supervisors are being interrogated one by one. Thanks to you, I'm practically a fugitive."

She straightened and blew a strand of red-gold hair from her eyes. "There's a reward offered for any information pertaining to your whereabouts. Isn't it against the law to pretend to be kidnapped?" Before he could answer her growled question, she moved around him to the passenger seat and yanked open the door.

Alex got a full view of her bottom this time as she bent over to retrieve something from under the seat. *Strange.* Denim had never made his mouth water before. . . .

"Something else I think you should know," she continued, backing out of the car and slamming the door. "If I help you, I'll be doing it for the factory and for my friends, not for you or because of your pathetic blackmailing attempts."

She piled a manila folder on top of the sacks he was balancing in his arms. Alex held it in place with his chin, totally besotted with the fireball quivering in front of him. If he hadn't had the bags, he would have pulled her into his arms and silenced her with a very long, pleasurable kiss.

Brooke Welch . . . woman extraordinaire.

"So this is the deal. You go into town and let the sheriff know you're okay, and I'll help you all that I can." She wrinkled her nose as she turned away—empty-handed. "You need a shower. You smell like fish!"

For a long, enjoyable moment, he watched her hips swing as she walked. She had her foot on the bottom step when he said very distinctly, "No."

Her back stiffened. He could almost feel her bristling as she hovered on the steps. Slowly she turned to look at him. She wasn't surprised by his answer, he realized, admiring her bluff.

"They're calling in the FBI," she added as if he hadn't spoken.

Alex believed her; she looked far too solemn to be lying. "That's too bad—and not my problem." It was going to be his secretary's problem when he finally reached her, but that wasn't something he wanted to share with Brooke at the moment. Or even in the next few days. The more he saw of her, the more certain he was of that.

"But . . . but—"

"Why don't we get these groceries put away?"
Alex advanced, and, like a skittish colt, she
scampered up the steps and into the cabin. He
followed and set the sacks on the counter before
turning to look at her. She was breathing hard,
and for a regrettable instant he saw a flicker of
fear in her eyes. His voice softened. "Relax. As
long as you play it cool, they won't know that
you have me."

Her voice shook slightly—more from anger
than fear, he suspected. "I don't *have* you!
You're free to go anytime you want. You can
even take my car!"

"I'm not going anywhere until I find out
what's going on at my factory, and I can't do
that if the entire town knows I'm here."

"Then why don't you stay somewhere else?"
she cried, sounding frustrated. "Why here?"

"I told you before, I like it here. And I like
your company."

"But I don't like you!"

"Don't you?" Alex taunted softly. "If I didn't
smell like fish, I'd show you what a liar you are."
He folded his arms to keep them from reaching
out for her. "You know what I think, Brooke? I
think you're scared."

Her whiskey-hot eyes flashed with scorn. "I'm
not afraid of you. If you wanted to hurt me,
you've had plenty of opportunities."

"That's not what I'm talking about. You're
afraid of *us*."

"There *is* no us!"

Alex began to unfasten his shirt, watching as her gaze dipped down and her eyes widened in alarm. "There is, or will be. Sooner or later." Hesitating long enough to let her imagination soar, he finished unbuttoning his shirt and turned, flinging over his shoulder, "I'm going to take a shower. There's fish on the grill—do you mind checking on it for me?"

He left her standing in the kitchen, her face a comic mixture of confusion, panic, and disappointment.

It was the disappointment that put a spring in his step. Once in the bathroom, Alex forced himself to concentrate on what he should do about this new information. *FBI, huh?* It sounded like Gloria had really gone too far this time. He hoped when this was all over that she learned her lesson.

In the meantime, his first priority was to contact someone and let them know he was okay, so they could call off the heat. To do that, he needed to get that charger for his phone from the hotel room so that he could make the call when Brooke wasn't around. It wasn't exactly chivalrous of him to keep fooling her, but he didn't think she'd hang around just for the hell of it once the threat was gone. No, she was too frightened of what was happening between them.

Standing beneath the cold spray, Alex chuckled, imagining Brooke's reaction when he told her what they had to do.

Chapter Fourteen

Brooke felt the feathery touch of fingers against her neck. She shivered and jerked away, adjusting the rearview mirror until she could glare at Alex, who lay curled in the backseat. "Stop that! You want someone to see you?"

"I hardly think anyone could see my fingers in the dark from another vehicle," he argued.

The sight of his slow, sexy smile curled her toes. She ground her teeth and took a deep breath, wondering how much longer she would be able to resist his charms—and her raging hormones. Both were equally difficult to control, and getting more difficult by the hour. He reminded her of lava creeping down the sides of a volcano: sizzling hot and unstoppable.

165

"This was a bad idea, you know. If we get stopped while you're in the car, then you're busted."

"So are you."

Oh, he was quick. Brooke clenched her jaw. And lethal. Ruthless. Manipulative—with a rock for a heart. "You forget, this is my town and these are my friends. They'd believe me over you any day." If she were a mean, spiteful person, she would add that most of the people in Quicksilver already disliked him.

"But the FBI would believe *me*."

Why? Brooke asked herself. Why did she bother to bluff with Alex? It never worked. "I hate you." The moment she said it, she winced. But pride kept her from retracting the rash, immature statement.

She should have known he'd find it amusing instead of painful. His husky chuckle fired her ears full of heat.

"You know what they say about love and hate. . . ."

Brooke seethed silently and prayed for a flat tire or something. Anything that would delay their arrival in Quicksilver and the task ahead. She'd argued until she'd gotten a bad case of heartburn, but Alex had remained stubbornly insistent that they retrieve his briefcase from his hotel room. Daisy's file had been a disappointment; it held no letter of resignation, and no forwarding address.

Up ahead, the city lights of Quicksilver came into sight. Brooke unconsciously slowed the

Pinto. Her reluctance didn't go unnoticed.

"I've got all night if *you've* got all night," Alex remarked from the backseat. His voice deepened as he added, "Although I can think of several things I'd rather be doing."

She flicked him a look that should have cleaved him in two. He grinned. It had taken her a while to realize it, but Brooke now understood: Alex Bradshaw *enjoyed* getting her riled. He seemed to revel in it.

It was baffling . . . and disturbing.

But then, everything about Alex disturbed her.

She jumped as his warm breath tickled her ear. She took her hand from the wheel and tried to wave him away. "Get down! Are you crazy?"

"I haven't been *down* since I met you," he whispered huskily. "And yes, I'm crazy. You make me crazy."

Her mother would have called him a silver-tongued devil. And she would have been right, Brooke mused, straining to concentrate on the road and not on the hot tongue circling her ear. When his teeth captured her earlobe and tugged gently, Brooke sucked in a sharp gasp and stomped the gas pedal.

Alex flew backward onto the seat.

Brooke giggled at his startled expression, watching him in the rearview mirror. His eyes suddenly narrowed in warning.

"I can take a hint," he said.

"Good."

"But sooner or later we'll be back at the cabin."

Feeling reckless, Brooke arched a brow in the mirror. "So?"

"So . . . payback's a bitch."

Suppressing a shiver at the promise in his eyes, Brooke slowed the Pinto and made the turn leading into town. "You'd better get down out of sight. We're here."

A few moments later she pulled in front of room 205 at the Quicksilver Motel. The row of fifteen rooms faced the road; a sign announcing VACANCIES hung above the office located on the end. Alex had checked into room 208, but they'd both decided it would be wise to scout the area on the off chance that someone was watching the room. Personally Brooke doubted that was the case. Why would the police watch his room? It wasn't likely a kidnapper would return to Alex's room to get his clothes and briefcase. Nobody could be that stupid.

She winced.

"How's it look?" Alex asked, keeping his head down.

Brooke carefully scanned the area. Nothing but empty cars and a giggling couple embracing in the darkened doorway of room 215. They could be undercover police, she supposed, biting her lip as she watched them. She let out a sigh of relief when they finally opened the door and disappeared inside.

"Coast is clear," she announced in an undertone. She reached through the window and opened the door from the outside, leaning forward so that Alex could squeeze between the seats.

Like a shadow, he hurried to his room and slipped inside. The moments seemed to drag by. Brooke kept watch, tapping her nails nervously against the steering wheel.

The thought slipped in as thoughts sometimes did when the mind was given time to think. Slowly she stopped tapping her nails and grew utterly still.

If she left right now, Alex would have a hard time proving that she'd kidnapped him.

If she left right now, he might be angry enough at her desertion to fire her, but at least she wouldn't go to jail.

But if she left right now, Alex would likely be discovered and his cover would be blown. Whoever was stealing from the company would probably either clear out or cover their tracks so they'd never be caught. Alex would be forced to bring in that auditor, and the factory might be closed for an indefinite period of time.

To add insult to injury, he'd probably be forced to replace all of the supervisors if the audit revealed nothing.

Immersed in her dilemma, Brooke was surprised by a sudden, blinding light in her face. She tried to shield her eyes with her hands and bumped her funny bone against the door panel. "Ouch!"

"Brooke? Little Brooke Welch? Is that you? What in the world are you doing out here?"

It was Sheriff Snider, Brooke realized, uncertain whether she should be relieved or alarmed. It could have been one of those agents Dixie had mentioned with a list of tricky questions she really didn't want to answer. Brooke had read somewhere that they were trained to detect a lie by watching someone's facial expressions.

She'd never been good at lying.

"Could you point that light elsewhere, Sheriff?"

"Oh, sorry." He flipped the switch.

Brooke blinked. White spots still danced before her eyes. She hoped her vision cleared before she had to drive again.

"So what are you doing here, Brooke? This seems an unlikely place for a girl like you. Lose your air-conditioning or something?" He followed his questions with his usual friendly smile, but Brooke had a paranoid thing going and couldn't seem to shake it.

She felt as if GUILT were written in big block letters on her forehead. Thinking quickly, she said, "Dee ran off, so I thought—"

"You didn't know?" Sheriff Snider exclaimed, hitching up his pants and looking concerned. "She went to Vegas with that new boyfriend of hers. Heard they were getting married."

Was there anyone who didn't know? Brooke wondered ruefully. She gave the sheriff a wan—and she hoped worried—smile. "I knew she left with him, but I was hoping they hadn't gone far."

"Now, Brooke. You know Dee Dee's a big girl.

She can take care of herself. It's time you live your own life, have some fun. Get yourself a fellow." His brow lowered ominously as he added, "Someone worthier than that Lotus character. He's a womanizer."

Didn't she know it!

"Your daddy wouldn't have liked that guy, I'm thinking."

Brooke bit her lip. She had to agree.

"By the way, there's a fellow in from Amarillo, wants to have a word with you. I think he's talked to all the supervisors except you. You have heard about Alex Bradshaw, haven't you?"

Nodding, Brooke said, "Duncan told me."

"Seems the young Bradshaw's been sick and they're all worried about him."

"Sick?" Alex was sick? He didn't look sick! "Um, what's wrong with him, do you know?"

"I'm thinkin' it's not anything serious, or they would have sent someone besides that private investigator."

A private investigator. Not FBI. Brooke was so happy she could have kissed the sheriff. "Well, you tell him to come by and see me tomorrow, okay?" She wouldn't be home, of course, but Sheriff Snider wouldn't know that. Now that she knew the mystery man's occupation, she also realized she didn't have to talk to him.

It was most certainly best that she didn't. She might be tempted to do something irrational, like throw herself on his mercy before she did something regrettable—like sleeping with the man who was now waving cheerfully at her from the hotel door.

Brooke swallowed a shriek and quickly tore her gaze away from her reckless, crazy boss. Was he trying to get caught? Was he making the mistake a lot of foolish people made by thinking Sheriff Snider was another Barney Fife?

Just as she feared, her strange reaction didn't go unnoticed. Sheriff Snider frowned and glanced sharply behind him. Brooke held her breath and followed his gaze, slumping against the seat when she saw that the doorway Alex had been standing in seconds before was now empty again.

Slowly she closed her eyes, vowing to kill him.

"Everything all right, Brooke?" Sheriff Snider asked gruffly. "You're not in trouble or anything, are you? Because if you are, you know me and your daddy were good friends, and there ain't nothing I wouldn't do for you—"

"I'm fine, Sheriff Snider. I'm just fine. In fact, I need to get back home in case Dee calls." She managed a grateful smile as she started the engine and curled her fingers around the gearshift. "Thanks, Sheriff."

Holding her smile in the hope that Alex was watching through the hotel window, Brooke waved at Sheriff Snider and backed out of the parking space. She hummed softly as she headed to the burger joint for a milk shake. A tall, thick milk shake that would take her a good fifteen or twenty minutes to consume.

Let Alex sweat, she thought with a wicked grin. Let him sit there and wonder if she was coming back for him or running out for good. After nearly giving her a heart attack, he deserved to sweat and worry.

At the drive-up burger joint, Brooke ordered an extra-large chocolate malt. When it arrived she began to sip very slowly, watching people and wondering if Dee and Cliff were husband and wife yet, and whether Alex was sweating or cursing or both.

After twenty minutes she set her empty cup on the tray beneath the speaker and drove slowly back to the hotel.

Not a cruiser in sight. The place looked deserted.

She pulled in front of room 205 and honked the horn. If Alex could be careless, then so could she, she decided with a smug smile. *He'd* be furious for a change, and *she'd* be amused.

Five minutes later Brooke's smug smile faded and she began to worry. Why didn't he come out? Had something happened to him? Was he truly sick, as Sheriff Snider had indicated? Although he appeared healthy—very healthy—he had mentioned something about occasional headaches. . . .

She let another few minutes crawl by before she got out of the car and knocked on the door. When no one answered, she tried the knob.

It was unlocked.

Imagining the worst, she pushed open the

173

door and rushed inside. "Alex? Alex, are you in here?"

The only thing that kept the room from total darkness was the light shining through a gap in the curtains. It cast a silvery line across the double bed.

"Alex?"

She was grabbed from behind, one steely arm clamping around her waist and a big hand closing over her mouth. She was hauled against a hard, warm male body.

Brooke froze, her nose quivering as she inhaled the faint odor of fish. Alex, she thought instantly, relaxing against him. She felt the hard length of him pressed against her backside, hot and throbbing. The man was *always* hot and throbbing. But then, so was she when he was around. . . .

His hand slowly tunneled beneath her shirt and closed over her breast. She arched against him, her breath hissing between her tightly clenched teeth. Against her ear, Alex whispered huskily, "I told you payback was a bitch, didn't I?"

Chapter Fifteen

He thought rubbing the pad of his thumb across her nipple was payback?

Brooke let out a ragged breath, melting against him as a riot of sensation ricocheted through her. She allowed the moment of insanity to stretch because . . . well, because it felt so damned good!

She immediately tensed again as he began to walk her toward the bed, his thumb moving relentlessly against her hard nipple. He shifted his other hand down to lie against her belly, causing her to clench her stomach in reaction to the heat of his hand.

When they reached the bed he turned her

around in his arms and pushed her gently backward.

Brooke fell onto the neatly made bed because her legs wouldn't work. Her arms wouldn't either, for that matter. Why else would they reach out for him when she should be pushing him away? He was her boss—another power wielder like Kyle. Not only her boss, but the very man who had blackmailed her as casually as he might order a pizza.

But reach she did, and into her arms he came, every rock-hard inch of him pressed along her body like a hot, steaming iron against cotton. He locked that power mouth onto hers and proceeded to make her mindless with wanting him, so mindless she didn't even care when he raked her top up to expose her surging breasts, and when his hot mouth searched for and found her nipple, she closed her eyes and groaned instead of shouting for him to stop.

And when he closed his teeth gently over that shameless point thrusting upward for attention, she didn't berate him as she should have. *Oh, no.* She clutched his head and pressed his mouth harder against her flushed, aching breast, shameless in her need.

This was what she wanted, and she knew he wanted it, too.

Why not? Why not just forget who he was and get lost in his arms—his very strong, very irresistible arms? Rid herself once and for all of that tingling throbbing he'd caused from the moment they'd met?

Right now, Brooke couldn't think of one single reason not to go ahead and just do it.

So she stopped thinking, and started feeling and enjoying and participating. . . .

As Scarlett O'Hara had declared, tomorrow was another day.

Alex was in heaven.

She was a perfect fit—for his hands, his mouth, and that part of him that throbbed and threatened to burst the strong denim of his jeans.

She cradled his length as if she'd been custom-made for him and him alone, closing around him and pulsing against him until he had to grit his teeth to keep from snarling like a wild animal.

Her essence, a mysterious, womanly scent, called to him like one jungle beast to another. She smelled of a summer breeze and sunflowers, but beneath those more obvious scents, Alex was lured by the sweet smell of desire.

She wanted him.

Brooke Welch, of no-man's-land, wanted *him*. He could smell it, sense it, and feel it.

The knowledge caused his heart to flood with a mingling of pride and pure, arrogant male satisfaction. To find the one woman who could make him forget everything but the moment at hand, and then have her arching and writhing with need beneath him, was the ultimate fantasy come true.

He wanted to make the most of it. To make

her pant and whine like a woman with an itch, and snarl and growl like an animal in heat.

He also wanted to make the moments last, to draw them out and make slow, sweet love to her so that when it was over and done she couldn't forget. He wanted to make her feel cherished. Make her aware of how precious she was, of how very unique he thought her to be, and of how privileged he felt just being with her now . . . this close.

But Brooke, it seemed, entertained no such womanly thoughts of a leisurely hour of love-making. She tugged his head up and reached for the buttons on his new shirt with a zeal that was uniquely Brooke. Alex rose, straddling her to give her better access. Through the faint light from the window, he looked into her liquid amber eyes and saw an uncensored hunger that stole his breath.

This fiery woman beneath him on the bed meant business.

"Get out of your clothes," she commanded in a husky whisper. "Before I rip them off."

The sound of her husky voice and the touch of her frantic fingers against his skin as she fought with his buttons were enough to make Alex growl a warning: "If you plan to change your mind, you've got about five seconds."

A button popped from his shirt, landing on the floor with a *ping*. Her penetrating gaze never wavered from his. "One . . . two," she chanted. Another button came undone, then another. He inhaled sharply as her knuckles grazed his stomach. "Three . . . four . . . five." Her small, perky breasts rose and fell with each agitated breath she took. "Now let's get naked."

Alex gave a laugh that ended on a groan as she finished the last button and splayed her hands across his chest. She raised her head and trailed her tongue from one nipple to the other, lingering to nibble and suck each peak as he had done to her moments before. Her hard, pebbled nipples scraped his belly.

He prudently grabbed her wrists and held her away, his voice now hoarse from the strain of holding back. "If you keep doing that, you'll be counting even less when I'm finally inside you."

Her eyes glazed over, proving to Alex what he'd only suspected—and hoped: Brooke loved pillow talk. It was a good thing, too, because he was in the mood to talk it.

But while Brooke might have been distracted by desire, her witty tongue wasn't. Above her glazed eyes, she arched a pert brow and drawled breathlessly, "I'm beginning to wonder if we're ever going to get to that part."

Alex grinned, slowly shrugging his shirt from his shoulders. He reached out, lifted her up, and single-handedly drew her tank top over her head, exposing her bare breasts to his hungry gaze. No . . . Brooke definitely had no need for a bra.

She was magnificently formed, with firm, just-the-right-size breasts topped by dark, jutting nipples. He closed his hands over the quivering mounds, watching her as she arched and closed her eyes, her obvious pleasure becoming his own.

With her eyes closed, she tucked her lip between her teeth as he rolled her nipples between his fingers. Blindly she reached for the button on his jeans, unfastened it, and slowly opened his zipper, drawing it down inch by torturous inch.

Alex filled his hands with her breasts and watched her tense, flushed face. He tried not to think about what she was doing, because he hadn't been kidding when he hinted to her that he didn't have much control left in reserve.

She didn't stop until he'd sprung completely free of his confinement.

The shock of her fingers curling around him made Alex let out a harsh gasp and surge forward. He nearly exploded in her hand, baring his teeth as he fought for control. The minx was fire and temptation beyond anything he could imagine.

For the second time, Alex grasped her arms and held her away from him to save himself and her from certain disappointment. Her fierce frown made him smile. He kissed her fingertips, then drew her finger into his mouth and sucked hard.

Her eyes widened in surprise.

"The fun has only just begun," he whispered, still smiling. He reached for the snap on her jeans and flicked it open. Mocking her earlier torture, he slowly drew the zipper along the track until he glimpsed the top of her skimpy panties.

The white scrap of silk was hardly enough to cover the soft vee of red-gold curls his fingers yearned to touch.

But not yet. Now that she wasn't touching him, he was ready to extend the foreplay. He wanted to explore every inch of her firm, trembling body. Taste her skin, nibble and lick every hollow and curve.

Find her secret places. All women had secret places, Alex had discovered long ago, but not all were willing to share the knowledge with a partner.

Before this night was up, Alex vowed he would know Brooke's secret places. Each and every one of them.

And he would start right now.

He drew her jeans along her thighs, down to her knees, and onto her ankles before tossing them to the floor. When she tried to reach for him, he shook his head, his smile both rueful and tender. "No, don't. Trust me, you don't want to touch me right now."

Her sultry gaze dropped to his hard, jutting length. He watched, fascinated, as her swollen lips moved.

"I don't?"

Disappointment had never sounded so sweet to Alex. "No, you don't. He hooked his fingers in the tops of her panties and edged them down the path her jeans had taken. "I want to see all of you . . . touch all of you."

She licked her lips, her breath coming faster as she watched him through heavy-lidded eyes. "And then it's my turn?"

"Yes." The word came out on a satisfied sigh as Alex drew his gaze slowly along her body. She was a tiny thing, but there was nothing tiny about her sex appeal.

"I want to taste you," Alex said hoarsely. He didn't add that he'd never wanted anything more in his life, but the thought was there. He knew instinctively that her flower held the sweetest nectar in the garden.

Brooke, apparently, was innocent enough to misconstrue his words. She reached for him with eager arms to pull his mouth to hers.

Alex gently pushed her back and shook his head. "No, not that kind of tasting." He placed the tip of his finger in the center of her red-gold curls. Her startled cry as she arched her hips against his hand nearly drowned out his next words. "I want to taste *you.*"

But she heard. Her eyes, so dark and luminous with desire, flooded with confusion. She glanced at his hand, then back to his face. Comprehension slowly dawned. "You . . . you mean you want to—"

"Yes."

The air between them became hushed with tension.

Alex took advantage of her silence. He lifted her ankle and nibbled his way along her leg to her silken inner thigh. Once there, he paused to look at her.

She stared back at him, her eyes huge and eloquent with apprehension . . . and anticipation.

Close to exploding again, Alex took several ragged breaths before moving up to place his hungry lips where the nectar was the sweetest.

Her fingers grabbed frantically at his head, first trying to pull him away. Alex ignored her; it wasn't hard to do, for he was having the time of his life.

She was exactly as he'd thought—sweeter than the sweetest honey. Hot and throbbing against his lips.

But after a few seconds she no longer tugged at his hair. She pressed him close, squirming and bucking beneath him. Alex held her firmly, relentless in his quest to bring her the ultimate sexual pleasure.

Within moments she began to shudder and spasm, crying his name.

It was a beautiful sound, and every bit as satisfying as he thought it would be.

When her shudders gave way to trembling, Alex moved his body over her, kissing his way along her navel, then latching onto a quivering, turgid nipple. Although he ached to bury himself inside her, he tempered his need, taking his time until he finally reached her mouth.

Her whimper of gratitude inflamed his already ignited senses. He could wait no longer. He shifted his hips and came to rest between her thighs as if he'd been there a thousand times.

A perfect fit, just as he had instinctively known it would be. Brooke transcended everything and anything he'd imagined—

"Wait."

That single, breathlessly whispered word froze Alex from head to toe. With remarkable control, he kept that one quivering, pulsing, hard part of him from ignoring her and plunging ahead.

Wait? Was she serious? Wait—now? He was poised at the gates of heaven and she wanted him to wait?

"You have to use a condom."

Protection. Alex gave his burning forehead a mental slap. Of course she wanted a condom! He was a stickler for those himself, and until tonight he never would have considered making love without one.

Until tonight and Brooke.

It was a sobering thought.

Then his next thought obliterated his first one.

He didn't have a condom.

For a while after his divorce from April, he'd kept a condom in his billfold like a lot of red-blooded males, hoping to get lucky with the right girl. It had finally worn through the package and he'd thrown it in the trash.

After April, he hadn't cared much for courtship or sex, finding it safer and more satisfying to bury himself in his work.

Until Brooke.

And she wanted a condom. Her baby sister

was pregnant, so of course she'd want a condom. She hardly knew him—knew nothing of his sexual habits—so of course she'd want a condom. In this day and age, anyone with any sense at all would want to use a condom. Under normal circumstances—which had been far too few since April—using a condom would have been as natural as breathing to him.

Alex moaned, burying his sweaty forehead against her neck. Unbelievable. Incredible. Totally inexcusable.

He owned a condom factory, and didn't have a condom.

Embarrassed, frustrated, his voice muffled, he said the damning words: "I don't have one." Then, not bothering to hide his desperation, he added, "Aren't you on the pill?" It didn't solve the problem of disease, but he trusted her—although he didn't know why—and knew due to the recent battery of tests his doctor had performed that he was clean as a whistle.

He felt the negative shake of her head against his shoulder before she whispered, "I don't do this kind of thing . . . very often."

His rueful chuckle sadly lacked humor, and his voice literally squeaked with frustration. "I own a damned condom factory and you work there, but between us we don't have a condom."

Alex didn't realize he'd said something wrong until she went still and stiff beneath him. Her voice startled him with its clarity.

"Thanks for reminding me. And before you waste your breath trying to persuade me, *boss man*, I don't intend to go any further without protection. So get off of me."

Alex was too surprised to resist the sudden shove. He rolled over, landing on his back. Bewildered, he lay there as she rose from the bed and gathered her clothing.

Boss man. He discovered he much preferred *hotshot* or *lover boy. Boss man* was something he never wanted to hear from Brooke's lips. He'd known from the start he wouldn't like it.

"You just had to go and screw things up again," she said, stepping into her tiny silk panties and jerking them over her hips.

It wasn't easy, but Alex managed to ignore the sharp throbbing in his groin. God, she was beautiful! Quashing his desire for the moment, he said, "You can't keep pretending I'm not who I am, Brooke." When she flashed him an *Oh yeah?* look, he added in a hard voice, "I'm Alex Bradshaw. I can't change who I am."

She zipped her jeans and snapped them.

The rest of her remained deliciously, arousingly bare as she stood straight, planted her hands on her hips, and looked him in the eye. At the sight of her pointed nipples, he had to clench his hands to keep them from reaching out.

"I wish you could," she said in a tone that left him convinced she meant it. "I really . . . wish . . . you could."

Chapter Sixteen

Alex studied the closed bedroom door a long moment before he flipped open his briefcase. Extracting his cell phone charger, he tiptoed across the room and plugged it in, then retrieved his cell phone from his boot. He connected the two and, quiet as a mouse, slid the phone out of sight behind a dusty, fake potted fern in the corner of the room.

He hadn't dared use the phone at the motel in case the police were monitoring it. Well, by morning the cell phone would be charged and ready. He could call Gloria. She in turn would alert the local authorities and they would call off the search. Sooner or later Brooke would realize they were no longer looking for him, but by that time he hoped she would be involved enough in his investigation to want to stay and help him.

That was, if she got over wanting to strangle him.

An image of her standing by the bed, bare-breasted and trembling, flashed through his mind. Heat shot to his groin like white-hot lightning. He felt as if he'd been sizzled and fried.

Hell, no—that wasn't right, because he was still sizzling! He'd been so close to sinking into her eager warmth when she'd whispered those words.

You have to use a condom.

Alex closed his eyes. How close he'd been to babbling like a sex-starved idiot, telling her he'd recently been tested for everything under the sun, assuring her that if a baby resulted in their union, he would gladly marry her.

Gladly? Alex wiped his hand over his face and took a deep breath. *Okay.* Yes, he was losing his head over Brooke. She was the freshest, most invigorating woman he'd ever met. *Oh, and don't forget the sexiest, most arousing . . .*

He wanted her so badly his teeth ached.

And if that meant he had to use underhanded means to keep her around, then he would. Once she fell in love with him, she'd forgive him for his dastardly deeds.

Wouldn't she?

He grinned foolishly behind his hand, trying to imagine Brooke in a forgiving mood, especially when she discovered he'd never intended to press charges. Hell, the way she turned him on now—when she was furious most of the time—he dared not imagine how he'd react to Brooke when she was in a loving mood.

Tonight at the hotel her mood had been almost . . . savage. Once she'd acknowledged her desire, she'd surpassed his wildest expectations. And though she might have fooled herself into believing she was angry because she'd come to her senses, she hadn't fooled Alex.

Brooke had been angry because their lovemaking had stopped short of consummation.

Alex glanced at the box of condoms sitting beside his briefcase—the ones Brooke had brought him from the factory, at his request, along with Daisy's useless file. He didn't try to kid himself into thinking he'd have a chance to use them now, but just in case, it was comforting to know they were there.

Lots of them.

In the meantime, for as long as he could, he'd keep her so distracted she'd forget that *he* was now the hunter, and she the hunted.

Hmm. He liked the sound of that. Hunter. Yes, he was hunting . . . for love. Just shy of two days after meeting Brooke, he suspected she was the one woman he wouldn't and couldn't forget. And like any good hunter, he would use every call known to man to lure his game, including the most natural lure: sexual desire.

After tonight she'd left him in no doubt she

was hot for him—almost as hot as he was for her.

He couldn't wait to get burned.

Brooke had never been more miserable in her life.

She lay propped on her pillow in the bedroom, studying the far wall and wishing she had a stack of plates or a few cracked cups to chunk at it.

Okay, so she lied. She wanted a *case* of cups or several stacks of plates. More than a dozen. It scared her, this craving for the sound of shattering china.

He must hate her now.

Or worse, think she was the biggest tease in the entire world. He'd never know the truth: that it had taken an enormous amount of willpower to shove him away.

But how could she not? How could she risk pregnancy—or disease—after she'd pounded warnings into Dee's head a thousand times? She'd be worse than a hypocrite; she'd be a fool. Ten times more a fool than Dee.

At least Dee professed to love Cliff, while *she* barely even liked Alex. Lust, that was all it was and ever would be between them. She wasn't naive enough to think a big man like Alex could be serious about someone like her—a lowly factory worker. He probably had tons of spoiled, gorgeous socialites lounging on his arm when he wasn't being kidnapped by one of his deranged supervisors.

Not that she wasn't talented and special. Why, she possessed talents that would make Alex lift those beautiful, sexy black brows in surprise. Brooke scowled at the wall. As if he'd be impressed by her talent for solving problems among her crew—which had gotten her the job as supervisor. He probably wouldn't even be impressed by her ability to perform miracles under pressure, like the time Susannah Createn had decided to have her third child right there on the floor of the factory. While everyone else panicked and ran in circles, she had calmly called the ambulance, then proceeded to deliver the baby, who wouldn't wait.

The memory made her smile. Susannah had even named the baby after her, and still talked about the event as if Brooke had performed a miracle.

Brooke flopped onto her stomach and pressed her cheek against the musty-smelling pillow. She felt selfish and mean for leaving him in that . . . that gloriously aroused state. Worse, she was still aching as if she'd never experienced the most intense satisfaction of her life!

The plain fact was that she'd wanted to feel him inside her in the worst way, wanted to hear him cry her name, growl with pleasure. Alex had done things to her she could scarcely recall now without blushing, yet she'd still wanted it all, every amazing, silken inch of him.

She'd been warned by the other women at the factory what abstinence could do to a person. Oh, she had certainly rued the day she'd confessed that she hadn't had sex since her single, disappointing encounter in the backseat of a Thunderbird during her senior year of high school.

She'd kept her abstinence a secret until last year at the factory Christmas party. Tipsy from too much alcoholic punch, she'd spilled the beans to her friends and coworkers and had regretted it ever since.

The women—mostly married or engaged— had decided to make Brooke their own special project by helping her get laid. Condoms had appeared in her purse, her pockets, and her car. Neon blue, hot pink, lime green . . . the list grew so endless that Brooke had decided to start a collection. It seemed such a waste to throw them away.

She never thought she'd use them, because the sad fact was, she didn't *want* to have sex. Most of the men she knew, she knew very well, since childhood. The others were married or otherwise taken. And last but not least, she'd been determined to set a good example for her baby sister.

Then Kyle Lotus, the married, handsome plant manager who kept the married women sighing wistfully and the single ones hoping, got a divorce. He began to play the field, with Brooke being his first choice. Encouraged by her peers to give it a go, Brooke was at first flattered by her superior's attention.

She agreed to go on a date with him.

One date turned into two, and two into several dozen. Just when Brooke began to relax and believe she'd found someone compatible—someone she might eventually want to develop an intimate relationship with—she found out he was also dating Connie Reeves.

And Dana Kilworth, and Sabrina Ann Hayes, whom everyone knew enjoyed a variety of bed partners . . .

Brooke squeezed her eyes shut at the memory. It was her friends' attitudes, when they gazed at her with open pity, that had been the ultimate humiliation. Her pride had suffered a rotten blow, slightly redeemed by the knowledge that she wasn't in love with Kyle, wasn't even all that attracted to him.

In fact, she couldn't remember a single date when she'd been tempted to have sex with him, although he'd indicated a willingness from the get-go.

With Alex it was instantaneous, spontaneous, and mind-blowing from the moment they met. The embarrassing, humiliating part came later, after the searing fire died enough to let rational thought creep in.

Why Alex? He was her boss—just one of many reasons to avoid him! Her experience with Kyle had taught her that dating the boss wasn't a good idea. In fact, it was a rotten idea.

Not that Alex had said anything about dating. He hadn't tried anything that subtle, and she wasn't foolish enough to think he was interested in anything but sex.

The memory of his lovemaking shimmered

through her. She tightened her arms around the pillow and tried not to imagine how the rest of it would have gone.

It was no use. She could think of little else.

In the wee hours of the morning, Alex awoke to the beep of his watch alarm. He tiptoed to the cell phone, unplugged it from the charger, and slipped outside. He wanted to make the call now because he didn't know when he'd get the opportunity after Brooke awakened.

Gloria answered on the second ring, as if she'd been waiting for his call. Alex smiled faintly at the sound of her croaking, anxious voice.

"Gloria? It's Alex—"

"Alex! Where in the heck are you? Are you all right? Oh, God, have they hurt you? I tried to convince those idiots you've been kidnapped, but they wouldn't take me seriously!"

"Gloria—"

"I figured they'd just kill you to shut you up, maybe bury you someplace out in those god-forsaken woods. But I guess those rats didn't know that *I* knew what was going on, too!"

"Gloria, it's not like—"

"How did you get away? Do they know you're calling?" Alex heard Gloria suck in a horrified breath before she said, "They aren't . . . they aren't holding you hostage for money, are they? People like that are crazy, Alex, so you have to be careful! If they suspect that someone else knows what they're up to, they might go ahead and kill you!"

Alex pinched the bridge of his nose and bowed his head. He let her ramble furiously for another moment before he broke in. "I haven't been kidnapped, Gloria."

"What?"

He imagined her surprised—and probably, if she were honest, slightly disappointed—expression. "I said that I have not been kidnapped."

"Then . . . then why didn't you call? And don't think you can fool me, Alex. I heard that woman talking in the background! Are they making you say this, Alex? If they are, just say yes."

"No. They aren't—nobody's making me say anything. I'm free to go and do as I please, and I have not been kidnapped." How many more times would he have to say it to convince her? "I haven't called because my phone went dead and I couldn't get to another phone. Now, you have to notify the authorities and let them know that I'm not lost, and that I'd prefer to remain incognito in Quicksilver. Tell them—*make* them understand that I don't want my cover blown."

"Your *cover* blown?" Gloria said in a squeak. "Alex! You're not a trained cop! You can't just go around conducting secret investigations like . . . like James Bond, or something! These people could be dangerous!"

Alex couldn't resist a laugh, thinking of Brooke and her fake pistol. "They're not dangerous, believe me."

"Are you sure, Alex? Positively sure?"

"Positively sure, Gloria. I've got to go. I'll try

to keep in touch, but don't panic if you don't hear from me for a few days. I've found the perfect vacation spot near the factory, and I've got someone helping me investigate Daisy's claim of an embezzling scheme."

"Oh. You mean the woman I heard in the background the last time you called?"

"Yes. She's one of our supervisors. Brooke Welch."

"Are you sure you can trust her, Alex?"

His hesitation lasted a nanosecond. "Yes. I'm sure." No need to explain to Gloria about his threat of pressing charges, or Brooke's reluctance in the matter. She'd come around. "Gloria . . . there's a leak in the break room at the factory. I want you to get a crew on it Monday."

"If you're planning to remain incognito, won't that make people suspicious?"

"If you get someone on this quickly, they'll just assume I ordered the repairs before I disappeared." Alex checked the front door before he continued. "Also, I want you and Derrick to go over the company handbook and get it updated ASAP. Tell him to use the boilerplate of our other factory handbooks." Derrick was Gloria's assistant, a sharp college graduate working his way up the corporate ladder. Gloria worked him relentlessly.

"Yes, sir, boss. Anything else?"

Alex stifled a sigh at her flippant tone. He supposed she deserved to be insubordinate after she'd spent the last forty-eight hours believing he'd been kidnapped. Twisting around, he eyed the back of Brooke's dusty Pinto. "Yes, there is something else. Ask Derrick to call around to the salvage yards and see if he can find a set of hubcaps for a seventy-two model Ford Pinto."

"Excuse me? Did you say *hubcaps?*"

Grinning at her squeaky tone, Alex said, "Yes, hubcaps. Used hubcaps, like the kind you see on automobiles. Originals."

"For a Ford Pinto."

"A *seventy-two* model Ford Pinto," Alex corrected.

Silence reined. His odd request had stunned his secretary, as he had known it would.

"Alex . . . are you okay? Are the headaches—"

"I haven't had a headache since I arrived." Well, maybe a small one, but that had gradually disappeared.

"Are you certain you're okay? Is this . . . is this about Brooke Welch?"

Nothing subtle about Gloria, Alex mused dryly. He hesitated, but finally saw no harm in admitting the truth. "Yes, it's about her. I like her." Mild for what he really felt, but he didn't have time to get into it now.

"Oh."

Once again, he had stunned the unstunnable Gloria Coltrain. Chuckling, Alex promised to call her back in a day or two, and hung up. He flipped the phone shut and headed for the cabin. Curiosity would just about kill Gloria, but he figured he owed her one.

As he bounced up the steps, he sensed someone watching him. He glanced up to find

Brooke standing in the doorway. She looked heavy-eyed from sleep and gloriously tousled, but there was nothing sleepy about the gaze focused on the boot he'd slipped the phone into seconds before.

Alex braced himself for the storm and tried to keep his eyes where they belonged—which was *not* on her agitated chest. She probably wouldn't fold her arms like that, Alex found himself musing, if she knew what it did to him.

"You were on the phone."

No doubt about it: she had seen him.

Chapter Seventeen

Brooke wasn't certain if she should be furious about his deception, or elated.

She decided to be furious first—in case there was no reason to be elated. "Who were you talking to?"

He was silhouetted by the rising sun, and his expression remained frustratingly elusive as he finally lifted his gaze and leveled it on her face. "My secretary."

A sprig of hope blossomed in Brooke's breast. She moved a tiny step forward until she was in his shadow and didn't have to squint to look at him. "So you've changed your mind?"

"No. Only Gloria knows where I am, and she's not talking."

That little sprig of hope shriveled and died. To hide her disappointment, she went back to being furious. She did it to keep herself in line; it certainly didn't deter Alex! "What kind of man keeps a phone in his boot?"

His teeth flashed in an easy, boyish grin. "The kind who loses them?"

"You're crazy," Brooke muttered, wondering how long he'd been awake. Obviously long enough to look well rested and hopelessly attractive.

"Maybe." His gaze dropped along her body, leaving heat in its wake. When he finally looked at her again, his eyes had darkened, and his voice had deepened. "Maybe I am at that."

Brooke let out a disgusted sigh, moving her arms to cover the telltale points of her nipples. She didn't normally need a bra, but lately she'd been needing one a lot. "Do you ever think about anything else?"

His gaze widened comically. "*Is* there anything else?"

"You sound like a teenager."

"I feel like a teenager. You make me feel like one."

Brooke tossed her head and shot him an exasperated look. "That's the cheesiest line I've ever heard."

"It's the truth."

"Like hell."

"Want me to show you?" He stepped forward.

She stepped backward quickly. "No! What I want you to do is stop . . . stop—"

"Turning you on?"

"You're not turning me on!"

"I'm not?"

Before she could back out of his way, he reached out and peeled her arms from her chest. He spread them wide. She knew without looking down that her nipples were hard.

"Hmm." He studied her breasts until they began to ache. "It's about seventy-five degrees out here, so you can't be cold. . . ."

"Oh, shut up!" Brooke jerked her arms free and whirled away from him, breathing hard. This insanity had to stop. Either he stopped tormenting her, or she would gladly go to jail.

She rushed to the stove and began making coffee, mentally deciding which pan she'd use if he came after her. The iron skillet might cause too much damage, but the small, lightweight pot nestled inside it would do nicely. She grabbed the handle and banged it onto the stovetop so that it would be within easy reach.

He'd had a cell phone all along! The realization made her seethe anew. If she had known about the phone, she could have called Dee the first night. Of course Dee wouldn't have answered, since she was off marrying Cliff, but Brooke might have figured things out a lot quicker if she had known Dee wasn't home.

Then she wouldn't have had to spend the night with her tormenting boss.

The sound of the bathroom door closing gave Brooke an opportunity to relax her vigil. When she heard the shower, she gave way and leaned against the counter, pressing her flushed, heated face into her palms. Again she asked herself why she fought it, and again she came up with ten good reasons not to sleep with Alex.

Jeopardize her integrity for a few moments of rapture? *Nah.* She was a grown woman, not the hormonally charged teenager she had accused Alex of resembling.

Risk getting fired when he finished with her? She had already been passed over for a promotion she deserved because of her relationship with Kyle. Definitely not smart.

Take the chance of getting her heart broken? Brooke paused over that one, letting her hands fall to her sides. She stared out the little window above the sink at the placid lake beyond. Was this turning into more for her than just a physical attraction? If it was, then she was a bigger fool than she'd first thought.

To fall in love with a successful, drop-dead-gorgeous man like Alex would take enormous courage, and courage wasn't something she had in abundance—when it came to romance.

"I'm hungry. How about you?"

At the sound of his voice, Brooke gave a start. She hadn't heard the shower stop or the bathroom door opening, she'd been so immersed in her thoughts. Slowly she turned around and feasted her eyes on the sight of his damp chest and wet hair.

As usual, he'd read her mind.

* * *

They ate breakfast on the back patio over-looking the lake at a small table her daddy had taken great pleasure in making. He'd built houses for a living, but making furniture had been his true love. He'd talked of pursuing the hobby when he retired. . . .

Brooke swallowed a pang of loss along with the last bite of her western omelet. She flashed the man seated opposite her a disgruntled glance he couldn't fail to miss.

"You don't like my cooking?"

"It was delicious," she snapped ungraciously. And it was, which was the problem. There were too many attractive things about Alex Brad-shaw. And now she had discovered that he could cook. "Is there anything you don't know how to do?"

"Is there anything that doesn't make you an-gry?" he returned pleasantly, smearing another slice of toast with the homemade orange mar-malade Brooke had found in the pantry.

Her mother had loved to can jellies, pre-serves, pickles, and all sorts of colorful relishes that she gave away at Christmas. Brooke blinked the blur from her eyes and straightened her spine. She shouldn't have come here, know-ing the painful reminders would be all around her.

"Would you mind telling me what you know about the other supervisors? That is, if it doesn't make you angry. . . ."

Brooke made a face at him, pulling her gaze away from the strong, tanned column of his throat. "Why should I mind ratting on my friends and coworkers? I've only known them most of my life. Went to school with them, shared their joys and their sorrows, listened to their problems—"

Alex held up his hand, slanting her a dry look. "Why don't we make a deal? For the duration of the present conversation, I'll keep my hands and my eyes to myself, and you put the sarcasm on hold."

"And the sexual innuendos?"

"You can keep making those."

"I—" She clamped her lips together at his wicked grin. Her fingers curled tightly around her fork. In a million years she wouldn't tell him that even without the touching, looking, and innuendos, it disturbed her just being this close to him—looking at him. Aroused her, distracted her.

"Okay, I'll try." She didn't sound confident that she could do it, which made him keep on grinning. The man was impossible. "But I'm warning you, I draw the line at talking about their sex lives."

"You know about their sex lives?"

Brooke smiled at his astonished expression. "It's a small town and a small factory. I've been told I have a knack for listening."

"So you're Safe and Secure's Dear Abby?"

She shook her head. "No. Dear Abby gives advice, and I mostly just listen. I don't think I've had enough life experience to be giving much advice." When she saw his eyes light with interest, she hastened to add, "Don't even think about interrogating *me*."

"You're one of the supervisors," he pointed out.

"But *I'm* not under suspicion." When he continued to stare at her, she scowled. "Think about it, Alex. If I were the guilty one, do you think I'd be here?" She laughed shortly. "I would never have returned when I left yesterday!"

"Maybe, but here's another scenario. What if you were in cahoots with the others at the factory? Wouldn't it make more sense for you to be here, keeping an eye on me—distracting me—while they clear away the evidence?"

Brooke leaned back in her chair, staring him straight in the eye. Softly she challenged, "If you really believe that, then why aren't you storming the factory instead of pestering me?"

"Because I don't believe it, and I like pestering you."

"A typical 'bad boy' answer," Brooke drawled.

Alex looked surprised by her description. "I think my ex-wife would disagree with you. She thinks I'm boring, a workalcoholic with nothing on my mind but money."

"But that didn't stop her from *taking* your money."

"So you've heard the rumors."

Brooke shrugged. "When you have money, you sacrifice privacy."

"Well, there's a little twist to that rumor that

most people don't know," Alex said, staring off in the direction of the lake.

"And I suppose you're going to share such a well-kept secret with little ol' me." When he gave her a look that reminded her of their deal to lay sarcasm and seduction aside, Brooke relented. "Sorry, it's a habit."

"The fact is, she didn't take the money and run. I gave it to her."

"Why?"

"Because I felt I owed it to her. I *was* boring, and I was a workaholic. No question about it."

"And are you obsessed with money?"

He smiled faintly. "No, but since I worked all the time, it stands to reason that I would make money."

Miraculously, Brooke felt the ever-present tension between them ease a bit. "So you're a self-professed workaholic. I didn't know they took vacations." She was probing, and he was likely to tell her to mind her own business, but he didn't. Instead he frowned, his gray-green gaze once again focused on the lake.

"A few months ago I began to get these mysterious headaches. The doctor seemed to think I needed a vacation."

"Sheriff Snider mentioned you were sick."

He glanced at her. "Sheriff Snider?"

"The tall man standing by my car last night when you went bonkers and started waving at me? The one wearing the sheriff's uniform and a big mean gun?" *Oops. Sarcasm again.* Brooke bit her lip and tried to look sorry.

"That's two you owe me." He continued to stare at her so long that Brooke began to squirm. Finally he said, "They're right: you do have a talent for pulling out confessions."

Brooke bristled. "I don't *pull* them out of people. They just start talking. Believe me, there are some things I'd rather not hear."

"Speaking of which, we got sidetracked, didn't we? Tell me about the supervisors. You can start with Tailor Black."

"You know their names?" She wouldn't have thought he'd known the location of the factory, much less the names of his supervisors!

Alex steepled his hands, smiling at her shocked reaction. "If I were the jackass you think I am, then I'd keep quiet instead of telling you that I have their files in my briefcase."

"Including mine?" The thought unsettled her, although she couldn't fathom why. Alex already knew things about her—intimate things—that would never be in her personnel file.

She hoped. He could now easily scribble in the words *big tease* beside her name. Brooke cringed inwardly at the reminder and thrust the thought from her mind. She hadn't thought about protection any more than he had. They'd both been swept away by—

"Brooke? Where did you go?"

Absolutely nowhere she cared to share with him. "Um, I was thinking about Tailor Black. He's a typical family man, and his wife works at the factory with him. He's got one grown son, and seems pretty happy most of the time."

"Nice house?"

Brooke closed her eyes, trying to remember the last time she'd seen it, which had been . . . at a barbecue last summer. "Medium income range, two-car garage, aboveground pool. Nothing fancy."

"Car?"

"Cars," Brooke corrected. "He drives a ninety Cutlass, and his wife drives a station wagon they've had for years."

"Vacations?"

"Nothing extravagant. They went on their first cruise this year, but I know they cashed in an insurance policy for that."

"How do you know?"

She grinned. "Because Theo George works at their insurance company, and his sister works—"

"At the factory," Alex concluded with a chuckle.

"Right on. Theo's sister thought it was just a waste of good money."

"I guess gossip is a part of life in a small town."

"About as predictable as Treva's menu at the diner." Brooke sighed, lifting her face to the light breeze that began to stir. "I think you can mark Tailor off your list of suspects. The man's as honest as they come."

"How about Dixie Comford?"

"Married with children. Her husband works for the telephone company and makes decent money, and she's a very good friend. I don't think she would get involved in anything illegal." To her relief, Alex nodded and left it at that. "Next?"

"Leroy Coast."

"Nice family man, recently promoted to Level B supervisor." Her lips tightened briefly before she forced herself to relax again. "He's a good, honest man, and he deserved the promotion." It was the truth. But *she* had deserved a promotion, too.

"I guess that leaves our most obvious suspect, Kyle Lotus."

She couldn't help her spontaneous reaction. She stiffened, and those sharp gray-green eyes of his saw the movement. They narrowed in sudden speculation—or was it suspicion? Hoping to bluff her way out of it, she shrugged and said, "He's the plant manager—as you probably already know."

"Married?"

"Divorced."

"Children?"

"No."

"House?"

"Apartment." Brooke knew she was fumbling, knew that instead of her volunteering the answers, he was having to pull them out of her, and knew that her hot face was a dead giveaway, but she couldn't help it. She did not want to talk about Kyle Lotus with Alex.

"Is he the reason you're in denial about us?" he asked softly.

And now she knew *why* she didn't want to discuss Kyle with Alex. Desperately she pretended ignorance. "I don't know what you're talking about."

"I think you do."

Needing her defense, Brooke broke their no-sarcasm, no-seduction pact. Thrusting her chin out, she said in a growl. "Since you're so certain you know what you're talking about, why don't *you* tell *me?*"

"Was he your lover?"

Brooke's jaw dropped at his outrageously personal question. But the thing that shocked her the most was the blatant jealousy in his voice.

Even more amazing was the rush of pleasure she felt on hearing it.

Chapter Eighteen

A rosy, telltale flush on her face, evasive eyes, evasive answers . . . no, Alex decided, Brooke Welch wasn't good at subterfuge. Another facet of her personality uncovered.

And in the process of uncovering this facet, he'd discovered one of his own he hadn't realized existed: jealousy. He tried to think of a single time in the past when he might have been jealous of his ex-wife and another man . . . and couldn't. He'd always thought jealousy was a weak, useless emotion, a sign of insecurity.

Yet there was no mistaking the identity of the emotion raging through him now. Perhaps it was the primitive surroundings that brought out his baser male instincts, made him want to snatch her to his chest and growl out, "You're mine, understand?"

Oh, that would go over well, Alex thought with an inward chuckle. He suspected Brooke would squelch his macho feeling of ownership in a heartbeat, using that rapier tongue of hers.

He watched her now as she stared at him in that arousing, defiant way she had. He speculated on just how deep her involvement with Kyle Lotus was. Questions surfaced, questions he felt a burning need to have answered by the woman sitting across from him.

"Tell me about him," he commanded.

She titled that stubborn little chin higher and narrowed her eyes. "He's good at his job, and generally well liked. He's handsome and outgoing, and he drives a cherry red sixty-five model Corvette—totally restored."

Her beautiful amber eyes never wavered, but Alex detected an odd sheen in them.

"He carries breath spray in his pocket, and keeps a spare key to his apartment taped above his door." Her eyes darted to the lake, then back to his face, brighter than ever as she finished bitterly, "If you want to know the size of his penis, I'm afraid you'll have to ask him—or one of his countless girlfriends."

If Alex had disliked Kyle Lotus before, he came close to hating him now. "He hurt you."

Brooke shook her head. "Only my pride."

"How?"

She hesitated, fixing her gaze on her empty plate. "I guess I thought I was special."

"And you found out he was dating someone else?"

"More than one someone."

"Ouch."

"Yes, ouch." She met his gaze, her expression somber. "Getting involved with Kyle was a stupid thing to do."

"Because he's your boss?"

"Yes!"

That single, sharply hissed answer made Alex flinch. He planned to override her fears about getting involved with the boss, but right now he had one last question to ask about Lotus. "Brooke . . . do you think Lotus is behind this?"

Her eyes widened. "You're asking me that question, knowing how I feel about him?" She laughed. "I can hardly be trusted to be unbiased!"

"I trust you." And surprisingly, he did. Brooke didn't strike him as the vengeful type. Yes, she was hot-tempered, but there was a vulnerable sweetness about her anger that he couldn't explain even to himself.

"Why?"

"Because you came back from town when you could have left me here. Because you didn't send Elijah into town to explain everything—"

"Jail can be a powerful motivator," Brooke inserted dryly.

"True, but we both know you could have told Sheriff Snider I was in the hotel room. I think it would have been difficult to convince him I'd been kidnapped if he had found me there."

When she dropped her gaze abruptly, Alex reached out and tilted her chin. He searched her face as he asked, "So why didn't you?"

For a long moment, she didn't answer. Finally she said, "I . . . don't know."

Brooke spent the rest of the day cleaning the dusty cabin, stacking wood, and straightening the tiny shed where her father had kept his fishing equipment.

Every step she took, Alex was right beside her, helping and generally keeping her tense and edgy. By the time night fell, Brooke didn't have to pretend to be exhausted when she informed Alex she was going to bed early.

To her surprise—and slight disappointment—he didn't argue, and despite the heart-pounding knowledge that he lay stretched out before the fireplace on the other side of the door, Brooke slept soundly.

She awakened early Monday morning, tiptoeing around Alex's sleeping form. Once in town, she drove to her house, made a quick pot of coffee, and drank two cups while she dressed for work.

Brandy normally made it to the factory by eight o'clock, and Brooke had every intention of beating the tech there so that she could replace Hugo before she found it missing. She didn't relish trying to explain to the technician why she had taken the test model.

Twenty minutes later Brooke pulled into the parking lot at Safe & Secure and cut the engine.

Her tense shoulders relaxed slightly when a quick scan of the parking lot failed to reveal Brandy's green Toyota. *Good*. She'd made it.

The lab where Brandy worked was located next to Kyle's office, and had once served as a utility closet. Kyle had converted the room into a small lab six months earlier, hiring the twenty-four-year-old divorcée to test the condoms at random for quality and resilience. The weekly results of her testing were faxed to the Bradshaw Corporation.

Another senseless Bradshaw demand, Brooke mused as she used her master key to open the door to the darkened room. Kyle had been furious over the new order, claiming the money that it cost to run the lab could have been put to better use, such as replacing old equipment, which would in turn increase production, or fixing the leaky roof. . . .

Brooke couldn't have agreed more. She was doubly certain that Sonny, the janitor, would agree with Kyle's assessment. He was the one who spent hours mopping water from the break room floor when it rained, and it was those rainy days when his arthritis pained him the most.

Deciding against turning on a light, Brooke felt her way through the room in search of the metal table where she'd snatched Hugo last Friday from his exalted resting place.

Her shin found it first.

Swearing beneath her breath, she withdrew the plastic model from her pocket and used her fingers to find the screw sticking up from the table. When she found it, she spent another frustrating few moments trying to line up the threads with the bottom opening in Hugo.

Finally she got it. Turning Hugo around and around, she quickly began to screw the model onto the tabletop.

The overhead fluorescent came on, blinding Brooke for an instant.

She froze, her startled gaze focused on her hands, which clutched the oversize penis. Slowly she closed her eyes. This can't be happening, she thought, wishing she had a deep, dark hole to jump into.

"Well, well, well," Kyle Lotus drawled from the doorway. "If it isn't our cool little tigress, Brooke Welch."

Hearing her name on his lips motivated Brooke. She finished the job and stepped away, her insolent gaze taking in the slim, blond-haired, blue-eyed man lounging in the doorway. He was dressed in a light gray summer suit, the blazing white of his shirt emphasizing his artificial tan.

Kyle Lotus was a handsome man, but he couldn't hold a candle to Alex's raw sex appeal and candid personality.

Finally she lifted her eyes to his face, trying not to remember how close she'd come to becoming another meaningless notch on his belt. Coolly she said, "What are you doing here so early? It's not ten o'clock yet."

Her jibe about his late hours hit pay dirt. He

stiffened, his eyes narrowing to threatening slits.

"Never mind about me. The big question is, what are *you* doing?" He nodded at Hugo, his leering smile making her skin crawl. "If you're that desperate, I can give you some phone numbers."

Brooke closed her hands into fists, her temper rising. "Look, you little—"

"Brooke!" Brandy exclaimed, appearing behind Kyle. Pushing him aside, she approached Hugo, throwing Brooke a conspiratorial wink. "Oh, good. You fixed him. You said you could do it, and you did. Thanks a bunch."

Kyle darted a suspicious gaze between the two before pushing away from the door. He gave his blond head a disgusted shake before disappearing.

Brandy closed the door and locked it behind him.

"Whew!" She wiped a hand over her brow in an exaggerated gesture of relief. "He's been a bear lately, hasn't he? I think this thing with Bradshaw has him in a tailspin."

Brooke tried to sound casual as she said, "Why is that?"

"Oh, I don't know. I guess he's worried about what will happen to the factory if something happens to Bradshaw." She shrugged, glancing at Brooke with unconcealed curiosity. "So now that he's gone—what *were* you doing with Hugo?"

"It's a long story—and I promise to tell it to

you sometime—but right now I've got to run. Thanks for sticking up for me."

Leaving Brandy openmouthed and staring after her, Brooke hurried from the room. She had a million things to do before she headed back to the cabin that evening. A shiver of anticipation stole over her at the thought of seeing Alex again.

As she passed the break room, she heard the pounding of a hammer and the muted sound of male voices. Frowning, she backtracked and peeked inside.

A man dressed in dingy coveralls stood balanced at the top of a ladder; he was replacing the water-stained ceiling tiles with new ones.

Unsettled, Brooke continued along the hall past the small offices housing the supervisors. So Alex was having the leak fixed. If he thought to score brownie points, he would be sadly disappointed. Fixing the leak was something that should have been done a long time ago—without her prompting.

Still . . . Sonny would be tickled that he wouldn't have to mop the break room floor when it rained. Maybe she'd thank Alex, after all, Brooke mused. Cook a special dinner for him, buy a bottle of wine to go with it. Lost in her forbidden fantasy, she didn't notice the shadow rounding the corner of the hall in front of her.

She ran smack into Leroy Coast, the supervisor who had gotten the promotion she should have gotten. As he steadied her, she smiled brightly into his dark brown eyes. Leroy was nice. It wasn't his fault Kyle Lotus was a sore loser.

"Oops! Sorry, Leroy. Guess I wasn't watching where I was going."

"I'll say. You looked like you were in another world." Leroy dropped his hands, his smile a blinding flash in his broad, brown face. "How are things going with you?"

"Fine. And you?"

"Great. I'm looking forward to my vacation next week."

"Going anyplace special?" Brooke asked politely.

"Yeah, we're going to Disneyland. The kids are really looking forward to it."

"Hmm. Sounds expensive." Brooke could have kicked herself. As a longtime employee and family man, Leroy was the last person to be taken in by the likes of Kyle Lotus.

"We've been saving for a while, and since we'll be staying with my brother and his family, we won't be out hotel expenses." His quick and easy grin flashed again as he patted his paunch. "More money left to spend on food and fun."

Brooke felt ashamed of herself. "Well, I hope you have a good time, Leroy."

"Thanks, Brooke."

After he'd gone, Brooke ducked into her cubbyhole of an office for a quick breather. She had to calm down, stop suspecting everyone—stop asking personal questions she had no business asking before someone became suspicious. Alex had instructed her to keep her eyes and ears open, not to interrogate each and every supervisor.

Kyle was the main suspect—the one in a position to rip the company off. She had no reason to think the others knew of his scheme or were involved in any way. They were her friends. She'd worked with many of them for the past six—

"There you are!" Dixie Comford cried, startling a guilty shriek out of Brooke. "You've got some explaining to do, girlfriend."

Dixie's chiding words sailed right over Brooke's head, because Brooke's attention had been snared by the huge diamond on Dixie's finger.

A very big, very expensive-looking diamond.

Chapter Nineteen

"Wanna know what I think?" Dixie asked, popping the tab on her diet cola. She had grabbed a package of sugar-laden doughnuts from the vending machine and sat across from Brooke at one of the tables in the break room.

The workers had gone, leaving behind a shiny new ceiling. Brooke shook her head at Dixie's question, trying to concentrate on what her friend was saying instead of what she was wearing on her finger. A rock that size had to cost thousands of dollars. What if Dixie did know what Kyle was doing, and had accepted a bribe to keep quiet? What if Leroy had as well? What if everyone knew but her? The ugly possibility made her face burn.

"Well, since you asked . . . I think Bradshaw's hiding out right here in Quicksilver."

Brooke nearly spewed her fruit drink across the table. Trying to appear casual, she dabbed at her mouth and cleared her throat. "Why . . . why would he do that?"

Dixie leaned forward. "To spy on us. To catch us slacking on the job." As if she'd conjured him by talking about him, Dixie glanced uneasily around the deserted break room. "Like I'm doing right now."

"Dixie . . . you're on an official break right now," Brooke gently reminded her. "Every employee is entitled to a fifteen—"

"I know that, but think about it, Brooke. If the rumors about Bradshaw cleaning house are true, then he'll be looking for an excuse to fire us."

Stifling an irritated sigh, Brooke said, "He'd have to have a better excuse than that, Dixie. Besides, maybe the rumors aren't true. Maybe Kyle circulated that particular rumor to get us riled, keep us on our toes." In fact, the more Brooke thought about it, the more it sounded like something Kyle would do. And if the others knew that Kyle was stealing from the company, then maligning Alex would definitely serve Kyle's purpose.

"Sounds like you're taking up for that son of a bitch," Dixie accused.

"He's not so—" Brooke censored herself abruptly. She'd nearly said, *He's not so bad.* How disastrous would that be? And why was she taking up for that blackmailing, ruthless shark? "What I mean is, we've never met him, yet we've condemned him already. Maybe we're not being fair."

"Well," Dixie drawled in a disgusted tone, "you're easy. He fixes a measly leak in the break room and suddenly he's a hero. Which brings me back to my earlier suspicion. Bradshaw's supposed to be missing. Who do you suppose ordered the maintenance?"

"Maybe he ordered it before he disappeared," Brooke answered automatically. She glanced at her watch. Dixie had five minutes left on her break. It was now or never—and Brooke had to know. Taking a deep breath, she focused on the rock on Dixie's hand. "Wow, I've never seen you wear that ring before. Where did you get it?"

Dixie's guilty flush made Brooke's mouth go dry. Flipping her permed hair over her shoulder in a defiant gesture, Dixie said, "I bought it for myself—for an anniversary present. God knows Rick would never buy me anything!"

Spots danced before Brooke's eyes. She had to blink to focus on the hand Dixie thrust out.

"Looks real, doesn't it?" Dixie laughed at her shocked expression. "It's cubic zirconia! As if I could afford anything else on *my* salary!"

Brooke slumped in her chair, her relief so great it left her weak. Dixie didn't know, because if Dixie knew, she would tell Brooke . . . wouldn't she?

Oh, God, was she really suspicious of Dixie?

It was all Alex's fault for bringing on this ridiculous paranoia!

When darkness fell and Brooke hadn't returned, Alex began to get edgy. He waited for her on the porch in the old rocker, trying to relax and enjoy the peaceful night.

It was no use. Without Brooke, the place was dull as dirt, just as she'd predicted. He was used to action, to facing constant challenge and making split-second decisions.

But it didn't take him long to figure out it wasn't the daily grind of the business world that he missed; it was Brooke. Her personality—full of vitality and fierce energy—was like a drug he couldn't resist. The more he saw of her, the more he wanted to see until he ached physically with the need.

She was amazing, stunning, irresistible, and refreshingly honest. When she focused on something, she was like an avalanche.

Headlights cut through the dark, winding road to the cabin. Alex dropped his booted feet from the porch railing and stood. His muscles bunched with tension; his blood began to pound in his ears as he prepared his libido to spend another night in agonizing, close proximity to a woman he wanted to ravish.

He noticed something wrong the moment she stepped out of the car. It wasn't like Brooke to move slowly for anything, but this time she didn't hurry.

And she didn't slam the car door.

Alex watched her approach, her head down, one hand jammed into the pocket of her jeans and the other clutching a white sack. She climbed the steps as if each foot weighed a ton, then stopped on the porch. Without preamble, she handed him the sack. He caught a whiff of sweet-and-sour pork and soy sauce.

"One of the packing machines went down, so we had to pack the rest of the shipment by hand. That's why I'm late, and that's why I'm tired. So if you'll excuse me, I'm going to soak in a hot bath. Your interrogation will have to wait."

She moved by him and disappeared into the cabin. Alex stared after her in silence. He'd never seen her look so desolate and weary. Guilt nagged at him. While he'd spent the day in peaceful relaxation, Brooke had spent an obviously hard day at the factory. *His* factory, the one he'd been too busy to inspect these past six months.

The sound of running water gave him an idea. There *was* something he could do for Brooke. She might not appreciate his offer at first, but with a little coaxing, Alex thought she would come around.

He quickly lit a small fire in the grate and gathered a couple of plates from the cupboard, setting them by the fire with the cartons of Chinese cuisine. Moving to the bathroom door, Alex waited until he heard the screech of the old faucets as she turned off the water. He knocked lightly. "Brooke?"

"Who else?"

He grinned at her wisecrack answer. Apparently she was getting her second wind. "Do you have bubbles in your bath?"

"What?"

"Bubbles."

There was a long silence before she said suspiciously, "Yes, I do. Why?"

"Because I'm coming in." Before she could protest, he opened the door and slipped inside the tiny bathroom.

She shrieked and sank beneath the mound of bubbles until the only things visible were the dark pools of her eyes and the cap of her strawberry blond hair. "Alex! what the hell are you doing?"

Calmly as you please, Alex picked up the bar of soap from the rim of the tub and gently tugged the washcloth from her hands. "I'm going to wash your back."

"You . . . are . . . not!" she said in a hiss, trying to snatch the washcloth back. "Get out! I'm not in the mood for your games tonight."

"No games." Alex knelt beside the tub and briskly rubbed the soap on the washcloth until it formed a rich lather. "Now turn around," he ordered.

"Go away!"

"Turn around."

"I won't."

It was a pity he had to resort to threats, Alex thought as he narrowed his eyes on her flushed face. "If you don't turn around . . . I'll start with what I can reach." His gaze dipped to the glistening tops of her breasts rising and falling beneath the bubbles.

She must have realized how determined he was, for after a slight hesitation, she huffed and turned her back on him.

He eyed the rigid curve of her spine and wondered what the hell he was thinking. She was gorgeous. Perfect. Tempting. His hands trembled as he lifted the washcloth and brought it to the smooth slope of her shoulder. Her audible hiss set his groin on fire. Setting his jaw, he tried to think of something besides the glistening honey-tinted skin beneath his hands, and what he knew lay just beyond his vision.

"Your skin feels like satin," he couldn't resist saying.

"That's just the soap."

Her tart answer made him smile. He abandoned the washcloth and smoothed the soap across her shoulders with his hands, wanting—needing—the contact. She arched her back and he followed the movement along her spine until it disappeared into the water.

"I hope you're having fun."

The slightly husky sound of her voice made him groan inwardly. "I am. Do you want me to stop?"

She waited a telling heartbeat before she said, "Yes."

"Why?"

"Why do you always ask why? You know why."

"I want to hear you say it."

"You're sadistic."

Alex soaped his other hand and began to knead her tense shoulder muscles. She sighed and surrendered, tilting her head from left to right to give him better access.

"Okay, so you're pretty good at this," she said grudgingly. "I hope you don't expect me to return the favor."

"It's not a favor."

She tensed again. "What do you mean?"

"I should have inspected the factory months ago."

She twisted around to look at him, and Alex just managed to keep his eyes on her face instead of the delicious frontal view she unwittingly displayed by her movement. "Is this another one of your devious schemes to get me into bed?"

Her candor amused him, as always. He smiled and shook his head. "No, it's not. Scout's honor." His voice deepened as he said in a growl, "Now do me a favor and turn around so that I can continue being a good Boy Scout."

"Oh." Her face turned scarlet as she realized what he meant. She covered herself and swung around, presenting her back again. "Sorry."

He rinsed her back and reached for a towel, spreading it wide in front of him. "Now stand up."

She surprised him by obeying. He wrapped the towel around her and lifted her into his arms, chuckling at her startled shriek.

"Alex . . . what are you doing?"

"Taking you to the bedroom so that I can ravish you, what else?" When she stiffened in his arms, he relented. "Just kidding."

He strode to the fire and set her gently on the blankets he'd spread out earlier. She clutched the towel, her eyes huge and apprehensive as she watched him settle before her.

Alex tugged her foot into his lap and began to massage it, well aware of what she was thinking. He wondered if she would be disappointed when she found out she was wrong. He sincerely hoped so. In fact, he was counting on it.

After a long moment of watching him, she began to relax. "I could get addicted to this."

So could he. He kept his head bent, working his fingers between her toes, then onto the pad of her foot. She rewarded him with a pleasurable groan that turned him inside out. It would be so easy to work his way slowly up, rip the towel aside, and press her into the blankets. . . .

"Alex?"

Alex gave a start and looked up—his mistake. Her eyes had grown soft and sleepy, giving her a sexy look that locked the air in his lungs. "Hmm?" was all he could manage. He was thinking about the box of condoms on the counter.

"That feels sooooo good," she purred.

Desperate to distract himself, he took her other foot and began to massage it. The fire was hot against his side, but there were other parts of him flaming up as well. She had small feet and tiny toes . . . painted a blush pink that reminded him of the color of her areolae. *Hell.* Even her *feet* turned him on!

Perhaps it was time to move on to the next stage of his pampering.

He dropped her foot and reached blindly for a box of the Chinese food on the hearth.

"Alex? Is something wrong?"

"What could be wrong?" Avoiding the flushed, half-naked vixen beside him, he fumbled with the flap on the box, finally tearing it open. He forked sweet-and-sour pork onto a plate, added a heap of fried rice, and handed her the feast—all without looking at her. When she took it, he fixed his own plate and ate without tasting.

She was beautiful. Gorgeous. He didn't have to look at her to know these things. All he had to do was close his eyes and a sharp, desire-inducing image of her filled his mind.

"Something *is* wrong."

Her soft, concerned voice rippled through Alex like a current of electricity. "I think maybe it would be a good idea for you to put your clothes on now," he said hoarsely.

A small, revealing silence followed his statement.

"Alex . . . I can't forget that you're my—"

He cut her off before she could finish. "Just get dressed, will you?"

"Fine." She put her plate aside and scrambled to her feet, nearly losing her towel in the process.

Alex clenched his jaw and prayed for strength. He wanted to reach out and snatch her into his arms, kiss her senseless, caress her until she was mindless.

Until she forgot who he was.

"Just remember—you're the one who started this."

She was angry, and Alex couldn't blame her. She was also right.

He heard the bedroom door slam, then open again.

"Thanks for the foot rub!" she shouted, slamming the door again.

Chapter Twenty

"I want you to get into Lotus's office and make copies of every piece of paper you can find. Inventories, expense sheets, anything that looks interesting."

Leaning against the counter the next morning, Brooke stared at Alex over the rim of her coffee cup. "Have you lost your mind? If Kyle catches me in his office, he'll not only fire me—in which case I'd be no help to you—he'll probably have me arrested! Besides, Alex, do you really think Kyle would keep records in his office of anything that could incriminate him?"

Alex shrugged. "Probably not, but I want those copies anyway."

Brooke set her cup on the counter and folded

her arms, ready to do battle. She'd had a rough night, and Alex looked no better. Something had to change. The tension between them was giving her a headache. "Why don't you just confront Kyle about your suspicions? You're the boss—you can then go through his files yourself—*if* he's stupid enough to keep anything incriminating."

"Even crooks keep records."

"And if we don't find anything in his office?" Brooke drawled, heavy on the sarcasm. "Do we then break into his apartment?"

"Why break in when you could use the spare key he keeps over his door?" Alex retorted.

"It's still breaking and entering!" she sputtered.

"Not if you get an invitation."

He was dead serious. Brooke couldn't believe what she was hearing. And it hurt. Hurt more than it had a right to hurt. "You want me to . . . to *offer* myself to Kyle just to get into his apartment?"

His jaw tensed—she could see the motion from where she was standing.

"I'm not asking you to sleep with him."

"Well, *that's* a relief." She studied the hard, purposeful glint in his eyes for a moment before saying softly, "You want to catch him pretty badly, don't you?"

He didn't try to deny it. "Yes."

"Why?"

"Because he's stealing my money." He began

to walk toward her, holding her gaze. "He's also maligned my character."

She sucked in a sharp breath as he kept coming. When he reached her, he slipped an arm around her waist and brought her flush against him in a possessive gesture that strummed an answering chord inside her. She automatically gripped his shoulders as her knees threatened to buckle.

The man was flat-out potent.

His voice lowered to a harsh whisper. "And because he's the reason for that barbed-wire fence you keep around you."

Brooke licked her lips. "What . . . what if it turns out the fax Daisy sent you was a hoax?"

His brow rose as if he hadn't considered that possibility. "I don't think it was a hoax, but even if it is, Lotus is finished anyway."

"Don't you think that's rather unprofessional to fire someone because you're jealous?" It was a cheap shot, but Brooke had to do something to ease the heightened tension before she did something reckless—like lean in for a kiss, as she ached to do.

He smiled, a slow, wicked smile that should have warned Brooke she was in over her head. "Don't *you* think it's unprofessional to want to kiss your boss?"

"What makes you think—"

"You keep staring at my mouth."

"That doesn't mean—"

His lips touched hers all too briefly, sparking a flame in her belly. Brooke sighed, wrapped her arms around his neck, and leaned her forehead against his. She was a pitifully weak person, she decided, disgusted with herself. "Yes," she whispered. "It *is* unprofessional. And unethical, and a big, fat mistake."

"Why is it a mistake?"

Because when playtime is over, you'll go back to that big office in the sky and I'll be left here nursing a broken heart.

The truth of her thoughts frightened and saddened her. Alex Bradshaw *could* break her heart—of that she was now certain.

If she let him.

But she wasn't planning on letting him. Without Dee, her life would be empty enough. If she let herself get involved with Alex for an all-too-brief time, then she feared the emptiness would be unbearable. No, casual affairs weren't for her. She wanted something lasting. . . .

Something she didn't think she could have with Alex. They were worlds apart. It wouldn't work. He'd grow tired of her. The list went on and on.

Gathering her courage, she dropped her arms from around his neck. "I should get to work."

Reluctantly he stepped back and let her by. "You should wait until tonight to get those papers," he said.

"Right. Tonight." Brooke flipped her hair behind her ear and scorched him with one of her go-to-hell looks. "And who's going to bail me out of jail if I get caught?"

"You won't get caught."

He sounded so confident of her abilities that Brooke had to squelch a surge of pleasure. "This should earn me a promotion." She wasn't kidding.

"I'll need someone to take Lotus's place when this is over," Alex said.

A warm glow swept over Brooke when she realized *he* wasn't kidding, either.

But by the time she arrived at Safe & Secure, the glow had faded and a curious ache had settled in her chest. If she'd had any glorified ideas about Alex's feelings toward her, she had none now. He'd all but promised her Kyle's position when this was over.

Not a promise a man would make if he were thinking about whisking a woman away into the sunset.

Alex wanted to call her back the moment she left.

What was he thinking? Was he, in some perverse way, testing her loyalty by asking her to search Kyle's office? What if he *was* placing her in danger? From what he'd learned about Lotus, he didn't think the man was dangerous . . . just devious and clever.

But what if he was? If anything happened to Brooke because of something he'd forced her to do, he'd never forgive himself.

"I see that you're still alive and kicking."

Alex turned to find Elijah standing at the edge of the porch. He smiled ruefully at the knowing look in the older man's eyes. "Yes, I am. Barely."

"She cuts deep sometimes."

"That she does. Care for a cup of coffee?"

"Wouldn't mind at all."

Elijah settled onto the rocker on the porch as Alex went inside to get the coffee. When he returned, Elijah had produced a piece of wood and was whittling away.

"Mighty nice prison you got here," he commented.

"Yes, it is." Alex chuckled at Elijah's dry humor. It reminded him of Brooke's.

"Seems to me you could just walk right on down that road there. Shouldn't take you more than a couple of hours to reach town."

"I could," Alex conceded, realizing the old man was fishing for information. He decided it couldn't hurt to give it to him. "But Brooke and I have an agreement."

"Oh?"

Alex watched Elijah work the knife as he contemplated how much he'd tell him. Again he couldn't see the harm. "I've got a little trouble at the factory, and Brooke's helping me investigate."

"You mean you sent her in to spy?" Elijah glanced up sharply. "That don't sound like my Brooklyn. Spying on her own people." He shook his head. "Nope, that sure don't sound like Brooke. Makes me wonder how you convinced her to do such a thing."

The conversation had taken a drastic turn, Alex realized, admiring the man's skill with both the wood and the word. He found himself on the defensive. "A little harmless blackmail—"

"Blackmail ain't never *harmless*, son."

"Neither is kidnapping," Alex retorted, stung by the older man's rebuke.

Elijah paused and studied the point of his knife thoughtfully. Finally he pointed it at Alex. "Have you asked her what happened to her parents?" he demanded.

The sudden shift again caught Alex off guard, as did the man's hard, penetrating gaze. "No, I haven't."

"So if you don't care nothing about getting to know her, what *do* you want?"

Alex floundered. "Company. I like her company." It wasn't a lie, but it wasn't the entire truth, either. "And I *do* plan on getting to know her better."

Snorting in disbelief, Elijah said, "I wasn't born yesterday, you know. I know what you're after, and Brooke ain't a loose woman."

"I never assumed she was," Alex said stiffly.

"She's tough on the outside, but soft as cotton on the inside."

"I've noticed."

"If someone were to get inside to the soft part, they could do some damage, I reckon."

Surprisingly, Alex understood what Elijah was trying to tell him. "She's a remarkable woman. I would never do anything to hurt her."

"Now you're talkin'." Elijah held out his cup. "I'll take another shot, if you've got it."

When Alex returned from filling his cup, Elijah motioned for him to take a seat on the steps.

"Now tell me what you think my sly little nephew's up to," he demanded.

Alex frowned. "I'm afraid I don't—"

"Kyle Lotus is who I'm talking about. That's who's causing the trouble, ain't it?"

Shock jolted through Alex. "Lotus is your nephew? Brooke never mentioned—"

"She doesn't know," Elijah said. "When I found out he was back in town a few years back, I didn't see fit to mention the relation to Brooke. Didn't want her to think she had to be nice to him on my account."

"I take it you're not too fond of your nephew?"

"You take it right, son. He's my sister's young'un. She lives north of Shreveport, Louisiana, and he ain't been back to see her in five years. She writes to me now and then, askin' about him." Elijah settled back in the rocker and began to whittle again. He had the look of someone remembering something very unpleasant. "Last year I went to find out for myself why he ain't been to see his mama. Little fart looked right through me as if I wasn't there. Told me to mind my own business."

"And what did you tell your sister?"

"I told her he was doing just fine, and staying busy."

They shared a look of complete understanding.

Alex braced his back against the porch post and took a sip of his coffee. "What can you tell me about Lotus?"

"Just stuff my sister's told me over the years through her letters. Seems he had a little trouble in college, something about selling copies of a test he wasn't supposed to have. After that, he switched jobs pretty regular for one reason or the other until he hooked up with Donaldson and got the job as plant manager." Elijah paused in his whittling to cock a brow at Alex. "I'm still speculating on how he got the job, with his past history and all."

"I think I can solve that mystery. I've got his file, and it's as clean as a whistle."

"Ah. Falsified his credentials, did he?" Elijah shook his head. "Donaldson never did have good business sense. I'm surprised he managed to hold on to the factory as long as he did. So what do you suppose Kyle's up to?"

"Embezzling company money." After their interesting exchange, Alex was certain of it now. When he caught the weasel, he was going to find Daisy and reinstate her, then give her a nice, fat bonus.

"I'm not surprised, and while I hate to break my sister's heart, that little fart needs taking down."

"I agree."

"Mighty smart of you to keep low, too. Mae's always bragging about how clever Kyle is. If he knew you were snooping around, you can bet he'd make himself clean as a whistle before you got to him. So you're Batman and Brooke's playing Robin, huh?"

Alex chuckled. "Something like that."

"And in the meantime, you get to vacation right here, and enjoy Brooke's delightful company in the evenings."

"You make me sound selfish."

"I might think so, if I didn't know Brooke like I do. She's having the time of her life; she just don't know it yet."

"How can you be so sure?"

"Well, when was the last time she chopped wood?"

Thinking back, Alex said, "Saturday. Right after she talked to you."

"Uh-huh. And how many dishes has she broken since you first met her?"

He shook his head. "None that I know of, although she did mention something about wanting to." Instead she'd chopped enough wood to last a week.

"Well, there you go. There's your proof plain as day."

Or as dark as night. Alex scratched his head. "I'm not following you."

"When Brooke's upset about something, she has a tendency to take action. Chopping wood, breaking dishes, driving fast . . . Everybody has their own unique way of dealing with stress. Me, I whittle, or take a walk."

"And Brooke . . . smashes things."

"Yep. Been that way since her folks died. What do you do?"

"I work."

"Wonder it doesn't give you headaches."

Alex gave a start at his uncanny statement.

"As a matter of fact, it does. About Brooke. Do you think—"

Elijah waved him to a stop. "You got questions about Brooke, you can ask Brooke. She keeps her nose out of my business, and I keep mine out of hers."

After delivering that bold-faced lie, Elijah got to his feet with groans and grunts and headed down the path. After a few yards, he paused and turned around.

"Don't worry about Kyle. He's too cowardly to be dangerous. Oh, and don't shame an old man by telling Brooke he's my nephew."

"I won't, and thanks, Elijah, for your help."

"Just treat my little girl right, you hear?"

"Yes, sir."

Long after he'd gone, Alex remained on the steps and pondered their conversation. He had some thinking to do, and this was just the place to do it.

Chapter Twenty-one

The secretary's office lay in shadow. Brooke glanced one last time down the deserted hall before she slipped inside. She turned on the copy machine so that it could be warming up before she ventured to the door of Kyle's office.

It was locked, of course.

Silently she flipped on her pencil-size flashlight and began searching through the secretary's desk drawers. She knew Peggy kept a set of keys to Kyle's office; it was just a matter of finding them.

The first two drawers yielded nothing of interest, but with the third one she hit pay dirt. Lying on top of a small ledger book were the keys. Brooke gathered them and started to close the drawer. She paused, shining the light on the little leather-bound book. Probably a date book and nothing more.

Before she could change her mind, Brooke flipped it open to take a peek inside. It *was* a date book, but instead of appointments and reminders, Peggy had written numbers on each page. Frowning, Brooke flipped to the front of the book. CUSTOMER COMPLAINTS. Her brows rose as she flipped back through the pages dating from the first of January.

According to Peggy's records, there were a lot of customer complaints in the past few months, logged in volume instead of individually.

Dee could have easily been one of them, Brooke thought, closing the book and shutting the drawer. More than a little disturbed by the find, she found the key to Kyle's office and went inside, closing the door softly behind her.

She spent the next hour and a half making copies of anything that looked remotely interesting or suspicious. Finally, when she had a stack a half-inch thick, she turned off the copier, locked Kyle's office, and returned to her cubbyhole. She placed a few harmless schedule sheets on top of the stack to camouflage the evidence in case she ran into anyone on her way out.

An hour later, back at the cabin, feeling very much like an accomplice in a robbery, Brooke sat across from Alex at the kitchen table as he sorted through the booty she'd stolen. Finally she could stand the suspense no longer. "Well?" she demanded. "Is there anything there?"

Alex frowned and shook his head. "If there is, I'm not seeing it. But then, we knew he was clever, didn't we?"

Brooke let out an explosive breath. "Maybe there's nothing to find."

He gave her a hard look. "So you think Daisy was lying?"

Picturing Daisy's sweet, honest face, Brooke reluctantly shook her head. "No, if Daisy said something was going on, then something was going on. She's as honest as the day is long." When he kept staring at her, but remained silent, she groaned. "I guess this means we go to plan B."

"You have a better idea?" he challenged.

She wished she did! The thought of being nice to Kyle turned her stomach. A little desperately, she asked, "What makes you think he'll go out with me again?"

Slowly his gaze traveled over her. By the time his eyes returned to her face, they had darkened with desire. She shivered.

"Kyle's a thief, not a fool," he stated softly.

Flushing at his compliment, Brooke laughed. "You've got cabin fever. I'm just an ordinary woman . . . a nasty-tempered one at that. It isn't likely that Kyle's forgotten."

He reached across and unfastened the first three buttons of her blouse, brushing his knuckles boldly across her breasts. "Oh, there's nothing ordinary about you, Brooke Welch. Not a single thing."

"I guess . . ." Brooke hastily cleared the huskiness from her voice and tried again. "I guess this is my cue to go to bed." When he lifted an interested brow, she couldn't help chuckling. He was impossible.

And very, very tempting.

She fled the room while she still had the necessary willpower.

Wednesday Kyle was out of town, so it wasn't until Thursday that Brooke was able to make her move on the plant manager. But unbeknownst to Alex, her plans had changed. She lured Kyle in much the same way she'd nearly snagged Cliff—only this time the story was about Alex Bradshaw, and the information she claimed to have concerned the thing dearest to Kyle's heart: Safe & Secure's future.

Unable to resist her mysterious lure, he agreed to meet her at Treva's Diner Friday night at seven o'clock—which meant he wouldn't be at his apartment.

Brooke would be there, though. If she got caught, she would simply pretend she'd gotten confused about the meeting place. She would make up something about Alex Bradshaw and then get the hell out.

Her plan was so simple it frightened her. By the time the five o'clock whistle blew, her teeth were chattering with nervous tension.

Nancy Drew she wasn't.

She drove straight to her house and took a long, hot shower, hoping it would settle her nerves.

It didn't work.

When she emerged from the bathroom, she checked her messages on the answering machine and discovered that Dee had called the day before. She and Cliff were honeymooning in Vegas—and Brooke was not to worry.

Brooke collapsed on the bed and stared at the ceiling, stunned to realize she hadn't thought of her sister in days. Alex had taken Dee's place in her thoughts. When she wasn't thinking of Alex, she was thinking of her reaction to Alex.

Another surprising realization was that although she resisted temptation because Alex was her boss, she rarely thought of him as her boss. No, when she thought of Alex, it was in a very physical way.

But he *was* her boss.

She could quit.

The absurd suggestion made her laugh out loud.

Throw her job and her future away, just to satisfy her lustful cravings for her boss? *Ha! Not in this lifetime.* Besides, it wasn't just her job she was trying to protect; it was her heart. It was best if she kept reminding herself of that.

Alex had hinted strongly that she might take Kyle's place when this was over. If she got the job, she didn't want any misunderstanding about why she'd gotten it.

Another excellent reason why she shouldn't

give in to her cravings for Alex Bradshaw.

Feeling suddenly drained, Brooke hauled herself from the bed and got dressed. She brushed her hair, her teeth, and put on some mascara. Finally it was time to go. Kyle's apartment was a five-minute drive from her house, and the route would take her by Treva's Diner, so she'd be able to see if his car was there.

He'd wait for her at Treva's no longer than twenty minutes, Brooke guessed. If she'd hooked him with her lure, he would call her from a pay phone, possibly drive over to her house. That would take up another fifteen minutes.

She had thirty-five, forty minutes, tops, to go through his personal files and get out.

On the drive over, she went down a mental list of charges Kyle could bring against her if he caught her snooping around his apartment. Invasion of privacy, theft, breaking and entering— if he could convince Sheriff Snider she wasn't invited—to name a few. She was certain there were other charges she hadn't thought of. On the other hand, what was a little breaking and entering when she had a kidnapping charge hanging over her head?

The key was exactly where she'd told Alex it would be, taped above the door. Casting a guilty glance left and right, she quickly unlocked the door and replaced the key. Once inside, she secured the lock. If Kyle came home, she would hear his key in the lock.

It would be precious little warning, but thieves couldn't be choosy.

The layout of the apartment was simple and easily maneuvered even in the dark. There was a living room, a small state-of-the-art kitchen, a bedroom, a bathroom, and another small room Brooke knew Kyle used as a combination library/office.

It was the room that Brooke knew housed the filing cabinet.

She turned on the desk lamp and hurried to the metal cabinet, yanking at the handle so hard she broke a nail. *Locked!* Frustrated, she began searching through his desk drawers for a key, as she'd done in Peggy's office.

The only thing she found was an assortment of condoms and an interesting little attachment she was certain she didn't want to touch, let alone identify.

Willing herself to calm down and think, she systematically lifted every object on his desk, from a smoke-tinted pencil holder to a glass paperweight.

She found the key taped beneath the elegant green desk lamp. Thank God for Kyle's penchant for losing keys! Breathing a sigh of relief, she opened the filing cabinet and began to leaf through the files. She dismissed the ones labeled RECEIPTS, HOUSEHOLD ACCOUNTS, BILLS PAID, BILLS DUE.

Nothing of interest in the first drawer.

She quickly opened the second drawer and flipped through the folders. One folder in particular snagged her attention: LANDCO SYNTHET-ICS, INC. Frowning, Brooke withdrew the file. It contained a dozen or so order sheets and figures from a company she didn't recognize. Though it meant nothing to her, it might mean something to Alex. She took the sheets out, folded them, and placed them on the edge of Kyle's desk. Once she was finished gathering information, she would hide them inside her jacket.

Pulling open the top drawer, Brooke took a few sheets from several folders and placed them in the Landco file so that at first glance, Kyle wouldn't notice anything amiss. She paused to take a quick peek at her watch, hesitating. There was one last file drawer to search, but Kyle had been at the restaurant a full twenty minutes now.

Should she play it safe and get out before Kyle returned? Biting her lip, she stared at the closed drawer. What if this was the drawer that contained the answers? It would be a waste to pass up the opportunity to look inside after taking such a risk.

A distinct clicking noise snagged her attention.

She drew in a sharp gasp, recognizing the sound of a key in the lock, followed by the low murmur of voices.

Kyle was back, and from the sound of it, he wasn't alone.

Glancing wildly around, Brooke searched for a suitable hiding place. It took her only a second to realize that if she remained in his office, she would be trapped.

Snapping off the light, she darted into the bedroom just as the front door swung open. Soundlessly she dived under the bed and scooted along the carpet until she reached the middle. She worked on breathing slowly and quietly.

What now? she wondered. Wait until Kyle slept, then try to sneak out? How long would that be? It was Friday night, not normally an early night for a popular, single man.

Brooke swallowed a groan. She *knew* she wasn't Nancy Drew material! Instead of wasting time trying to decide if she should continue searching, she should have left while she had the opportunity.

The voices grew closer, louder. Brooke breathed shallowly and listened.

"I wonder what happened to her?" a female voice asked, sounding worried.

Brandy Clevenger! What was she doing in Kyle's apartment? The technician had stressed to Brooke on more than one occasion that she didn't know what other women saw in Kyle.

"Chances are she was lying anyway," Kyle said. "After the way that PI drilled me about her, I think our little ice princess has made someone very suspicious. She was probably hoping to pick my brain."

"Whatever she's done, she couldn't have picked a better time," Brandy responded with a nasty little chuckle.

"Exactly."

Brooke really hated the way he said *exactly*. What were they talking about? Why would the PI drill Kyle about her, when Kyle was the one under investigation? Granted, Dixie had mentioned the PI was asking everyone questions, but Kyle made it sound as if she'd been singled out.

"It must be something serious for that guy to travel all the way back to Quicksilver," Kyle said as if to himself.

The bedsprings suddenly creaked and sagged, startling Brooke. Her nose came into contact with cold iron. Prudently she turned her head to the side. If they moved around much, she'd be wearing squares on her face in the morning. . . .

"Hmm. Enough of business," Brandy purred throatily. "Let's get down to a different kind of business."

"Good idea. Did you bring the good ones?"

"Of course."

Good ones? Brooke swallowed quietly, praying they weren't talking about what she thought they were talking about. Risky or not, there was no way in hell she was going to stay under the bed while they . . . they—

"You don't think I'd be stupid enough to use our own, do you?"

Brandy's laugh sent shivers down Brooke's spine. What did she mean by that remark? The bed dipped again, bringing the springs perilously close to her check. Brooke squeezed her eyes tightly shut, anticipating having her face crushed.

"You're so hard," Brandy whispered—unfortunately loud enough for Brooke to hear.

She also heard the rustle of clothing, and the sound of a zipper. Dear God, they were going to do it right on top of her. She was going to kill Alex for this!

"Hmm, I missed you."

"Me, too. It makes me crazy to think of you with those other women."

"Appearances, my dear." There was a groan and a grunt, and more rustling and creaking. Kyle was breathless by the time he added, "They mean nothing."

"Not even little ol' Brooke?"

"*Especially* not her. I'm not an expert, but I'd say that woman has serious problems."

"Oh?"

Brooke's thoughts exactly!

"She's dysfunctional. Sexually. I think she might even be a virgin. Or maybe she prefers toys to the real thing. You saw for yourself the way she was handling that ridiculously oversize test model."

Despite the fact that the couple rolling around on the bed had no idea she lay listening beneath them, Brooke's face flamed with humiliation. She was *not* dysfunctional! Just because she had instinctively sensed that Kyle was a rat and hadn't jumped into bed with him, he assumed she was dysfunctional. A cheap stab at salvaging his ego.

Wasn't it?

"What do you care?" Brandy asked, her voice laced with unmistakable jealousy. "You went out with her so people wouldn't become suspicious about *us*, right?"

Kyle was quick to respond. "Right, darling. Same as the others. Pretty soon we won't have to worry about appearances . . . *or* money."

Mulling over Kyle's last statement, Brooke nearly shrieked out loud as an earsplitting alarm began to sound.

"What the hell?"

It was Kyle, and he sounded frustrated. The bed squeaked as the couple leaped to their feet. Brooke let out a sigh as the springs moved away from her face. Clothes rustled; zippers were zipped in haste.

"Sounds like the building's fire alarm!"

"It does . . . guess we should check it out."

Brooke couldn't believe her good luck! Their voices faded, and a few seconds later she heard the front door open and close. Knowing there wasn't a second to waste, she scrambled out from under the bed and made a dash for the door.

Just before she reached for the knob, it began to turn.

Chapter Twenty-two

She froze in place, staring in horror as the door slowly swung open. Her hastily constructed explanation died in her throat as she recognized the figure standing in the doorway.

"Alex!" she had to nearly shout over the raucous sound of the fire alarm. "What . . . how . . ."

He grinned at her stunned expression. "I borrowed Elijah's horse."

He was joking, of course, because Elijah didn't have a horse. But he owned an old, temperamental Ford pickup that jarred a person's teeth loose. She knew from experience.

"Actually, Elijah gave me a ride," Alex confirmed.

"But . . . but why?" To spy on her? To find out if she was really friend or foe? After what she'd heard Kyle say, Brooke couldn't help wondering if Alex's apparent trust in her was all a sham—and had been all along.

His eyes darkened with an undefined emotion. "Because I hated the thought of you being here, alone, with Lotus. When I saw Lotus going upstairs with a strange woman, it didn't take me long to figure out that something was wrong."

"So after throwing me to the wolves, you had second thoughts and decided to rescue me."

Ignoring her sarcasm, he gestured to the door. "We'd better go before they figure out it was a false alarm."

"But they'll see us—"

"Not if we take the fire escape down. Elijah's waiting in the alley."

Brooke allowed herself to be tugged through the door and along the hall. She had questions, but she realized that now was not the time for asking. With the fire alarm blasting in her ear, she followed Alex down the fire escape to the street below.

She smelled burning motor oil before she spotted Elijah's black truck idling in the alley. Smoke billowed from the tailpipe; punctuated occasionally by a loud backfire.

Her old friend gave her a toothy grin, as if he were thoroughly enjoying himself. He reached across the seat to open the passenger door, throwing it wide. Brooke climbed in and scooted to the middle; Alex quickly climbed in beside her. He slammed the door, but it popped open again. With a muffled curse, he opened it again and slammed it harder.

This time it stayed shut.

It was a tight fit, leaving Brooke no room to pull away from Alex. Her thigh pressed against him, and their shoulders touched. She placed her hands in her lap and ignored the contact. Or tried to.

They had cleared the alley and bounced onto the main street in front of the apartments before Brooke remembered the papers she'd left on Kyle's desk.

"Damn!"

At her furious curse, Elijah hit the brakes, nearly sending Brooke through the cracked windshield. She braced herself against the dashboard, noticing that Alex had to do the same. "I've got to go back inside."

"Out of the question." Alex sounded adamant.

Brooke bristled at his bossy tone. "I found some papers you might be interested in seeing, but Kyle came in . . . and I left them lying on his desk. He'll know someone's been there!"

"You're not going back."

In the distance, Brooke heard the wail of a fire truck. Howie, the town's fire chief, was going to be madder than hell to find out it was a false alarm. She didn't relish running into Howie any more than she relished running into Kyle or Brandy, but after what she'd had to endure . . .

She ignored Alex's stubborn glare and turned

to Elijah. "Let me out, and wait here for me."

"You're not going back!" Alex said growling.

"I'm not on the clock right now, Bradshaw. Besides, *you're* the one who sent me in there—have you forgotten?"

"No, I haven't forgotten, which is precisely why I'm not letting you go back."

Stunned by his answer, Brooke froze. Was this Alex's offhand way of apologizing?

Elijah steered the old truck to the side of the road as the fire truck drew closer. Brooke looked at Alex as she asked cautiously, "What do you mean?"

"I mean that I shouldn't have sent you in the first place. It could have been dangerous."

Was this the real reason? Brooke wondered. Or did Alex have second thoughts only when he realized he couldn't witness the conversation between herself and Kyle? Kyle had said the PI had returned to Quicksilver with the specific purpose of asking more questions about *her.*

She'd caught Alex talking to his secretary. He could easily have instructed the PI to return. In fact, as head of the company, he was very likely the one who had ordered his return.

A queer feeling settled in her chest. It was hurt, she realized. The knowledge that Alex didn't trust her hurt, which was absurd, really. She'd kidnapped him. Of course he didn't trust her.

But he also knew the reason she'd kidnapped him, and that it had been an honest mistake. Still . . . breaking the law was breaking the law, and someone who would break the law wasn't generally someone who could be trusted.

Unfortunately, knowing that didn't ease the hurt.

Something was bothering her, Alex realized shortly after they arrived back at the cabin. Elijah had dropped them off at her car, which she'd parked on a side street out of sight of Kyle's apartment. They'd stopped for burgers on the way out of town.

Brooke hadn't touched hers.

Yes, something was definitely bothering her. And she was keeping something from him. It was there in her eyes, which were normally so expressive. Now they were shadowed and intense, black as night with zero visibility.

His jaw clenched when he thought of what might have happened if Kyle had caught her in his apartment. The thought of that bastard touching Brooke made him want to smash something. He was mostly angry with himself for being such a selfish brute.

He dipped a cold french fry in ketchup and popped it into his mouth, noticing that she hadn't touched her fries, either. "So you had no idea Kyle was seeing Brandy."

Brooke shook her head. "None. In fact, I was under the impression she didn't particularly care for Kyle."

"Tell me again what they said while you were under the bed."

"Are you hoping my story will change?"

Alex was tempted to reach across the table and haul her onto his lap for that snide remark. Reluctantly he quelled the urge. "No, I'm just trying to make sense of the conversation."

"Well, listen up, because this is the last time I'm repeating it. I heard the key in the lock, so I made a dash for the bedroom and hid under the bed. They came into the bedroom and Brandy suggested they get down to business. Kyle asked Brandy if she'd brought the condoms. They began to make out and the fire alarm went off. End of sex, end of Nancy Drew's disastrous attempt to ransack Kyle's apartment."

"How did that make you feel, hearing your exboyfriend making out with another woman?"

Her eyes finally came alive. They sparkled with disbelief and anger. "You think I was *jealous?*"

"Were you?" Alex countered.

"If I were," she drawled bitingly, "it certainly isn't any of your business."

Speaking of jealousy . . . Alex rose and went around the table. He brought her to her feet and closed his arms around her, trapping her against his heated body. "I need to know. Is it over between you and Lotus?"

Her fiery gaze clashed with his at close range. The impact made Alex's knees weak.

"Why do you want to know?" she taunted. "Are you looking for reassurance because you think eventually I'll give in and . . . and—"

"Make love with me?" Alex slowly, erotically

rotated his hips against hers, watching the awareness, mingled with alarm, flare in her eyes. "Have the time of your life? Is that what you're afraid of, Brooke? That you'll enjoy yourself too much?"

"Of all the conceited—"

"Don't change the subject," he interrupted in a low growl. "You want to as much as I do, don't you?" Again he moved his hips against hers, leaving her in no doubt the state of his arousal.

"Let me go."

He did, satisfied to see that she had to grab the top of her chair for support. He had to go one step further and sit down.

Why had she lied?

As Brooke tossed and turned, seeking sleep, she also sought an answer to her impulsive decision to remain silent about her discoveries.

If her suspicions proved true, Alex believed she was involved; if he found out she had lied about the conversation between Brandy and Kyle, he'd be convinced.

So why had she lied? True, she didn't know if the Landco folder she'd found in Kyle's filing cabinet held any merit in the investigation, but she also didn't know that it *didn't*.

And she had not only forgotten to grab the file, she had pretended to forget what the file contained.

Forgetting the file had been an honest blunder. Forgetting about Landco Synthetics was deliberate.

He hadn't believed her. She'd seen it in his eyes, a glimpse of disbelief . . . and a glimmer of suspicion.

Brooke sniffed. *So?* What did she care what he thought? Apparently Alex had suspected her all along, or he wouldn't have sent that nosy PI back to Quicksilver to ask more questions about her.

It was pride, she decided with a sigh. Her blasted stubborn pride had prompted her to keep quiet. All along Alex had obviously suspected her, watched her, and waited for her to stumble. Yet he'd sent her in to do his dirty work . . . hoping he'd catch them making plans together? She bit her lip, ignoring the curious pain in her heart. Had it been Alex's plan to storm the apartment after she and Kyle arrived? To catch them in a compromising situation? Or to sneak in and eavesdrop on their conversation?

Well, he must have been disappointed when he'd seen Brandy and Kyle heading into the building. It was Brooke's first pleasant thought all evening, the possibility that Alex had been disappointed. He and that nasty suspicious mind deserved to be disappointed.

Tomorrow, when her temper had cooled and her hurt had eased, she'd tell him the truth, share her own suspicions about what was going on, and confront him about the PI asking questions. It was time she and Alex came to an understanding. She wasn't an angel, but she wasn't a thief, either.

But first she was going to have a little talk with Brandy Clevenger. . . .

Chapter Twenty-three

The cabin was empty and silent when Alex awoke Saturday morning. A quick search confirmed that Brooke had once again tiptoed by him and escaped.

Alex frowned as he made coffee in the ancient percolator. Last night she'd mentioned nothing about working today. In fact, he was fairly certain she'd left out a lot of things last night.

Today he intended to find out just what she was hiding.

He jumped as his cell phone rang inside his boot, then grinned ruefully. After a week, he'd gotten used to the peace and quiet. Enjoyed it so much that he debated about not answering the insistent ring.

In the end he couldn't resist. He snatched it from his boot and pushed a button.

"I thought you might want to know that you're dealing with a lunatic," Gloria announced.

What happened to "Hello"? Alex wondered. "Gloria. Good morning."

His secretary ignored his dry greeting. "Aren't you worried?" she demanded. "Did you know that she was under a shrink's care?"

Calmly, Alex watched the clear bubble on top of the percolator and braced himself for another overly dramatic conversation with Gloria. "Let me guess: you're talking about Brooke Welch?"

"Of *course* I'm talking about Brooke Welch! The girl's a loose cannon, Alex. Her parents were shot in a convenience store six years ago. That's when she started seeing the shrink."

"Imagine that," Alex drawled sarcastically. "She's a victim of a violent crime and had to have therapy. What a weak woman." He *tsk-tsk*ed.

Gloria fell silent for a moment. Finally she said, "I'm worried about you, that's all. I thought you should know the woman has some unresolved issues that could make her dangerous. She dropped her therapy after one week— telling her psychologist to shove his practice where the sun doesn't shine."

Alex tightened his fingers on the phone, holding on to his temper by a small margin. "I take it you didn't get this information from the Internet."

"No, I sent Luther."

Closing his eyes, Alex counted silently to ten before he trusted himself to speak. "Let me get this straight. You knew that I didn't want anyone to know that I was here, yet you sent in a PI to ask questions."

"I didn't see the harm," Gloria said defensively. "In fact, I thought it added credence to your disappearance."

"If it hadn't been for you and your overactive imagination, I wouldn't have disappeared."

The reminder sailed over Gloria's head. "You've been ill, Alex. I was afraid you might not be . . . well, that you're not using your head."

It wasn't difficult to read between the lines. Gloria meant he might not be using the *right* head, and Alex had to admit there was a smidgen of truth in her words. Nothing he cared to admit, however. "Brooke may have some past issues—which are understandable, considering what you told me about her parents—but she's not a thief. I'd bet the boat on that."

"Or the factory?" Gloria needled. "Did you know that she was involved with Kyle Lotus, who is the—"

"I know who Lotus is," Alex said in a growl. Just the mention of the man's name curled his fist. "And I'm pretty sure he's our man."

"Hmm."

The not-so-subtle syllable prompted Alex to

defend Brooke. "She's not involved with Lotus now."

"Are you positive?"

"Yes, I'm positive!" Alex snapped. "The next time Luther contacts you, tell him to get the hell out of Quicksilver before he blows my cover."

"Fine. I will." Gloria sniffed. "I was only looking out for you."

Alex softened at her hurt tone. "I know, I know. But do me a favor, will you? Let me look out for myself."

He hung up the phone and poured himself a cup of coffee. Eventually he began to chuckle as he thought about Gloria's ridiculous suspicions. Though at first he'd harbored a few suspicions about Brooke, he knew now that she was incapable of being a party to something as dishonest as embezzling money.

The only thing she was guilty of stealing was his heart.

Brooke stumbled to a halt in her doorway, clutching the doorknob and staring at the mountains and mountains of boxes in her living room.

Boxes of Safe & Secure condoms from the factory.

Someone's idea of a sick joke?

Cautiously she stepped inside and closed the door. She locked it out of habit, her incredulous gaze glued to the mirage in her living room.

She kicked a box with her toe—SUPER RIBBED FOR THE ULTIMATE SEXUAL PLEASURE. She nudged another box, twisting it around to read the stamped letters on the side. GLOW IN THE DARK FOR THE ULTIMATE FANTASY FUN.

Not a mirage.

Her mouth dry, Brooke tore open a box and scrambled through the packages, tearing one open.

It was indeed a condom—neon pink—with Safe & Secure's inscription on the package.

As bizarre as it sounded, someone had broken into her home and filled her living room with condoms from the factory.

Why?

It was a big question, and a burning one. Why would someone do this? Brooke found it hard to believe someone would go to this much trouble for a joke.

On shaky legs, Brooke wound her way through the boxes until she reached the kitchen. She yanked out a chair at the table and sat.

It was a setup, Brooke thought, forcing her stunned mind to think. It had to be a setup, and she didn't have to guess long to figure out who had done the setting up.

Kyle Lotus and his cohort, Brandy Clevenger.

When Kyle had found the papers on his desk, he must have put two and two together and figured out she'd been in his apartment. It wouldn't be difficult, and Kyle was anything but stupid. The meeting she didn't keep, the misplaced papers, the fire alarm with no fire . . . no, it wouldn't be difficult to figure out that someone was onto him.

So he was trying to turn the tables, was he? Brooke narrowed her eyes, fighting the urge to deplete her stash of chipped plates by crashing them into the sink. What Kyle didn't know was that she was working with Alex, and Alex already knew his game.

Brooke sucked in a slow gasp, remembering that Alex didn't know everything. He didn't know of the mysterious conversation between Brandy and Kyle about the condoms and the money, and he didn't know the contents of the file she'd found locked away in Kyle's filing cabinet.

He also didn't know about the little book she'd found in the new secretary's desk, the one where she'd kept count of the customer complaints.

The clues were adding up, but last night the hurt had been too fresh. She hadn't felt very generous toward Alex after finding out he'd sent a PI to ask questions about her.

Today was a little better, and she had planned to tell him everything later, to share her thoughts on how Kyle was stealing from the factory.

Immediately after she told him—after she'd proved to him that she wasn't involved—she was going to regain her dignity by handing him her resignation. If he wanted her to continue working for him, then he was going to have to do some mighty convincing apologizing.

At least, that had been her plan before she walked through her front door and found a shipment of condoms in her living room.

Alex would believe her. Of course he'd believe her. The whole setup was so blatantly obvious, he'd probably laugh until he cried over Kyle's pitiful attempt to make her out to look like a thief.

Brooke nibbled on her fingernail. In the meantime, she had to get back to Alex and explain before Kyle reported the theft and pointed a finger in her direction, because she'd much rather explain this whole silly misunderstanding to Alex face-to-face and *not* through the bars of a jail cell. Together they'd plan the next step in bringing Kyle down.

Grabbing her purse, Brooke leaped over boxes and dashed to the front door. She had the presence of mind to take a careful look through the windowpanes before opening the door. She half expected to see Sheriff Snider striding up the walk with a search warrant in his hand.

The way her luck had been going, it wouldn't be a surprise.

She didn't see Sheriff Snider, but what she did see made her freeze.

A dark, late-model sedan was parked across the street from her house. The car itself might not have given her pause, but the man inside holding a pair of binoculars to his face gave her plenty of pause.

And he was looking in her direction.

"I don't believe it," Brooke muttered, swallowing hard. It had to be the PI who'd been asking questions, because she would have recognized either of the local cops or Sheriff Snider. Besides, she doubted if they knew how to do a stakeout—which was exactly what the PI was doing.

Staking her out. Spying on her.

If she'd had any doubts before about Alex's lack of trust in her, she had none now.

Fear receded, and anger—familiar and welcome for a change—returned. Brooke jerked open the door and stepped outside, careful not to glance in the man's direction. She took her time locking the door and walking to her car. She even managed to whistle as if she hadn't kidnapped Alex Bradshaw, stolen files from the factory, broken into Kyle's apartment, and now held a shipment of stolen condoms in her house.

Still whistling, she started the Pinto and backed out of her driveway. As she drove slowly down the residential street, a casual glance in the rearview mirror told her the sedan had moved in behind her. She cruised over to Main Street and followed it until she reached the city limits.

The moment she passed the sign welcoming folks to Quicksilver, Oklahoma, she put the pedal to the metal. The powerful 302 Boss engine roared to life.

Allowing herself a savage, victorious grin, Brooke rolled down the window and let the wind rush over her as she left the sedan behind.

Before long, the car was nothing more than a speck in her rearview mirror. He'd never catch her, she thought smugly.

Her smug smile died an instant death at the sight of the flashing lights that moved in behind her with lightning speed. With a groan and a curse, Brooke slowed the Pinto and pulled onto the shoulder.

There was only one car in town that could match the Boss's speed.

Brooke's heart began a heavy pounding as she watched Sheriff Snider unfold his tall form from the cruiser. But instead of coming her way, he turned and reached into the car. When he emerged again, he was holding . . . Brooke squinted, then ground out a curse as she recognized the object.

Her hubcap.

Chapter Twenty-four

What a day. Make that What a week. Brooke amended, cutting the engine and leaning her hot face against the steering wheel. Dee would never believe how incredibly crazy her life had become.

She kidnapped a man who refused to be *un*kidnapped.

Her house—her childhood home—was filled with condoms because her thieving boss—her immediate boss—was determined to put everyone at the factory out of a job and frame her in the process.

And to top it all, she had to share her one and only haven with a man who kept her in a perpetual state of intense arousal. A man she should be running *from*, and not *to*. Not that she had anyplace else to go.

Brooke turned her head slightly, her gaze landing on the warped hubcap on the seat beside her. For the second time in a week, the damned thing had nearly caused her to have heart failure.

Well, this was one aspect of her out-of-control life that she could fix, she determined, snatching it up and climbing out of the car. A few good whacks with a sledgehammer should do it—and make her feel better in the process. She'd beat it into shape and *weld* it on, if necessary.

And if it fell off again, she would leave it on the side of the road for good.

Gripping the hubcap, she skirted the front porch and marched to the backyard, glad to notice that Alex was conspicuously absent. *Good.* Maybe he'd gone to visit Elijah and she'd be left in peace for a while, free of him and his spying PI—and not a very good one at that, letting her see him. Apparently Alex didn't have the guts to tell her to her face that he didn't trust her.

Slamming the hubcap onto the chopping block and ignoring the strange, unwanted ache in her heart, she stomped to the small storage shed where her father had kept his fishing equipment and various woodworking tools.

Inside the dim interior of the shed, she found a sledgehammer lying on a shelf. It was nice and heavy . . . just what she needed to pound some respect into that ornery old hubcap. She emerged from the shed with the hammer and returned to the chopping block. Lifting the hammer high, she aimed for the warped side of the hubcap.

A splash from the lake halted her downward swing.

Brooke glanced in that direction, thinking the ducks that inhabited the lake had taken flight, or a particularly large bass had jumped to catch a dragonfly. If her father were alive, she thought wistfully, he'd race to get his fishing equipment.

It wasn't ducks, or a big fish flopping.

It was Alex.

As she watched, openmouthed and breathless, he rose from the water and waded to shore, slinging his wet hair from his face.

Naked. Dripping. Tanned and glistening. Muscled and magnificent. Adonis rising from the water, gorgeous and sexy enough to make any woman swoon.

Including herself.

A wave of dizziness washed over Brooke, reminding her that it was time she gave her lungs the air they needed. She inhaled slowly, then exhaled, unable to look away. Just breathe, she commanded herself, staring at the breathtaking sight walking in her direction.

He looked up and saw her, and even from a distance of twenty yards or so, she saw his interest.

He kept right on coming, brazen in his naked state. And with good reason, Brooke thought with a gulp. He had plenty to be proud of. . . .

The hammer slipped from her numb fingers, narrowly missing her toes as it thumped to the ground. Brooke reached blindly to the stump behind her and found the hubcap. She grabbed it and thrust it between them just as he reached her. "Cover yourself," she croaked, handing him the hubcap.

He took the hubcap, his gaze hot enough to evaporate the water drops clinging to his thick black eyelashes. The sun, warm and bright, made the air between them shimmer with heat as they continued to watch each other.

It was happening, Brooke thought. That *thing* she'd been fighting—avoiding, trying to ignore. The irreversible . . . inevitable conclusion. And it had nothing to do with Safe & Secure condoms, the factory, or the fact that Alex was her boss.

She knew that now—had probably known it all along.

This was about her and Alex, and the powerful need they generated in each other—*for* each other. The consummation they both craved was long past due. Whether he trusted her or not, whether he loved her or not . . . none of these facts would change the inevitable.

"Here?" he asked softly, glancing at the thick green grass at their feet.

No need to pretend; she knew exactly what he meant. Her own voice a bare whisper of surrender, she said, "No. Inside."

Silently she turned and led the way inside the cabin. Alex closed and locked the door while

Brooke drew the curtains across the front window. The ceiling fan above them lazily stirred the cooler air and chilled the sheen of sweat on Brooke's neck and shoulders. But she couldn't blame her hardened nipples on the cooler air, and the dampness between her legs had nothing to do with sweat.

They turned to each other in the middle of the room, like boxers facing off before a fight. Both were breathing as if they'd already gone several rounds. Alex stood with one hand holding the hubcap in front of him, and the other hand clenched at his side.

"Take off your blouse," he ordered hoarsely.

Hands shaking, Brooke unbuttoned her blouse without taking her eyes from his. Her nerves were screaming with anticipation, but her mind could not ignore the unresolved issues that remained between them. She wanted *nothing* between them, including secrets.

"Someone left a shipment of condoms at my house," she announced breathlessly.

His gaze never wavered. "I don't give a damn if Lotus left a dozen dead bodies."

He sounded as if he meant it, and the fact that he had known instantly who was responsible warmed her. Brooke reached for another button. "Last night I didn't tell you everything."

"I know, and it doesn't matter."

Her fingers paused for an instant, then resumed. His eyes were an electric, sizzling gray-green, but she knew their darkening had nothing to do with anger. There was a tautness about his face that was as obvious and as old as time. The knowledge that she was responsible left her weak and shaken. "Don't you want to know what I didn't tell you?"

"Later. Take your blouse off."

He liked watching, and she liked him watching her. She was also just as eager as he to get on with it, but she wasn't finished.

Sliding her blouse from her shoulders, she let it fall to the floor. She stood, bare-breasted, trembling and aching in her jeans and running shoes. "I saw the PI watching me."

A flicker that might have been irritation or surprise flashed in his eyes, then was gone. "Gloria sent him. I'll explain later. Now get out of those jeans."

She supposed she should have been ashamed to believe him so easily, but she wasn't. He had instantly known Kyle had planted the condoms in her house. Wasn't it only fair that she believe Alex? And wasn't it time she stopped making excuses for something she wanted every bit as much as he did?

Her hands went obediently to the metal snap of her jeans. She undid them as she kicked off her shoes, then slowly slid her jeans and panties over her hips. When she'd kicked them away, she looked at him again. Her chin came up as her gaze dropped to the only thing left between them.

It was her turn to make demands.

"Now get rid of that hubcap," she said in a growl.

With an audible groan, followed by a husky chuckle that made her thighs quiver with shameless need, Alex sent the hubcap spinning onto the couch, revealing the proud jut of his arousal. He waited with his feet braced apart, his well-toned thighs taut with tension.

Watching her with eyes that seared her skin and left it tingling.

For several tense moments, they simply stared at each other. Finally Alex indicated his bedroll in front of the cold fireplace. "There?"

Brooke shook her head, feeling bold and brazen. She jerked her head in the direction of the kitchen. "On the counter."

He didn't seem shocked or surprised by her request. He reached her in four easy strides, stopping a mere inch away. Slowly he lifted his hand and cupped her face, lowering his mouth to hers in a tender, devouring kiss that buckled her knees. She had anticipated hunger, even savagery, something she could handle, something that would keep things in perspective.

He caught her against him, then lifted her in his arms. When they reached the countertop, he snatched up the box of condoms and headed for the bedroom. He smiled at her startled expression.

"You've got water in your ears," Brooke told him, winding her arms around his neck. "I said I wanted to do it on the counter—"

"I know what you said. I also know that you're expecting a few frenzied moments of down-and-dirty sex."

Brooke swallowed a gasp of surprise. "Aren't you? I mean, isn't that what we both want?"

"Maybe later. Right now I'm going to knock down a few fences."

His meaning sank in. Brooke began to struggle in his arms, fear streaking through her. "Alex, no! Put me down. I've . . . I've changed my mind."

He paused and kissed her again, that slow, tender kissing that made her feel all gooey inside. Shaky. Close to breaking apart. And very pliable.

He knows too much about me, Brooke thought, her inner fear escalating. She didn't want him to know her weaknesses, didn't want him busting down her defenses—her *fences*. It had taken six long years to build them, and she wasn't ready to take them down. Taking them down meant facing an overwhelming grief she wasn't ready to face. For Dee's sake, she had to remain strong.

But Dee was grown now, and married.

Brooke moaned at the ruthless reminder. "Alex . . . don't do this to me." She was begging, pleading, but right now she didn't care. "Let's just *do it*, and . . . and have a good time. It's silly to pretend emotions—"

"Who's pretending?" Alex set her gently on the bed, then quickly lowered himself beside her. He dropped the box of condoms by the side of the bed and turned to her. When she tried to rise, he closed his arms around her and held her tight.

She began to shake. The fence was beginning to wobble. *Damn him!* Despite the fact that he was forcing her to fall apart, she still wanted him, and he knew it. But it seemed Alex was going to have it his way . . . or no way at all.

It wasn't fair. He was supposed to prefer it her way! Instead he was turning into some kind of . . . of *gentleman* at the worst possible time. She wanted it down and dirty because down and dirty she could handle.

She feared gentle would tear her apart.

It was a clear case of fraud on his part, she decided, squirming in his arms.

His erection knocked against her. She heard him inhale with a sharp hiss. Desperate to turn the tables, she reached between them and closed her hand around his thick length. He throbbed and burned against her skin. Slowly she drew her hand down, then up, repeating the motion in an effort to make him forget about being a gentleman.

"It's not going to work, babe," he whispered against her neck—albeit in a strained tone. "I'm going to make slow, sweet love to you until the cows come home."

"No." Brooke searched for and found his nipple, nipping and sucking. Again he inhaled sharply.

"Yes." In retaliation, he pulled her head away from his chest and began to cover her face with tiny, tender little kisses. His mouth finally closed over hers. He eased his tongue inside and stroked her warmth with a lover's caress until she moaned.

The kiss went on and on, changing, growing deeper, hungrier, yet always sweet and tender. Brooke slipped her leg over his and thrust her pelvis forward, intent on taking what she wanted before he had the opportunity to complete his agenda.

He drew back with a regretful little chuckle.

"I hate you," she said in a hiss, burying her face in his shoulder. His chuckle turned into a laugh. Brooke took advantage of his distraction to slide from his arms and along his body. She reached her destination and closed her mouth over him before he realized her intent.

He growled and hastily lifted her up. "You little minx." And with that statement, he drew her nipple into his mouth and slowly drove her insane with the mastery of his tongue. Brooke buried her fingers in his hair, hanging on for dear life. He gave the same attention to the other breast, then proceeded to kiss her belly, her thighs, her knees, until finally he reached her feet.

Watching her through storm-dark eyes, he slowly drew her little toe into his mouth and sucked. Completely helpless now, Brooke could only watch as he continued to melt her defenses.

The man was magical. Incredible. Incomparable—not that she had much to compare him to. But she knew, instinctively, that Alex was an unselfish, wonderful lover.

And very, very stubborn.

When he'd thoroughly aroused all ten toes, he reached beside the bed for the condoms.

Brooke watched him, frowning as a memory nudged her desire-fogged brain. Something about the condoms, and Kyle and Brandy. With a jolt, she remembered. "Please, let me." She held out her hand for the condoms and Alex gave them to her. As she opened the box, she casually checked the date.

She managed to swallow a relieved sigh. She'd gotten the box from under the passenger seat, where a hopeful coworker had stuck them a long time ago, which meant they were probably safe to use. It was on the tip of her tongue to tell Alex now about her suspicions, but when she glanced up and saw him watching her so intently, she decided it could wait.

He looked more than ready to continue.

With a faint, playful smile, Brooke opened a grape-flavored condom and beckoned him closer. His eyes narrowed with suspicion.

"You're up to something," he said roughly.

Brooke didn't bother denying it. Her smile grew. "Yes."

"Minx."

She clucked her tongue. "Sticks and stones . . ." She curled her finger again, feeling reckless. "Now come here."

He edged closer, still eyeing her with suspicion. Brooke centered the condom on his pulsing, impressive length and slowly, teasingly, began to roll it down. His breath quickened.

Brooke bent forward as if to better view her task. Her tongue darted out, circling the quivering tip—so quickly he could do nothing but gasp.

Smiling at him, Brooke sat back on her heels and ran her tongue over her lips. "Yum, grape-flavored. One of our most popular varieties. Guaranteed to satisfy—"

With a very explicit oath, Alex smothered the rest of her words with his mouth and pressed her backward on the bed. Brooke gasped and braced her hands against his chest as he followed, her victory cut short as he pulled his mouth free and pinned her gaze beneath the blaze of his own.

"You, babe, are in deep trouble."

A threat had never sounded sweeter.

Chapter Twenty-five

Alex saw the anticipation in her eyes, and really, really hated to disappoint her. He knew what she thought. She thought she'd finally pushed him beyond control . . . and that mind-blowing tongue-twirling thing had been close.

But he had a little control left in reserve and he planned to utilize every inch of it. He wanted all of Brooke's attention, body and soul.

Speaking of inches, he'd never felt so full, so thick, and so damned hard. He was so close to her now that he could feel her literally pulsing against him—as if she were reaching out to draw him inside her. And if it was a sign of weakness that he had to grit his teeth—hard—

he didn't care because he didn't have much choice.

Her fingers curled against his chest as she stared at him with those hot, bone-melting eyes and whispered, "I'm waiting for my punishment."

Alex held her gaze and pressed very slowly against her until he felt her heat close around the very part of him she'd circled with her tongue. She tensed, her eyes flaring wider, her lips parting in joyous expectation.

"And you're going to get it," he promised softly, watching her reaction with intense pleasure, "but you're going to get it my way."

His smile was smug when she caught her breath in alarm. He pushed forward again, sinking a little deeper and desperately trying to think of anything other than how hot and tight she felt around him.

When she tried to trick him and surge forward, he anticipated the move and moved with her, holding back. "No, you don't, babe."

She pouted, her lips moist and inviting. "Why do we have to do this your way?"

"Because right now you're in no position to argue," Alex said huskily. "We'll do it your way later, I promise." Holding his position—with more effort than she would ever know—he captured her lips and moved his mouth seductively against her own. It was a kiss of tenderness, but she seemed to sense his inner struggle, for she whimpered and tried again to capture all of him.

Using one hand to hold her hips still, Alex trailed his lips along her jaw, onto her neck, and nibbled at her earlobe. "You taste so sweet," he whispered against her neck.

"Alex . . ."

He kissed her again—not the hungry, rough kissing he knew she wanted and expected, but devouring, soul-shattering kissing he knew she needed.

Brooke Welch had met her match.

"Alex . . . please!"

Alex thought of fishing, working out in the gym, poring over boring figures, and slowly, inch by teeth-gritting inch, sank into her welcoming body. When their bodies became one in the most torturous, sweetest way imaginable, he stopped.

Her nails pressed into the bunched muscles in his back as she ordered, "Don't stop."

"I won't, baby, I won't." And he didn't. At least, not for long. But he kept his strokes slow and easy as sweat pooled between his shoulder blades and his heart threatened to burst from his chest. He'd never been more determined to bring a woman to the height of ecstasy, and it had never been more difficult to hold back.

He watched her, and she watched him. As he nearly left her, then began the slow takeover again, he nuzzled his nose against hers. "We're making love," he stated gruffly.

She gave her head a slight shake, gasping as he sank into her to the hilt. "No . . . we're just having sex."

But she sounded doubtful. Alex smiled, tugging on her bottom lip with his teeth. Her breath feathered across his face. Her tongue darted out and traced his top lip and a low, keening moan rose from her throat.

She was close.

And so was he.

She began to tense around him, and deep inside her, Alex could feel her muscles contracting, grasping. Loving him.

At the moment of her release, Alex moved his mouth over hers, capturing her cry. She rose against him, pouring her soul into the kiss.

The fragile thread of his control snapped.

He followed her descent with a primitive growl, plunging deep as pleasure exploded inside him. He'd known it would be good with Brooke, but he'd never dreamed it would be this earth-shattering.

The reality stole his breath.

Against his ear, he heard Brooke whisper shakily, "I told you . . . the package said satisfaction guaranteed."

His chuckle came out sounding like a groan. "As we say in Texas, you, darling, are a hoot."

Alex rolled to his side and took her with him, holding her close as their breathing returned to normal.

He was still inside her, and he was still hard. He doubted that status would change as long as he held her. Stroking her damp hair, he enjoyed the feel of her heart beating against his, and her breath against his neck.

"So what do we do now?" she asked, stirring restlessly.

Alex tightened his hold, bracing himself for a struggle. "We talk."

"Talk? Oh, about the factory and—"

"No." Alex released a slow breath as he added, "About your parents, and how they died."

How could he? How could he bring up the painful subject of her parents' deaths right after she'd—they'd—experienced great sex?

Brooke tried to shove herself out of his arms, but he wasn't budging. He'd planned this, she realized with growing panic. He'd deliberately set out to lower her defenses so that he could move in for the kill.

Well, she wasn't going down without a fight, by God! "Let . . . me . . . go!"

"No."

He sounded almost sorry.

The bastard. "Look, Alex, I know you think you have to play this game and pretend you care, but honestly, you don't. Just let me up and—"

"You'll what?" he asked softly. "Break a few plates? Chop a cord or two of wood? Keep holding your grief inside until it rips you into little pieces?"

She moved again, and realized that he was still hard inside her.

A shudder shook her from head to toe. "You've been talking to Elijah."

"He dropped a clue or two, but the rest I figured out on my own."

"I don't want to talk about it," she insisted. "And you can't make me."

"Dee's grown now. You can let it go."

The sound of his tender, gentle words caused her eyes to water with hated tears. She had to get loose, run like hell before it was too late.

"It has nothing to do with Dee." It was a lie, but she didn't figure it was any of his business. And why he was attempting to *make* it his business remained a mystery to her.

"How did they die?"

Brooke clamped her lips tightly together and concentrated on ignoring him. It wasn't easy, considering that a part—a very pleasurable part—of his body was still attached to her own. And his scent . . . *God, his scent!* The man could market it and sell it as an aphrodisiac! She'd never realized that sunshine on a man's body had a smell. . . .

"Ignoring me won't work. I've got nowhere to go, so I can lie here as long as it takes."

She ground her teeth. He sounded so damned smug and serious. Desperate to distract him, she wedged her hand between them and began to scrape her nails along his chest in a slow, provocative journey downward.

"And *that* will only prolong the inevitable," Alex drawled with a soft gasp that proved he wasn't as calm as he seemed. "Did you cry even once when they died?"

The question made her eyes burn and her

chest grow tight, but she steadfastly ignored it. Instead she concentrated on changing the subject and his mind by tightening her inner muscles around him.

In response to her bold move, she felt him jerk inside her. A thrill darted through her and settled into her belly like a hot coal. Against her cheek, she felt the rhythm of his heart pick up speed. Brooke lifted her head and kissed him with an urgent, hungry passion, sensing victory.

He didn't deny her.

In one smooth roll, he came to his feet and cradled her in his arms. He paused long enough to pluck a condom from the box on the floor before striding into the kitchen.

A long sigh escaped Brooke as she continued to taste and nibble his neck. Now, she thought, they would get down to business and leave all of the emotional garbage behind.

He sat her on the counter and moved between her legs. Brooke threw her head back and closed her eyes, listening to the sound of him ripping open a new condom.

It was music to her ears.

Her thighs quivered in shameless expectation. She was insatiable . . . how could she be this eager when they'd only just finished moments before?

"Brace yourself," he ordered hoarsely, grabbing her thighs.

Brooke placed her hands on the counter behind her, gasping as he entered her. Her tormentor was gone—replaced by a greedy, expert lover who knew exactly what he wanted and harbored no qualms about going after it, again and again, fast and furiously.

The tension inside her grew at an alarming rate, spinning out of control, shocking her with its intensity. Searching for an anchor against the gathering storm, Brooke wound her arms around his neck and buried her face against his chest. The ripples became pounding, pleasurable waves that swept her up and away.

She cried his name in a choked whisper, "Alex!"

It was a mistake.

Alex funneled his hand through her hair and lifted her head, continuing the pace without missing a beat, prolonging her pleasure. "Look at me."

The command couldn't be ignored. Brooke looked, watching his beautiful features grow rigid with his impending release. His eyes burned into hers, delved into her soul, stroked her heart as assuredly as he stroked her womanly core.

Brooke tried to look away, but found herself hypnotized by his gaze. He was telling her something without words.

He was telling her that he cared.

She didn't want to know. Had been desperately avoiding this moment.

Alex wouldn't allow her to ignore it. His eyes nearly closed as he began to climax, his strokes sinking deeper and with more force. Slowly he lowered his mouth onto hers.

Just before their lips met, he gasped her name.

Not with passion or triumphant satisfaction, but with aching, soul-wrenching tenderness.

In that split second, Brooke felt those old, weathered fences she'd taken such pains to erect crash to the ground.

Chapter Twenty-six

Alex tasted her salty tears and dared hope that he had succeeded in his quest. But he had no thoughts of gloating, because somewhere along the way, Brooke's pain had become his own.

Finally she broke the connection and pressed her warm forehead against his. Hot tears streaked down her cheeks and splattered onto his arms in a steady stream. Alex gently stroked her back and waited, wishing there was something he could do to ease her pain.

Her voice was surprisingly steady as she said, "My parents had this ritual . . . they always went out to eat on Saturday nights. Sometimes they caught the late show after dinner. That weekend I was home from college because I'd promised Dee I'd help her get ready for her first school dance. I remember that she was *so* excited."

She paused for a moment, as if to gather her strength. Alex's heart went out to her. He pressed his lips against her forehead, silently offering his support.

"If it hadn't been for that dance, Dee would have been with them."

A shudder shook her petite frame. Alex tightened his arms. He could almost feel the long-suppressed grief clawing its way out of her.

"Dad was trying to quit smoking, and they stopped at a convenience store—one of two that we have in town—to buy a pack of gum."

She looked at him, and Alex could see that in Brooke's case, time had not been her friend; her anger at the atrocity had grown instead of waned over the years.

"A pack of gum. That's all Dad wanted. Mom was waiting in the car. Apparently she got impatient and went in to investigate." Her fingers dug into his forearms, but Alex doubted she noticed. "She walked in on the robbery—two local boys high on coke, with previous records as long as your arm. They—" Her voice broke, but she valiantly steadied it. "They panicked and shot her as she entered the store. Right through the . . . the heart. When Dad moved to go to her . . . they shot him in the back."

"I'm sorry." Alex swallowed a big, hard lump in his throat. Such an awful story . . . a horrendous crime committed against two innocent people. "I know it doesn't help, but I am sorry."

"No, it doesn't help," Brooke agreed, but she reached out and touched his cheek in a grateful gesture, seemingly oblivious to the constant flow of tears that continued to splatter his arms. "But thank you anyway. As hard as it is for me to admit it, I think I needed a good cry."

"Six years is a long time to go without crying."

Brooke shrugged, roughly wiping at her face. "I've cried plenty. I cried on Dee's first date because my dad wasn't there to scare the pants off of the boy."

"But *you* did." Alex was suddenly very certain of that. Her smile was a little sheepish and a lot on the naughty side. He felt his manhood leap in response; he quickly shamed it down.

"Yes, I did. Maybe too much. Her date brought her home at nine o'clock, and Dee didn't speak to me for a week." Her smile faded into sadness. "I cried at her graduation because my parents weren't there to see it. I cried when she left for college . . . for the same reason."

"Sounds like you did a damned fine job of raising her," Alex said gruffly. "Your parents would have been proud." Hell, *he* was proud!

She sniffled. "I don't think they'd be too happy about the current situation."

"It all turned out for the best, didn't it?" In fact, Alex made a mental note to send Dee and Cliff a nice wedding present. He had a lot to thank them for.

"We can only hope." Brooke worried her bottom lip with her teeth until Alex dived in to rescue it, soothing the hurt with his tongue. Her breath hitched in response to the provocative move.

"So . . . what do we do now?" she whispered between kisses and nibbles.

"Hmm. I have a few ideas. Wanna hear them?"

Her face still wet with tears, she laughed and put her hands between them. "I'm talking about the enormous amount of condoms at my house, and Kyle, the factory rat who put them there."

With a reluctant groan, Alex gathered her up from the counter and took her to the sofa, where he set her gently down again. He began to scoop up her clothing from the floor.

"If you insist on talking, you'd better get dressed first. You're messing with my concentration."

Her spontaneous giggle warmed his heart.

Over the next half hour as they ate a lunch of cold fried chicken and drank cans of ice-cold Coke, Brooke told Alex everything she had omitted earlier, and her suspicions about what she'd learned.

Then she listened as Alex told her his plan.

She had to admit that it sounded as if it might work, but there was just one teeny little part about his plan that caused her to hesitate.

She wiped her fingers on her napkin and took a swig of Coke. "So you really think once they arrest me for stealing the shipment of condoms and I'm in jail, Kyle will believe he's in the clear and get careless?"

"It could work. Especially if I show up and give him a clap on the back for catching you. Maybe even a promotion."

"You think he's that stupid?"

"No, I think he's that arrogant."

Brooke shook her head, having second thoughts. "I don't know. It all sounds a little drastic to me. I mean, not only is Sheriff Snider going to be madder than a wet hornet when he finds out you've been right here at the cabin all along, he's not going to appreciate us using him in our plan to trap Kyle."

Alex shrugged and dropped his gaze, reaching for another chicken leg. "Surely he'll understand when we explain everything to him."

"Where do you think he put the file? I doubt Kyle's stupid enough to keep it in his apartment after last night."

"We'll find it," Alex promised grimly. "After you're in jail and he thinks he's free of suspicion, I wouldn't be surprised if we found it on his coffee table."

"What if he catches you?"

His wicked smile heated her blood.

"Who said anything about me? I plan to stay right here and enjoy my vacation until it's time for me to make an appearance."

Brooke folded her arms and scowled at him. "Meanwhile, *I'll* be sleeping on a hard cot, urinating in an open toilet, and eating half-frozen TV dinners."

Alex came around the table and pulled her into his arms before she could gasp, nuzzling his lips against her neck. His low, masculine growl made her limp all over. "Believe me, I'd much rather you be here so that we could continue your therapy."

"You mean the sex." She felt him stiffen and immediately wished the callous words back.

"I told you, we were making love, not having—" He lifted his head and pinned her with a stern glare. "We'll continue our discussion when this is all over, understand?"

Drowning in the deep gray-green of his eyes, Brooke found herself whispering obediently, "Yes, sir."

She brushed aside the inner voice of caution urging her to beware of smooth-talking, smart-dressed men spouting promises.

Besides . . . why shouldn't she believe him?

Kyle didn't waste any time.

Two hours later, when Brooke pulled into the driveway of her family home, she didn't have to fake her nervous reaction on finding Sheriff Snider and Officer Duncan Gregory waiting for her. And why wouldn't she be nervous? Her living room was filled with stolen condoms, and although she knew she was innocent, they didn't. In fact, Alex's entire plan hinged on the fact that they would believe she'd stolen them.

The grim-faced men watched her as she got out of the car and walked in their direction.

"Sheriff Snider, Duncan." Brooke nodded

and stuck her hands in her jeans pockets, darting a nervous glance at the house. "Something tells me this isn't a social call."

Sheriff Snider frowned and asked sharply, "Why would you say that?"

"Well, you both look as if you've just discovered a dead body." Brooke feigned a sudden look of horror. "It's . . . it's not Dee, is it? Dear God—"

"No, no, gal, this ain't about Dee." Sheriff Snider cleared his throat and looked at the house before his shrewd gaze returned to her. "I've got a warrant to search your house."

This was the part of the plan that Brooke dreaded the most—allowing Sheriff Snider to believe that she was guilty. Muttering a quick prayer to the heavens above, Brooke threw herself into the part wholeheartedly, vowing to kick Alex's cute butt if Sheriff Snider didn't forgive her later.

Angling her chin defensively, Brooke asked, "May I see the warrant, please?" When he handed it to her, she took her time reading it. Finally she gave it back to him. "Well, I guess I can't stop you, can I?"

"No, you can't." Sheriff Snider motioned to Duncan, who gave a disbelieving shake of his head. "Come on, Duncan. Let's take a look inside."

They strode up the sidewalk to the front door, then moved aside for Brooke to unlock it.

"I want you to know," Sheriff Snider began, swinging the door wide, "that I don't believe a word Lotus told me—" He broke off, his gaze widening in shock at the boxes stacked in her living room.

Brooke felt her face heat, and she wished Alex were close enough to kick right now. Suddenly—and belatedly—she thought of a dozen different ways they could have trapped Kyle that didn't involve disappointing this good man.

But it was too late.

She had to drag the damning words out of her throat. "I'm . . . I'm sorry."

"If you needed money, you could have come to me." When she remained silent, he added, "You know I'm gonna have to take you in."

He was angry, and Brooke didn't blame him. Bowing her head, Brooke whispered with genuine shame, "Yes, I know." She heard the rattle of handcuffs, then Sheriff Snider's furious voice.

"We're not putting handcuffs on her, you fool! Take her to the patrol car and read her her rights. I'll stay and make an inventory of the . . . stolen goods, see if they match what Lotus says is missing."

Brooke went along docilely, glancing back once at Sheriff Snider. She winced at the naked anguish on his face. "I'm going to kill him," she muttered, referring to Alex.

Duncan, however, made his own interpretations.

"Now, Brooke, you don't need to be making things worse by threatening Lotus. I don't like the man myself, but he's got a job to do just like the rest of us. Stealing's wrong, no matter who's doing it."

She automatically ducked her head as he guided her into the backseat of his patrol car. As a child, she'd ridden with Sheriff Snider several times during his shift just for the sheer fun of it, and once to gather research for a term paper about the increasing dangers that officers faced each day, but she'd never ridden in the backseat.

Of course, she'd never before been a prisoner.

"This had better work, Bradshaw."

Duncan twisted around to look at her. "Did you say something?"

Brooke shook her head, unable to meet his questioning gaze. "I was just thinking that things certainly look different from the backseat of a patrol car."

"You wanna ride up front?"

Swallowing a hysterical giggle at his gracious offer, she declined. "Thanks, anyway."

As they pulled away from the curb, Brooke caught a flash of bright red from the corner of her eye. She squinted against the glare from the window. Her eyes narrowed further as she recognized the older-model Corvette and the driver behind the wheel.

It was Kyle Lotus, sitting in his parked car a few houses down, watching and gloating, Brooke presumed, arrogantly assuming he had cleverly diverted suspicion onto her. She fumed silently, resisting the childish urge to flip him the bird. *All in good time,* she chanted in her mind. *All in good time.*

Unless . . . unless Alex couldn't find the Landco file. If that happened, Brooke shuddered to imagine how they'd convince Sheriff Snider of the truth after her guilty behavior.

But Kyle wasn't the only one witnessing her humiliation, Brooke realized as they passed a dark sedan parked on her street.

So was the PI hired by the Bradshaw Corporation.

Chapter Twenty-seven

Farther down the street where Lotus was parked, Elijah and Alex sat in the old truck waiting for Lotus to leave. At the last moment Alex had impulsively decided to ride along, and as a precaution, he wore a faded baseball cap pulled low over his forehead, and a pair of ancient, wire-rimmed sunglasses Elijah had also uncovered from deep within his closet. The frames were bent and the lenses so scratched Alex had to continuously refocus his eyes, but all in all he thought it was a good disguise.

"He's leaving," Elijah said, pointing to the red Corvette pulling away from the curve.

Alex squinted through the scratched sunglasses and the bug-splattered, cracked windshield. The old man must have eyes like a hawk, he thought. "We'd better hurry before Luther follows her."

"I'm on it, Batman."

"I prefer James," Alex responded, imitating Sean Connery's distinct accent. "That's James Bond."

The motor backfired and bucked before leaping forward, nearly giving Alex whiplash. When Elijah pulled the truck alongside the sedan, Alex grabbed the knob and tried to roll down the window, intending to signal Luther before he could pull away; the knob came off in his hand. With a stifled curse lest he hurt the old man's feelings, he pitched the knob in the seat and grasped the inside door handle.

He had to give it three good shoves and a mighty kick before it came open. *Hell.* Didn't anyone in this town own a decent vehicle? he wondered. Ignoring Elijah's muffled chuckles, he got out and tapped on Luther's window.

The startled man gave a shriek and shrank back.

"Luther, it's me. Alex Bradshaw."

The window lowered at the speed of light, revealing Luther's long, thin face beneath the oversize Stetson he wore. His eyes bulged. "Alex? Is that really you?"

Alex lifted his glasses and arched a mocking brow. "In the flesh. Unlock the door and let me in." He turned and gave Elijah the signal to catch up with Kyle before trotting around to the passenger side.

Luther stared at Alex in disbelief as he climbed into the passenger seat. "Gloria said you fancied yourself as James Bond, but I didn't believe her. By God, you do, don't you?"

"I don't have time to talk about my secretary and her overactive imagination," Alex said dryly. "From now on you're working for me, not her."

"But she said—"

"Never mind what Gloria said. Suffice it to say you've been manipulated by a paranoid secretary. Now we've got a lot of work to do in a short amount of time. Elijah's going to keep Lotus busy for as long as he can, but since Lotus isn't too fond of his uncle—"

Mouth open in shock, Luther managed, "That old man is Kyle Lotus's uncle?"

Alex couldn't help grinning. "Missed that one, did ya? Yes, Kyle is Elijah's nephew. But he's not proud of the fact so he doesn't go around bragging about it. Get going. We're headed to Lotus's apartment—I'm sure you know where he lives."

Luther put the car in gear and pulled away from the curb. "I do, but why are we going there?"

"To search it."

"You mean, make an illegal search?"

"What other kind is there if you aren't a cop?" Alex retorted, his lips lifting at Luther's scandalized tone.

"I think you're barking up the wrong tree," Luther informed him smugly, making a left turn. "Brooke Welch is the person you're after."

"Is that so?"

The PI nodded vigorously. "Yes. A mysterious shipment of boxes arrived at her house in the wee hours this morning."

"Hmm." Alex couldn't resist playing with the PI. "I wonder what was in them?"

"Condoms!" Luther announced triumphantly. "From *your* factory."

"And just how would you know what's in those boxes?"

Luther clamped his lips tightly together, appearing to need all of his concentration to navigate the nearly deserted streets leading to Lotus's apartment.

But Alex was having too much fun to give the guy a break. "Luther? You didn't by any chance make one of those *illegal* searches, did you?"

Two blocks later, Luther finally confessed. "Okay, okay. I did go into her house, but only for a second. The suspense was driving me crazy. I had to know what was in those boxes."

Alex tensed. "Did you see who was driving the truck that delivered the shipment?"

"I would probably know him again if I saw him."

"Good. If all else fails, you might have to identify him for me."

"If all else fails," Luther repeated faintly. "Are you going to tell me what's going on?"

"Since you'll be the one making the illegal search, I guess it would only be fair to fill you in."

The PI swallowed hard. "I hope you've brought your checkbook, because this is going to cost you. I could lose my license over this."

"Well, then I guess you'll have to make sure you don't get caught. Otherwise, how will you spend all that money I'm going to pay you?"

In this instance, the promise of money didn't seem to mollify Luther. "Where will you be while I'm risking my butt?" he demanded, parking the sedan in front of the apartment building and cutting the engine.

"I'll be waiting in the car. Don't worry, I'll honk if Lotus appears."

Luther groaned. "I feel so much better knowing you're watching my back."

"I'm flattered. Now, here's what we're looking for. . . ."

"Are you sure you're comfortable?" Officer Gerald asked anxiously. "Because Sheriff Snider said you're not to be treated like a criminal."

Wisely hiding her amusement, Brooke glanced at the jail cot—now padded with a thick foam mattress covered with several quilts, and piled high with fluffy pillows. It looked more inviting than her bed at home.

She flashed Gerald, who had often been described as a slightly taller Danny DeVito, a grateful smile. "I'm fine, really."

"And the food? Is your steak too rare? Because if it is, I can send it back. Treva can give it another minute or two on the fire—"

"Gerald," Brooke inserted forcibly.

"Yes, ma'am?"

"Isn't there something you need to do?" She jerked her head at the toilet seat behind her, hoping he'd get the hint.

Gerald's face turned beet red. "Oh, right. I'll just pull the curtain for you, and leave you alone to do your, ah, business."

When the hastily strung sheet was firmly in place across the bars, Brooke sank onto the cot and glanced at the plate of food Gerald had brought from Treva's Diner.

She had requested a salad to mollify him, but he'd brought her a thick, juicy steak, a steaming baked potato heaped with butter and sour cream, and hot, crusty rolls. There was even a little crock of whipped butter and a dish of peach cobbler for dessert.

Too bad she wasn't hungry.

Her glance strayed from the queenly feast to the small television set, then to the half-open door. *So much for locked cells, hard cots, open toilets, and frozen TV dinners,* she thought, her lips twitching. *If Alex could see me now.*

Transferring the plate to the top of the television set, Brooke made herself comfortable on the cot and tucked her arms behind her head. She wondered what Alex was doing right now, and if everything was going the way he'd so carefully planned.

And if he felt as replete, yet drained, as she.

Her smile grew as she recalled every delicious detail of their lovemaking. Alex had not only knocked her fences down, he'd knocked her socks off. When she thought of how much time she'd wasted fighting her own feelings, she wanted to kick herself. Instead they could have been spending the evenings and nights making love. Hell, she could have taken a vacation and spent the days with him as well! So what if he was her boss? Secretaries married their bosses all the time—

Brooke came upright on the cot, sucking in a sharp, dismayed breath. *Whoa, girl. Nothing was said about love or marriage.*

The cautious voice was right; Alex had insisted they were making love . . . but he hadn't said *I love you.*

Thank God she hadn't made a fool of herself by confessing her own growing feelings for Alex.

Did she love him?

She frowned, easing back onto the pillows. It was a good question, and one she supposed she should be asking herself so that she could prepare her heart for the day Alex left town.

It didn't take her long to come to a conclusion: She did love Alex. Loved him so much it made her ache. It had to be love, because being in lust couldn't possibly make her heart throb at the thought of his leaving.

The way it was throbbing now.

Damn. Brooke bit her bottom lip, shaking her head. She'd gone and fallen in love with her boss. Not only inexcusable, but hopeless.

"Brooke? You decent?"

It was Sheriff Snider.

She sat up and tried to look suitably ashamed before answering, "Yes, I'm decent."

The sheet scrolled to one side and the cell door creaked as Sheriff Snider stepped into view, filling the tiny space with his imposing presence. He tipped his hat, but his face remained stern and censorious.

"I came to tell ya that I gave young Bradshaw a call and told him what we found. His secretary said he'd want to deal with this personally."

Brooke's heart skipped a beat, then settled into a slow, heavy *chug-chug*. She had to tilt her head to look at Sheriff Snider. "What, you mean they found Alex Bradshaw?" It wasn't in the plans, but she supposed Alex could have decided to make an early—

"Guess it's okay to tell ya, since you're, um . . ." Sheriff Snider trailed away and scratched his chin. His brows furrowed in a fierce frown. "He's *been* found. Never was lost, in fact. A couple days after he disappeared, his secretary called in and told us to call off the search. Said he was close by doing a little undercover work concerning the factory. We were told to keep quiet."

The day after . . .

Shock was a mild definition of what Brooke felt at the sheriff's revelation. Alex had lied to her. He'd deliberately, cruelly held the kidnapping charge over her head to keep her at the cabin, and to force her into helping him investigate.

He had *used* her, all the while steadily luring

her into his sensual web . . . to relieve his boredom? To prove that he could? After finding out the ugly truth, Brooke found it hard to believe that he cared. He could have told her the truth any number of times, but he hadn't. Instead he had bared her to the bone, revealing old wounds and forcing her to confront her grief over the loss of her parents.

She had been foolishly honest with him, but Alex obviously didn't believe in two-way streets.

"Brooke . . . ? Are you all right? You look pale all of a sudden."

"I'm . . . I'm fine." She resisted the urge to check her chest for blood. "Just peachy, but I'm a little tired. If . . . if you don't mind, I think I'll take a nap."

"Okay, but when Bradshaw gets here, I expect he'll want to talk to you."

"Yes. Yes, of course. I'll want to talk to him, too." *Talk. Shout. Curse.* She expected she'd be doing all three until her throat turned raw.

Her burning, furious gaze landed on the plate of food. With a snarl, she turned her back on it. Paper. Gerald had brought her a useless *paper* plate. What she wouldn't give for a good, breakable piece of china right now.

And Alex Bradshaw's head for target practice.

Chapter Twenty-eight

It wasn't a big surprise to Alex when Luther returned empty-handed. The tall Texan was shaking his head as he slid into the driver's seat. He removed his Stetson and wiped the sweat from his brow.

"Nothing about a Landco company in his files. There wasn't a key above his door, either," he added with an accusing frown. "But I did find the key to the file—taped to the underside of his desk."

"I certainly wouldn't have thought to look *there*," Alex drawled, thinking that Lotus and Gloria had something in common: they both watched too many movies. But Gloria would never do anything so obvious.

Maybe Lotus wasn't as smart as he thought.

Luther started the engine, glancing at Alex. "Where to next . . . boss?"

"Brandy Clevenger's house."

"That good-looking chick who tests the condoms? And what if she's there?"

"Then we'll bind her, gag her, and throw her in the closet until we're finished with our search." The PI looked shocked . . . until he realized Alex was kidding. "She ought to be at work by now anyway." He gave Luther directions to Brandy's house, and instructed him to hurry. He wanted this entire fiasco over and done with so that he could rescue Brooke from jail.

Afterward, he wanted to get her alone and naked, and after the heat of their bodies had cooled, he wanted to talk to her about weddings, honeymoons, and babies. More than ever, he felt she was the one and only woman for him.

Thinking of Brooke reminded him of something vitally important. He flipped open his cell phone and called Gloria. "Gloria, it's Alex."

"No kidding. I was just about to call you."

"Did you find the hubcaps I asked for?"

"No." She waited a cruel moment before adding, "But Derrick did. Mint condition."

"They've got to be the originals," Alex stressed.

"They are. Alex, are you all right? I haven't heard from Luther in a while."

"That's because he's with me, doing *impor-*

tant things instead of spying on Brooke Welch."
Now was the time for Gloria to apologize, he
thought.

He was wrong.

"Alex, I hate to tell you this, but Miss Welch
is in jail. Sheriff Snider called to report that
they found a shipment of Safe and Secure condoms stashed at her house. Apparently she's
been stealing the condoms and selling them
wholesale."

Alex moved the phone to his shoulder to relay
the directions Brooke had given him. "Make a
right at the light, then a left on Turnbeau Street.
It'll be the fourth house on the right."

Gloria's raised voice regained his attention.
"Alex? Did you hear what I said? Your thief has
been right under your nose all along."

His secretary's words evoked an erotic image
of Brooke moaning beneath him. The best part
was that it was a memory, not a fantasy.

"Look," Gloria continued in a soothing voice,
"don't beat yourself up over it, okay? You certainly aren't the first guy to be taken in by a
pretty face, and you probably won't be the last.
Take James Bond, for instance. Most of the
women he fell for ended up being spies sent to
kill him. Even Matt Dillon was tempted a few
times, although he always remained faithful to
Kitty."

"Gloria . . . what did you tell Sheriff Snider
when he called?"

She went silent for a moment, apparently
sensing the sudden tension in his voice. "Well,

I told him this sounded like something you'd want to deal with personally."

Out of respect for her sex, age, and loyalty, Alex held the phone away from his mouth so that she wouldn't hear his vicious curse. If Sheriff Snider had repeated Gloria's message to Brooke, he was in deep cow manure.

His secretary meant well, he reminded himself for what seemed like the thousandth time.

The reminder was getting old.

With great effort, he managed to say in a calm, controlled voice, "If *anyone* other than myself calls from Quicksilver again, do me a big favor."

"Name it," Gloria said, unsuspecting.

"Don't . . . answer . . . the . . . phone."

This time the silence lasted so long he thought she'd hung up. Finally he heard a long, dramatic, self-pitying sigh.

"Okay, Mr. Bradshaw. Silly of me to forget that I'm just a secretary."

As always, Alex felt a stab of guilt for hurting her feelings. And that pitiful sniff never failed to make him feel even worse. "You're more than a secretary. You're also my friend, but trust me, you don't know what's going on down here."

"Well, nobody *tells* me anything, so I have no choice but to rely on Luther to keep me informed, and he saw a truck deliver—"

"Gloria . . ."

For once in her life, Gloria heeded the warning and shut up.

Alex saw they had arrived at Brandy's house

and hurriedly ended the conversation. "Ship those hubcaps FedEx to the local post office here, will you? 'Bye, Gloria."

He disconnected the line and turned to Luther. "Let's get going. I promised Brooke I wouldn't leave her in that hellhole any longer than necessary."

If they didn't find the file, he knew he'd have no choice but to reveal himself and explain everything to the sheriff, and then they might lose the opportunity to prove how Lotus was embezzling factory money.

The thought made his lips tighten with determination.

Firing Lotus wouldn't be enough. He wanted to catch the bastard red-handed. After the trouble they'd gone to, he wouldn't be satisfied with anything less.

"So Alex sent you to keep me company?" Brooke asked Elijah as she flipped through the channels on the muted television. Acting on Sheriff Snider's orders, Gerald had added a VCR to her collection, along with several newly released movies bearing the logo of Family Video. She suspected that Brenda Pearson, the owner of the video store, had sent them over as an expression of her support.

She hated to be ungrateful, but after finding out about Alex's deception, she wasn't in the mood to do anything but brood.

With her blessing, Elijah helped himself to the cold steak and baked potato. He eyed her with shrewd, calculating eyes as he chewed. "I ain't on Bradshaw's payroll, Brooklyn. Now, you gonna tell your old friend what's bothering you? Your sour face reminds me of my first wife. That woman always looked as if she'd been eating green persimmons."

Brooke kept her gaze on the screen, but her mind was elsewhere. Out of politeness, she asked, "So why did you marry her in the first place?"

Elijah cleared his throat, and from the corner of her eyes, she saw him blush. Her interest perked.

"Um, it was a few days after we got hitched before I *noticed* her face. She was, um, um—"

"Stacked?" she supplied helpfully, surprised to find herself grinning at Elijah's obvious discomfort. "Elijah! I'm surprised at you. You never struck me as a chauvinist."

"I was seventeen," he explained hastily. "We were only married a couple of years."

"So you left her because she was ugly?"

Elijah looked offended. "Hell, no. I left her because I wasn't the only one who was attracted by her . . . her—"

"Breasts?" Brooke flashed him a mischievous grin, throwing his own words back at him: "It isn't as if I've never heard the word 'breasts' before."

"Speaking of chauvinists," Elijah said, grimacing, "I had the pleasure of detaining Kyle today."

Kyle. Not *that Lotus fella* but Kyle, as if Elijah

knew him. Acting on a sudden instinct, Brooke went fishing. "I wasn't aware that you knew Kyle." At Elijah's sudden guilty look, she turned off the television and sat up. "*Do* you know him?" When Elijah looked away and began to fidget, Brooke prompted, "Elijah? Is there something you're not telling me?"

Blowing out a sigh, Elijah confessed, "Yep, I know him. Not proud of it, but he's my sister's boy."

Brooke's jaw dropped. "Kyle's your *nephew?* And you never told me? But . . . but *why* would you not tell me?"

Elijah scowled. "Because he ain't worth mentioning, that's why. Ain't been back to see his poor mama since he left Shreveport. She keeps writin', asking about him, and I keep writin' back and lying to her. Today he kinda surprised me, though." He scratched his jaw as if still stunned. "Gave me a package to send to her, since he don't have her address. Said it was money for her birthday. He *claimed* he was comin' out to see me later this evening to get her address."

The flash of intuition hit Brooke hard. Kyle had no idea Elijah knew anything about the embezzling, or was involved in any way. Dry-mouthed with growing excitement, she jumped from the cot and grabbed the straps of Elijah's overalls.

He yelped in surprise. "Gal, you've got a bad habit of scaring the doodle out of me. You forget my heart ain't as strong as it once was."

"Sorry. Elijah, have you already mailed the package?"

"Hell, no! I don't have her address just floatin' around in my head, you know. My heart ain't the only thing failing. Sometimes I can't remember my *own* address."

"Elijah, you don't *have* an address," Brooke reminded him gently. "You have a post office box in town."

"Well, then I can't remember my box number half the time, when I remember to check it. I have to ask that smart-mouthed girl working at the post office—the one with the god-awful purple hair. She's got enough earrings in her ears to open a jewelry store."

Still holding his straps, she shook him lightly to get him back on track. "What did you do with the package?"

"It's out in the truck."

"Go get it!" she urged. "And hurry back. I think we may have found the evidence we need."

Still bemused by her excited outburst, Elijah went to get the package. Brooke paced her small cell and chewed her thumbnail to the quick.

When he returned, she said, "Open it."

Elijah frowned, staring at the package as if it contained something lethal. "Ain't that against the law?"

Suppressing an exasperated sigh, Brooke snatched the flat package from him and grabbed the tab.

But she found she couldn't open it, either.

326

She'd kidnapped Alex, had broken into Kyle's apartment, and confiscated files from the secretary's office.

Yet she couldn't open the package. It would be like tampering with evidence, or something along those lines, and if Kyle was smart enough, he'd realize it was a loophole he could jump through.

She didn't want him to have a loophole.

Scaring Elijah for the second time in a day, she shouted for Sheriff Snider. The sheriff could open it—*if* he had probable cause.

And that could be arranged.

When Sheriff Snider came running into the cell, Brooke handed the startled lawman the package—minus the return-address label she'd managed to peel off and stuff into her jeans pocket. "Do you have the authority to open this package if you think it contains something illegal?" she demanded.

Sheriff Snider nodded. "Yeah, but—"

"Well, *we* think you'd better open it." Brooke glanced at Elijah for support, relieved when he gave a vigorous shake of his head.

But the sheriff wasn't entirely convinced. "Where did you get this?"

Elijah answered. "A suspicious-looking fart—er, man dropped it by mistake. He didn't hear me calling after him, so I brought it here."

"Why didn't you give it to me when you came in?"

Brooke groaned inwardly. She knew better than to underestimate Sheriff Snider.

327

"Well, I meant to, but it plumb slipped my mind." Elijah scratched his head and looked convincingly disgusted. "I was just telling Brooklyn here that my memory ain't what it used to be. It's damned aggravating sometimes."

After another glance between the two, Sheriff Snider grabbed the tab and slowly peeled it away from the envelope.

Brooke and Elijah crowded close.

Chapter Twenty-nine

"There's nothing here."

At Luther's disappointed remark, Alex rose from his crouched position beside the sofa. "Well, she's got a nice supply of *Good Housekeeping* magazines."

Luther frowned as he surveyed the messy room. "Apparently she hasn't read them. Well, I guess that's the end of the road, boss."

"I think not. There's still his car."

"Wait a minute. Wait a damned minute! I draw the line at messin' with a man's wheels."

Alex sighed. "A car has a lot of hiding places." He headed for the door, but Luther was intent on arguing.

"If the man isn't stupid enough to leave that

329

file in his apartment or his girlfriend's place, do you really, actually think he'd be stupid enough to keep it in his car?"

The PI had a point, but Alex was just stubborn enough to keep his agreement to himself. Stubborn and frustrated. "He might. Come on, let's get out of here before Miss Clevenger returns."

Grumbling, Luther followed Alex from the cluttered apartment. Alex carefully locked the door behind him.

They drove to the factory in silence. Spotting Kyle's Corvette in the VIP parking slot, Alex instructed Luther to pull into the empty slot beside it. He looked carefully around to make certain the parking lot was empty.

When he was satisfied, he turned to Luther. "I'm going inside. Join me when you're finished."

"You mean, if someone doesn't catch me ransacking the boss's car and make a citizen's arrest first?" Luther drawled bitingly.

Alex shrugged. "Okay, *you* go in and keep everyone busy while *I* check the car. How hard can it be to break a window?"

"Break a—" Luther smothered a curse. "All right, I'll do the car. You keep them busy."

Reaching for the door handle, Alex said, "I'll be in Lotus's office. If you find the file, just nod. If you don't, put your hands in your pockets."

By the time Alex reached the entrance to the factory and looked back, Luther had used his impressive talents to open the driver's door of the Corvette. Alex gave Luther the thumbs-up sign and went inside, choosing not to speculate on just where Luther had learned his skills.

The lobby of the factory was a maze of partitioned walls divided by a carpeted hallway. Through several of the dividers he glimpsed family pictures tacked above computers. There were four cubbyholes in all, and all were empty. At this particular time of the day, the day-shift supervisors would probably be on the floor, he surmised, wishing he had time to check out Brooke's own personal work space.

At the end of the hallway, he came to a glass door with PLANT MANAGER, KYLE LOTUS stenciled in big black letters, but he knew from what Brooke had told him about the layout of the factory that he would have to go through the secretary to get to Lotus's office.

The door to the right of the office led to the testing lab where Brandy Clevenger worked—or made a show of working. Alex's mouth tightened. If Brooke's suspicions were right, he doubted Brandy did much testing these days.

Without knocking, Alex opened the door and barged into the secretary's office, catching Peggy Osmond by surprise. Her head came up sharply. She gave him a disapproving frown over the rim of her glasses. Middle-aged and full-figured, she reminded Alex of a librarian he'd had in grade school.

"May I help you?"

Anticipating her shock, Alex drawled, "I'm sure you can. I'm Alex Bradshaw—"

Her gasp interrupted his introduction. She leaped to her feet, knocking her glasses askew. Making a frantic grab for them, she caught them in midair and settled them onto her nose again. "Mr. . . . Mr. Bradshaw! We weren't expecting you . . . were we?" Her voice ended on a squeak.

Keeping in mind that Brooke believed Mrs. Osmond was an innocent pawn in Lotus's devious scheme, Alex forced a smile. "No, you weren't expecting me. I've just arrived by private jet after getting disappointing news about one of my supervisors." Despite himself, Alex was impressed with the way the lie rolled off his tongue.

Clutching her chest, Mrs. Osmond said, "You mean Brooke Welch? It's true, then? I just can't believe it! Brooke's such a hard worker, and a very likable person. Why, she worked two Saturdays in a row for my niece when her baby had pneumonia. So when Mr. Lotus told me, I thought to myself, 'There must be some mistake!' " She drew in a fortifying breath, her expression hopeful. "*Is* there a chance there's been a mistake?"

The secretary's reaction surprised Alex, and confirmed Brooke's insistence that Mrs. Osmond wasn't involved. "That's what I'm here to find out, ma'am. Would you inform your boss that I'm here?"

"Certainly, Mr. Bradshaw. I'll tell him right away." Plucking nervously at the opening of her pristine white, conservative blouse, the secretary jabbed at the intercom button. Her words came out in a breathless rush. "Mr. Lotus, Mr. Bradshaw is here to see you."

Lotus's disbelieving voice crackled over the speaker. "If this is your idea of a joke, I do *not* find it funny!"

Casting Alex an embarrassed glance, Mrs. Osmond said, "I'm not joking, sir." She paused significantly before adding, "He's waiting in my office."

The silence stretched for a few taut seconds before Lotus said in a low, angry snarl, "Get me off the speaker and pick up the phone."

As Alex looked on, the secretary's face turned pale, then red again as she listened to the dressing-down Alex was certain Lotus was giving her. Finally she nodded and replaced the phone. She looked at Alex, her expression reminding him of a wounded dog's.

"I'm sorry, Mr. Bradshaw. As I said, we . . . we weren't expecting you."

Alex nodded, holding on to his temper. "Quite all right. Thank you, Mrs. Osmond." With a polite nod at the flustered secretary, Alex entered Lotus's office.

Lotus jumped from his seat behind the desk and came forward, his face tight with the effort to keep a crocodile smile in place. He thrust out his hand. Alex shook it, not because he wanted to, but because he wasn't yet ready to rip Lotus to shreds.

He needed evidence first.

"Mr. Bradshaw! This is a surprise. I mean, I

know you're a busy man, so I wasn't expecting you to handle this little problem yourself." Lotus paused a beat, feigning concern. "This *is* about Brooke Welch, isn't it?"

"In a roundabout way," Alex drawled, disengaging his hand and giving it a subtle wipe against his jeans. Lotus was sweating. Alex hoped like hell he'd be sweating a lot more before the day was over.

"Sad thing, isn't it? She's been a supervisor here for going on six years." With a shake of his head, Lotus sighed. "Caught her red-handed, though, so I don't guess there's any doubt about her innocence."

Although he knew he shouldn't, Alex couldn't resist making the slimeball squirm a little. "Yeah, I guess there's no chance that someone's trying to frame her by dumping a shipment of condoms in her house, huh? Someone would have to be pretty desperate for that."

Lotus's smile faltered, then picked up again, his arrogance overriding his instincts. "Yeah, guess that's a little far-fetched. Have you talked to her?"

Alex shook his head, amazed at the man's confidence. "No, I thought I would get the scoop from you first." *Or lie, rather.*

"Good idea—"

"And take this opportunity to tour my factory," Alex added casually. "Starting with the testing lab."

The expression on Lotus's face was comical— a mixture of irritation and alarm. Alex suspected the irritation stemmed from the fact that he'd referred to it as *his* factory. It didn't take a genius to figure out the reason for his alarm.

Luther chose that moment to step inside the office. Both men glanced in his direction, Lotus in surprise, and Alex with expectation. When Luther stuffed his hands inside his pants pockets, Alex swallowed a frustrated oath. He hadn't found the file, which meant Alex would have to bluff his way through the next part of the plan in the hope of forcing Lotus into a confession.

Nodding at Luther, Alex said, "I believe you've met Luther."

"Yes, we've met." Lotus cast Luther a puzzled glance. "But I thought he'd left town."

Alex could have kissed the PI when Luther shrugged and said, "Thought I'd hang around awhile longer after I saw that truck delivering a shipment of boxes to Ms. Welch's house."

Lotus swallowed visibly. "You . . . you saw the truck?"

Luther's wicked smile would have scared a rattlesnake. "Yep, and I'd know that driver, too, if I happen to run into him again. Reckon he was on her payroll."

"Yes, he must have been," Lotus agreed quickly.

Alex could hardly contain his own feral smile. Without realizing it, Lotus had just confirmed that a man was driving the truck. After exchanging a smug look with Luther, Alex turned to Lotus. "I'd like to see the testing lab now, if you don't mind."

"Sure, sure. I'll just give Brandy a buzz and let her know we're coming—"

"Don't bother," Alex interjected in a steely but soft voice, halting Lotus's movement toward the phone. "It's just down the hall, isn't it?" Without waiting for Lotus to protest, Alex took the lead. Luther followed, with Lotus hastily bringing up the rear.

In the outer office, Alex paused at the secretary's desk. He gave her a warm, reassuring smile. "Mrs. Osmond, does this company offer an eight-hundred number for customer service?"

Her gaze darted to a second phone on her desk, then to Lotus. She gulped and focused on Alex. "Yes, sir. It's . . . it's routed through this office."

"And do you answer this phone?"

"Yes, sir."

"Do you keep an accounting of these calls?"

There was an audible curse behind him, and Alex was fairly certain it wasn't from Luther. "Mrs. Osmond?"

"I . . . I did at first, but last week Mr. Lotus ordered me to unplug the phone. He . . . he said the ringing interfered with his concentration."

"She doesn't mean—"

Alex held up his hand, silencing Lotus. "May I have the records of these phone calls?"

Avoiding the livid gaze of her immediate boss, Mrs. Osmond opened a drawer and withdrew the small book Brooke had described to Alex. Her hands were shaking as she held it out.

"I won't lose my job, will I, Mr. Bradshaw?"

"Of course not. As a matter of fact, you're getting a raise starting immediately."

Leaving the stunned secretary staring after him, Alex walked out of the office and made his way to the lab. Over Luther's smothered chuckling he could hear the sound of grinding teeth.

Kyle Lotus, it seemed, wasn't a happy camper.

Brandy Clevenger wasn't either when she looked up from her *In Style* magazine to find the PI and a strange man entering the lab, followed by her fire-breathing dragon of a boss.

In fact, she was so startled she dropped her magazine.

Alex wasted no time. "Miss Clevenger? I'm Alex Bradshaw." He grabbed her limp hand and gave it a shake, smiling into her shocked face. "And I think you've met Luther, here."

"Yes," she said faintly, glancing over his shoulder at Lotus hovering near the door. Her gaze turned faintly accusing.

From the corner of his eye, Alex saw Lotus shake his head as if he were silently denying any involvement in this unannounced visit. Alex kept his gaze locked on the lab tech. "I hope we're not interrupting your work."

Luther snickered.

Brandy still looked dazed. "No . . . no." She finally gathered her composure. Her chin came up in a defiant gesture. "I was on my break."

"Then I apologize for interrupting your break," Alex said with forced sincerity. "But I'm a little pressed for time . . . so if you don't mind, I'd like a quick demonstration of how you test the condoms." He glanced around the room with interest, his gaze landing on the familiar shape of the test model Brooke called Hugo. Above the table where Hugo reigned supreme were shelves stacked with boxes of condoms.

Scooping her magazine from the floor, Brandy glanced nervously from Lotus to Alex. "Certainly, Mr. Bradshaw." Licking her lips, she moved around him and approached the table. "As you can see, we use an oversize model of a . . . penis to test the durability of the condoms."

When she hesitated and glanced at the silently fuming Lotus, Alex ordered softly, "Show me."

He watched as Brandy retrieved a box of condoms from one of the lower shelves and opened it. She quickly sheathed the condom on the test model and stood aside.

Alex folded his arms. "Do another one." When Brandy reached into the open box, Alex stopped her with a tersely spoken, "Use a new box."

Brandy grabbed another box and took out a packaged condom. Her jerky movements betrayed her growing agitation as she removed the previous condom and replaced it with a new one. With a flourish, she placed her hands on her hips and stood back. She couldn't have been more obvious if she had shouted, "Satisfied?"

Lotus had been silent during the demonstration, but now he stepped forward with a relieved laugh. "As you can see, Safe and Secure continues to produce top-quality condoms. I congratulate you on an excellent investment."

Admitting defeat wasn't in Alex's vocabulary, and he wasn't about to add the term now. He had a couple of aces up his sleeve. Opening the book Mrs. Osmond had given him, he quickly leafed through it, then thrust it at Lotus. "If we produce top-quality condoms, then why do we receive so many complaints?"

Barely glancing at the book, Lotus handed it back. He shrugged, looking so damned smug Alex wanted to punch him. "Prank calls. Kids with nothing but time on their hands."

It was frustrating to know that Alex couldn't prove him wrong. The secretary had not taken names or specified the nature of the complaints; she'd just taken numbers—something he intended to rectify in the future. And without that file, he didn't have a leg to stand on.

"You saw for yourself," Lotus gloated. "These condoms are the best in the country."

"That's because they date from before Alex bought the factory," Brooke announced from the doorway.

They all turned as she sauntered into the room, followed by Elijah and Sheriff Snider.

She was a sight for sore eyes—and egos—Alex thought, letting his gaze drift from head to toe. The woman gave jeans a whole new look, and she certainly looked none the worse after spending a few hours in jail.

He was so busy ogling her that he nearly missed the box she pitched in his direction. He caught it before it smacked him in the face.

"Try those on for size. I found them in Dee's underwear drawer, and I think we *all* know the condition Dee's in right now—and who's to blame."

Lotus found his voice. His face filled with angry color. "I'm going to call security—"

"Settle down, boy," Sheriff Snider said in a growl, effectively shutting him up. "Let Brooke have her say."

Before Alex could open the box, Brooke plucked it from his fingers and thrust a flat package into his hands.

"Better yet, you hold this and *I'll* do the demonstration." She gave him a saucy wink that curled his toes and numbed his brain. "I'll bet Brandy forgot to show you Hugo's hidden talent."

Forget Hugo, Alex thought. *Forget the factory altogether.* He had a sudden, savage urge to clear the room and show Brooke *his* hidden talent.

He watched as Brooke slowly unrolled the condom over Hugo, reviving erotic memories only hours old. By the time she was finished, his erection was at full thrust.

He was very, very glad all eyes were on Brooke.

Chapter Thirty

Brooke carefully unrolled the condom over Hugo, glancing at Alex to confirm that he was watching; she didn't want him to miss the next step in the demonstration—one she was certain Brandy had conveniently left out.

Her fingers stilled at the familiar, heart-stopping expression on Alex's face. Her gaze dipped to below his waist, then jerked back to his face. Hot color flooded her cheeks.

Alex was aroused—*fully* aroused.

Slowly she looked at her hands curled around the base of the test model, and knew with a sudden certainty that he was remembering their lovemaking.

The heat from her face spread downward, encompassing her entire body. Reminding herself that she was furious with him, Brooke tried to concentrate on her task. It wasn't easy to ignore the thick sexual tension that seemed to connect them physically. Her hands shook with the effort.

Keeping her head bowed to hide her flushed face, Brooke placed her finger over the hidden button at Hugo's base as she explained, "When I push this button, air will fill the tip of the condom, simulating, um . . ." Her husky voice trailed away, and her face grew hotter. Sheriff Snider cleared his throat, and the PI stifled a laugh.

Brandy, Lotus, and Alex remained silent.

Brooke took a deep breath and pushed the button. Slowly air filled the tip of the condom. It burst with a soft pop. Forcing herself to look at Alex, she said, "Open the package. I think you'll find the evidence you've been looking for."

Lotus stepped forward as if to snatch the package from Alex. "That's tampering with U.S. mail!" he shouted, glaring at Elijah.

Sheriff Snider grabbed his arm and held him effortlessly. "You just stay still, Lotus. You're in enough trouble as it is."

"But you can't open my mail!"

"*I* can," Sheriff Snider said in a growl, staring hard at Lotus. "Especially if I suspect you're smuggling drugs."

"Smuggling—" Lotus sputtered to a halt, so

furious he could barely speak. "My lawyer will be talking to you."

"He knows where to find me." Unperturbed by Lotus's threat, the sheriff nodded at Alex. "Go ahead, Mr. Bradshaw. Take a look inside."

Holding her breath, Brooke watched Alex remove the contents and quickly scan the pages. When he finally looked up, his eyes were gleaming.

Brooke knew that gleam, and couldn't resist grinning. She'd save her fury for later. Right now she wanted to enjoy the satisfying conclusion.

"Landco Synthetics, Inc.," Alex stated, staring hard at Lotus. "Since when did I authorize this change? According to the invoices I receive, Safe and Secure is still contracted to purchase our latex from Superior, Inc., a company with an excellent reputation of long standing. Safe and Secure has been dealing with them since the beginning. Sounds like you've been practicing a little forgery, Lotus. Not only have you been buying inferior latex and pocketing the savings, you've been ruining this company's reputation."

Lotus strained against the sheriff's hold, looking frightened and desperate. "I can explain!"

Alex shrugged. "Explain to the sheriff—and the judge." His gaze met Brooke's. "And you might also want to explain how that shipment of condoms found its way into Brooke's house."

"She *stole* them!" Lotus screamed, unwilling

to give up. His face turned an alarming shade of purple. Alex clucked his tongue.

"I think not. You see, Brooke was gracious enough to let me stay at her cabin, and she's been keeping me company this past week and a half. She's hardly been out of my sight."

"You've . . . you've been *here*, in Quicksilver, all along?" Lotus said in a squeak. His lip curled as he looked at Brooke. "And you've been shacking up with him? How convenient."

Brooke was very glad Elijah was close enough to halt Alex's involuntary move toward Lotus.

"You're in enough trouble, Lotus," Alex said in a growl. "One more slur against Brooke and you'll be nursing a broken jaw."

"Or two," Sheriff Snider added ominously. "Now come along peacefully."

Lotus resisted. "I have the right to call—"

"You can call your damned lawyer when we get to the station." He yanked Lotus to the door, then turned to pin Brandy with a hard look. "You'd better come along, too, little lady. From what I hear, you were doing more than just following orders."

Brandy surprised Brooke by following docilely, leaving Brooke, Alex, and Elijah alone in the room. Elijah cleared his throat, glancing between the two.

"Guess I should be gettin' along, then."

Alex stepped forward and grasped Elijah's hand, his smile warm. "Thanks for your help. We couldn't have done it without you."

Elijah flushed at his praise and ducked his

head shyly. "You're just trying to make an old man feel useful, and don't think I don't know it." He jerked his head in Brooke's direction. "Brooklyn here's the one you should be thanking."

"Oh, I plan to," Alex drawled softly, with a hidden promise that made Brooke shiver.

Staunchly Brooke reminded herself of how Alex had lied and tricked her. A man who could act so ruthlessly couldn't be trusted, and she was nobody's fool. So when Elijah made to leave, she had every intention of following him.

Alex had other ideas. He caught her arm and held her until Elijah disappeared through the door.

"I've got to go back to Amarillo to start the recall proceedings on the defective condoms."

Her heart twisted painfully, but she managed a careless shrug. "It's your job, isn't it?" And his home. Not here, in Quicksilver, but hundreds of miles away in Amarillo.

"I'm coming back."

Again Brooke chose to misunderstand him. She decided it was much safer that way. "I suppose you'll have to, won't you? You'll need to find a replacement for Lotus." It would be a cold day in hell before she'd remind him that he'd practically promised her the position.

"Brooke." He paused and rifled his fingers through his hair as if searching for the right words. "I know you're probably angry because I lied to you, but—"

Brooke widened her eyes in feigned surprise,

her sarcasm as lethal as a snake bite. "Angry? Why would I be angry? After all, I had the time of my life, and because of your generous, *caring* therapy, I'm cured." She pulled free and spread her arms wide. "See? I don't have the slightest urge to break anything." It was true, too, but something was already breaking without her help: her heart.

Her smile felt brittle. "Besides, Alex, I'd be a hypocrite if I said I didn't enjoy the fantastic sex. You know, I think Lotus was right. I *did* have a hangup about sex, but you cured me of that, too. Now I can enjoy a healthy, normal sex life—"

His mouth stopped her taunting words. He kissed her long and hard, long enough to weaken her resistance and hard enough to almost make her forget her anger.

Almost. But not quite.

With a regretful moan she failed to stifle, she pulled free. The regret seeped into her husky voice. "You don't owe me anything, Alex. Not an explanation, not a commitment, not even a job. I helped you because the people who work at this factory are my friends, and I had sex with you because I wanted to. You didn't have to stoop to frightening me with threats."

"We didn't have *sex*, and you wouldn't have stayed."

Brooke ignored his first statement, and considered his second. Finally she shrugged. "Maybe I wouldn't have stayed at first . . . but I think I would have come back."

Alex lifted his hand as if to touch her face, but when she flinched, he let it fall to his side. His eyes were a steady, piercing gray-green. "I guess I didn't want to take that chance."

"Because you needed help in the investigation," she stated dully.

"No, damn it—"

The muffled ringing of his cell phone interrupted his passionate denial. With a four-letter oath, he reached into his boot and snatched it out.

As he barked into the phone, Brooke took the opportunity to escape. Why stay and torture herself? Alex obviously felt obligated, and it wasn't obligation she needed or wanted from him.

She'd just stepped through the door when the urgent sound of his voice stopped her.

"I'll be back in a few days. Meet me at the cabin."

With a heavy heart, Brooke ignored him and continued on.

The cabin needed a good cleaning. It had been months since she'd had the time, and the long weekend stretched ahead of her. When Dee and Cliff returned from their honeymoon, it would make a perfect retreat for the newlyweds.

Going there had nothing to do with Alex's promise to return, she told herself as she loaded the Pinto with cleaning supplies, lightbulbs, and fresh linens.

She wouldn't look for him, wouldn't expect

him to show, would not get her hopes up. Alex had been trying to be kind, and that was all. His life was in Amarillo, and hers was in Quicksilver. Yes, they'd had a great time, but she wasn't a gullible, love-struck teenager who believed that just because a man made love to a woman, he *loved* her.

Made love.

Brooke made the turn onto the dirt road leading to the cabin, mulling over her choice of words. To be honest, she had to admit that Alex was right—at least on her part. They *had* made love, beautiful, mind-blowing, tender love.

Not sex, but *love.*

Okay, so Alex was a considerate lover. He'd probably had plenty of experience—unlike herself—and knew that a woman enjoyed sex more when she believed the man cared about her. Even when she had insisted she wanted it down and dirty, he hadn't believed her.

And he'd been right on the nose.

She'd only been trying to keep her long-buried emotions where they hurt the least: stuffed deep into her heart. A soft, sappy smile spread over her face as she remembered his tender care in helping her face those tragic, painful emotions. The way he'd held her, and seemed to hurt with her.

Brooke quickly wiped the smile from her face and set her lips in a determined line. After she'd gotten to know him, she'd come to realize he wasn't the jerk everyone—including herself—

thought him to be. No denying that he was a gem among men.

But that didn't mean he loved her.

She'd come closer to believing that he felt guilty, thinking that she might have fallen in love with him. Yes, that was probably what he thought.

The possibility made her face burn with humiliation. Surely she hadn't been that obvious? Because she *was* in love with him—totally, helplessly in love with him.

The cabin came into sight. Brooke parked in her usual spot and cut the engine. She listened to the soothing quiet of the surrounding woods, comparing it to the noisy sounds of town life.

Maybe she'd sell the house and move to the cabin, she mused. It wasn't really that long a drive to the factory.

If she decided to keep her job.

Gathering a sack of supplies from the backseat, she took it inside, unloaded the cleaning products, then returned to the car for the blankets and linen.

A few yards from the Pinto, she ground to a startled halt, her gaze drifting from one hubcap to another. Slowly she circled the car, her amazement growing.

They looked exactly like her old hubcaps, only better. Shinier. Straighter. She stood back and planted her hands on her hips. Had she missed them earlier when she loaded the car? Brooke shook her head, dismissing the idea.

No, she wouldn't have missed them, even as preoccupied as she had been.

Which meant . . .

The creaking of a chair snagged her attention. She glanced up, her gaze widening. Alex sat in the rocker on the porch, looking right at home. He had his long, jeans-clad legs stretched out before him, and his booted feet planted on the porch railing.

He was watching her—intently.

The bottom dropped out of her stomach. He knees started to shake. With a concentrated effort, Brooke forced herself to breath in and out. Slowly. It was just Alex, and it had been only three days since she'd last seen him.

Three very long days. Three interminable days. Three torturous days.

He dropped his feet, but remained sitting. "Come here."

On shaky legs, Brooke approached the porch. She paused at the bottom step, unable to look away from his compelling gaze. She wanted to tell him that she couldn't continue their affair, that she just wasn't cut out for flings without strings.

His hand beckoned her closer.

Brooke obeyed. When she reached him, he lifted her up and settled her on his lap, her legs straddling his. Beneath her, she could feel every hard, pulsing inch of him.

Eyes locked with his, hands braced lightly against his chest, she waited, barely breathing. He splayed his hands on her thighs, and she could feel the potent heat of him right through her jeans.

"As I was saying," he began as if days hadn't passed since their last conversation, "it wasn't just your help with the investigation that I needed. I needed *you*. It wasn't long before I realized that I loved you."

Something wild and wonderful bloomed in Brooke's chest. In response to the joy filling her, she tightened her thighs against his arousal. He caught his breath sharply, a playful warning entering his eyes.

"Be still, or I won't be able to finish what I have to say," he said in a growl.

Brooke leaned forward and brushed her lips against his, whispering, "Then hurry, will ya?"

"Okay," he whispered back, chasing her mouth. "Will you marry me?"

"Yes."

"Can we have a baby right away?"

"Yes."

"Are you just saying this to get me to shut up?"

"Yes."

His deep, husky chuckle started an avalanche of ripples along Brooke's spine. She stopped running from him and let him capture her mouth. The kiss was slow, heated, and filled with expectation. She'd never, ever, tire of kissing him.

When he pulled away, she muttered a curse and tried to recapture his mouth. He cupped her face in his hands and held her still, his expression serious.

"I'm buying a new factory in Amarillo," he said. "I could use your expertise."

"Not a condom factory?" Brooke squeaked in dismay.

Alex grinned. "No, a *candy* factory."

"Now that's more like it. Chocolate?"

"You guessed it. So you'll come with me?"

"Yes."

"Brooke . . ."

"Hmm?"

"Are you doing that agreeing thing again?"

"Yes. Can we go inside now?"

Alex grabbed her hips and held her tight against his rock-hard arousal. "How about here?"

"Elijah—"

"Has gone to visit his sister in Shreveport."

Alarmed, Brooke sat up straight. "In that old truck? He'll never make it!"

He shook his head, smiling slightly. "He's test-driving a new Texas-edition Dodge truck."

"You didn't." But she saw that he had.

She melted against his chest and placed her lips near his ear. "I love you," she whispered, her fingers reaching stealthily between them in search of his belt buckle.

Laughing, he groaned and hugged her close. "You're a hoot."

"Yes."

Available January 2001   0-505-52412-0

THE WOLF OF HASKELL HALL

COLLEEN SHANNON

Enter a tumultuous world of thrilling sensuality and chilling terror, where nothing is as it seems, and where dreams and nightmares blend into heart-pounding encounters too enticing to be denied, too frightening to be forgotten. In our new line of gothics the most exciting writers of romance fiction explore dark secrets, forbidden desires, the hidden part of the psyche that is revealed only at the midnight hour and by . . .

Candleglow

Chapter One

Cornwall, England, 1878

Pain. Thirst. Hunger. The three demons ran alongside him in the gloom, dark harbingers leading him to a future more terribly beguiling with every step he took deeper into the moor.

Once, he had struggled against this fate. He'd traveled to the ends of the earth to avoid it. But neither the burning sands of the Sahara nor the bone-chilling cold of an Andean hut had quieted the call of blood to blood.

Such was the fate of his father.

And his father's father, back into the mists of time when Druids chanted and danced naked in the . . .

Moonlight.

He lifted his face to the siren call. Now that he accepted his family's curse as a blessing, the wanton moon no longer terrified him. Power surged through him with every alluring ray, making his senses acute to things no mere mortal could understand.

The taste of home upon his tongue with the salt damp of the marsh.

The feel of moss-covered ground beneath his bare feet, springy yet firm.

The touch of mist writhing like a woman's silken skin against his bare torso.

The sight of wild things darting about in the cover of darkness, secure that his flawed human eyes could not see the red glow of their heat. And sounds . . .

The laughter floated toward him, both a taunt and a temptation, drifting on the wind. He lifted his nose and sniffed. Through all the other smells of the fecund Cornish night, he caught the most seductive scent of all: woman. For an instant, he stood where he was, both grounded on the soil of home, yet lost in the dilemma of his kind. The remnants of humanity whispered in one ear—

—and demons howled in the other.

Louder, and far more seductive.

Pain . . . a stab so acute that it felt as if his rib cage must expand to hold the muscle and bone his frail human frame could not contain.

Thirst . . . His tongue, unbearably sensitive now, lapped out to taste a pond, but the thin water didn't have the texture and taste he craved.

Hunger . . . It twisted his guts into knots. He bent double, fighting the dark urges, but then the laughter came again. With it, the last of his humanity faded away, a pinprick disappearing into the dark maw of the night.

In one agile bound, he whirled and scaled the tall hedge separating him from his prey. Down, down the slope into the clearing, where the latest Haskell heiress galloped her horse in the moonlight. Her long silvery hair was a banner waving behind her in the stiff breeze, taunting him with the need to catch it and pull her out of the saddle. Unaware of him, she urged the white mare on to faster strides.

Not fast enough.

How easily he kept pace, power surging through him from the tips of his curving fingers to toes growing into claws.

Feet silent on the damp earth, he gained on her with every step.

And then, as he got close enough to leap, all his senses narrowed down to one driving urge.

The need to feed.

He was tensing to spring when he felt the Other bound into step beside him. They bared their fangs at one another, stiff neck hairs bristling as they growled. For an instant, they matched each other step for step, jostling for position as they battled over who would have first taste.

And then, as even her dull human senses

came alive to the danger, the woman looked over her shoulder. She screamed, trying to wheel her mount away from them.

But it was too late.

For her.

And for him . . .

Three Months Later

Delilah Hortense Haskell Trent drew the light curricle to a halt just inside the wrought-iron gates of Haskell Hall. Delilah and her two servants stared up at the odd mansion.

The Hall glowed like a sanctuary in the gloom illuminated by a half moon. Lights spilled from every window, as if the servants were determined to do their part to welcome the new mistress. But the bright displays only accentuated the building's sad state of decay.

It was a hodgepodge of architectural styles, from the simple Georgian pilasters and flat front of the central portion to the fussy Victorian wings on both sides, each capped with octagonal towers. Still, the overall effect might have been charmingly eccentric but for the sagging shutters, peeling double front doors, and moldering, ivy-covered stone that needed a good regrouting.

The gravel drive in front, however, was cleanly swept, and the grounds were immaculate.

"Blimey, she's a frowsy bitch, drawers a-droppin' round her knees at the first sign o' interest," came the ribald appraisal from Jeremy, Lil's groom, bodyguard, and favorite general nuisance.

Lil didn't even glance at him, for she'd long since given up trying to make him keep a civil tongue in his head. But he had other qualities she valued more than politesse.

As usual, Safira gave him a censorious look out of slanted, exotic eyes luminous against her burnished Jamaican skin. "Mon, ye have no need to stir up trouble before we even set foot inside the place."

"Trouble don't need stirrin' up here, me dusky beauty," Jeremy retorted. "It follows, bold like, right through the door with us. I can feel it in me bones."

This time, Safira didn't argue. Her lovely dark eyes got huge as she fingered the talisman at her throat and stared up at the Hall. "Mistress, the little bandy cock could be right, for once. Maybe we should turn around and catch the first boat back to America."

Lil spared them each an amused glance before she clicked her tongue to the horse. "Sometimes I'm not sure which of you is more superstitious, the voodoo priestess or the Cockney sailor who quit the sea because his captain had the temerity to bring his wife aboard."

Neither of them retorted with their usual spunk, so she left off her teasing. It was too late to turn back now. She was in England, the land of her mother's birth, for the first time, and she intended to enjoy every moment.

She had, after all, crossed an ocean to get here, drawn as much by curiosity as by duty. Without her presence, the tiny village of Haskell would fail, or so she was assured by Mr. Randall Cottoway, Esq., of Jasper, Diebold and Cottoway, London solicitors. The estate would be parceled off among various male relatives, the villagers and miners likely put out of work, if she did not stake her rightful claim to the inheritance. She, he'd informed her with typical lofty British superiority, was needed back in Cornwall. Surely—he'd made plain with a scornful glance around her mother's overly lavish drawing room—she could afford a few months and a few pounds to save the estate for future Haskell heirs.

"Such a bequest, coming down through the distaff side of the Haskell family, is highly unusual in English law," the solicitor had stated. "Because you are the last known female heir with Haskell blood, if you do not satisfy the terms of the inheritance by living on the property for six months, then everything will finally pass, after three centuries, into the male hands of several distant cousins related only to the patriarchal side of the family." He'd tipped his ridiculous bowler hat, left a packet of papers, and exited, obviously relieved that his duty was done and he could return to civilization.

Like her stoic Scottish father, Lil could be coaxed, she could be cajoled, she could be reasoned with. But she could never be bullied.

Challenged, however, was another matter.

So here she sat in her curricle under the hulking building that seemed to brood down at them. For a craven instant, she felt a quiver of unease shiver down her sword-straight spine. She had much of the sheer practicality of her stalwart father, and little of the flighty moodiness of her mother. However, as she stared up at the Hall, a strange foreboding niggled its way through her usual calm, as insidious as the gathering fog.

Had she done the right thing in coming here?

The doors burst open. Light flooded the darkness as smiling servants filed out. She had no time for regrets, or foolish fancies.

The next day, Lil sat in the salon partaking of that peculiar English ritual that had been the one legacy her mother seemed to cherish: high tea. Lil had never told her mother, since they always seemed to have plenty to argue about, but, like her father, Lil despised the taste of tea. However, since she had no wish to be considered more of a heathen American than she obviously already was to these people, she forced herself to drink it.

As she bit into a cucumber sandwich, Lil had to admit that no one knew better how to make gossip a high art than the English. Even the snooty Denver socialites who'd never accepted the Trents—their scandalous riches actually made, they'd whispered, by Mr. Trent's own hands—could take lessons in hypocrisy from these country ladies.

Mrs. Farquar of Farquar Hill gushed, "*So* brave of you to venture here across the sea, all the way to *Cornwall* from America. Of course, I make no doubt that even *our* desolate moors are positively *teeming* with social occasions compared to what you probably knew in . . . now, *what* was the name of that town you're from, my dear?"

Biting back the urge to tell the plump little busybody that Denver even had gaslights and paved streets, *really* it did, unlike the parts hereabout, Lil politely wiped the corners of her mouth with her linen napkin and responded, "Denver. Colorado."

"Oh yes," piped up Mrs. Farquar's horse-faced daughter, "you remember, Maman. That's where all the gold and silver miners moved after they made their fortunes."

Both ladies darted complacent looks at Lil out of the corners of their eyes.

It hadn't taken them long to investigate her background. How had they managed it so quickly in this backwater? Lil's teeth snapped down on a scone this time, but she managed to hold her tongue.

However, Jeremy, who'd been setting a new fire for them in the grate, had no such qualms. Dusting his hands off on his breeches, he said out of the corner of his mouth, "Aye, same place as many a pretty English rose went a-scoutin' fer a rich husband if she could get it, and a rich protector if she couldn't." Jeremy raked Miss Farquar with his wintry blue eyes. "Ye could try your luck, gel, but a man'd as lief mount a thoroughbred as a nag, and back ye'd be quick-like, puttin' down yer betters."

Both women goggled at him in shock.

Hiding a smile behind her napkin, Lil gave him a severe look over the linen. When her mouth was straight, she lowered the cloth, hoping her voice was sterner than her merry green eyes. "Jeremy, leave the room at once, and never speak to my guests so again!"

As usual, he read her like a book. He gave his cocky little half salute and strolled out with his peculiar, rolling gait, not in the least abashed.

"Well, *really*! How do you bear such a . . ." Mrs. Farquar's outrage stopped mid-spate as she stared at the door. Her daughter did likewise, and the looks on their faces made Lil swivel in her chair in alarm to see what horror stood there.

At first she could make out nothing in the dark hallway, but then the shadow moved into the room and resolved itself into a man.

A very tall, powerful man.

He wore work breeches and calf-high boots that molded his long legs, giving them an obscene clarity and beauty of power and form that would have made a lesser woman than Lil blush. His white lawn shirt was so thin that she could see the shadow of his chest hair, so she knew he must be dark. His face and hair were shaded under a broad-brimmed work hat. And his hands . . . she shivered as she stared at his hands.

Colleen Shannon

The nails were blunt and clean, but his long fingers had a tensile strength and . . . readiness expressed in every flagrantly male sinew of his indomitable frame. And when he walked into the room, he was silent despite his size. He flicked a short quirt against his leg, broadcasting dislike as if he had no more patience for the two gossips than Lil did. His rudeness in not removing his hat spoke loudly of his opinion of them.

Mother and daughter muttered excuses and fled, snapping the drawing room door closed behind them.

Only the sound of the fire crackled, but Lil refused to be intimidated by her own estate manager. For this man could be none other than Ian Griffith. "Why did you not knock, Mr. Griffith?" She glanced at the mantel clock. "You are early for our appointment."

"If you wish I'll go back out and return in five minutes—mistress." The deep, soft voice put a slight emphasis on the last word, and the intonation gave erotic meaning to the polite usage. Still, he did not remove his hat, and she had the peculiar feeling the omission was as much for his own protection as for hers.

Why would he be afraid of her gaze?

The urge to move her chair away from him almost overcame her, but instead, Lil tilted back her silvery head of fashionably coiffed hair and stared boldly up into the shadow of the hat, her own green gaze steady. She caught the glitter of eyes as he let them wander from her small, slipper-shod feet, up her green taffeta gown, past her full hips and small waist, to her generous bosom, pausing on the vee between her breasts before traveling on to her white throat. The glitter grew brighter as he watched the pulse pound there, but then he whacked the quirt hard against his leg as if to punish his own thoughts, and the glitter snuffed out like a light.

That was why he seemed so threatening, Lil instinctively realized. This man had the measured control of a leashed tiger. It would suffer you to feed it and train it and play with it, only so long as it pleased. But once that power was unleashed, and the wildness broke through. . . .

Nonsense. "Remove your hat, if you please." He was just a man, and she was no ninny to be so intimidated.

A sharp intake of breath betrayed his shock at the curt command, but he raised that large, capable hand and pulled off the hat.

It was her turn to gasp. His face was not conventionally handsome. His cheekbones were too high and exotically slanted, his blade of a nose too long, his lips too full and wide. And his eyes . . . she tried to delve into them and take the true measure of this man as she'd had to do so often since her father died, but the amber depths were too opaque and secretive to allow her in. They were fringed with long, dark lashes that would have looked feminine on a less primal face.

Curly midnight hair cascaded over his tanned brow, and long sideburns pointed like accusatory fingers down the sides of his strong, square jaw. As if to emphasize the obvious: *I grant favors, if I will it, but I never ask for them. Cross me at your peril.*

Every hackle on her body stood on end, and it was all she could do not to leap up and fire him on the spot just to avoid feeling so intimidated. Instead, she managed coolly, "Do you have the books ready for me to examine?"

"Yes, I do." He stalked to a cabinet against the wall and took out two black ledgers.

Lil rose and walked over to the Louis V desk in a place of pride in the middle of the room. The furnishings in the house were as eclectic as the facade, but there were a few priceless pieces, of which this was one. She sat down, expecting him to deposit the ledgers and move away.

Instead, he pulled up a chair. His nostrils flared as he obviously caught the subtle whiff of her perfume, and her own senses went on full alert. He didn't touch her anywhere as he leaned over her shoulder, but she felt his body heat and smelled a faint scent of something indefinable emanating from him, something earthy and primitive that raised her hackles again . . .

. . . and made her long for his touch to soothe them.

The neat columns, written in a bold dark hand, wavered before her gaze. She took a deep breath and tried to concentrate. But she felt the expanse of his shoulders so close that all she would have had to do was turn and she could investigate their width with her own tingling hands.

She leaped up, knocking over the gilded, spindle-legged chair. "Leave them with me. I will study them later, at my leisure."

An insolent smile tugged at the corners of those full lips as she fled back to her safe seat. She was too off balance to get up and slap it away, as her instincts urged.

"And the rest—mistress?" asked that deep, soft voice. "What of the new pump for the mine? The schoolroom in the village that needs a new roof, and—"

"Not today. I am . . . fatigued." Oh no. Next she'd make the age-old lady's excuse of the headache. Warily, she watched him rise, pick up the books, and come toward her. She almost leaped up to run, but he only veered around her to put the ledgers back.

To her intense relief, he put his hat back on and shielded her from those steady, unnerving amber eyes. "A true Haskell," he said with mild contempt. "I had hoped that somehow you might be different. Good afternoon." Turning on his heel, he stalked out, steps soundless even on the wood floor. The soles of his boots must be as soft as the shank.

Still . . . she had never met such an unsettling man. She pressed her hand to her hammering heart, vaguely aware that this strange pounding was not just arousal, or fear, or even excitement.

It was a combination of all three. She stood to pour herself a brandy with a shaking hand, thinking the spirits would soothe her agitated nerves. But the smooth burn of the liquor warmed her in unexpected places instead, reminding her of the way Ian Griffith walked, and talked.

And stared at her with secretive, burning eyes.

She tossed her glass into the fire, furious at her own weakness. She strode out of the room, vowing not to think of him again.

She broke her vow before she crossed the floor.

In the ensuing days, to Lil's relief, she didn't have to see Ian Griffith again. For over a week, she had her hands full with the household itself. The former owners had lavished money on the outbuildings, the stables, the greenhouse, even the old chapel on the grounds, but they'd been parsimonious with the interior. Every piece of furniture needed a good stripping and repolishing, every brass fixture needed shining, and the rugs and draperies . . . Lil sneezed just looking at them.

Lil had been unofficial chatelaine of her father's three Colorado homes since she was in her teens, and she knew much of running a household, even one almost as complicated as this. But here a mine, the enormous stables that held everything from broodmares to carriage horses to thoroughbreds, the village school, and even some of the shops were also Haskell-owned. For these, she needed her estate manager. But she refused to fetch him, and he seemed equally content not to come calling.

She wondered where he lived. She wondered if he was married. She wondered why he seemed to dislike the Haskells. And then she wondered, to her own fury, why she bothered wondering.

When the house is ready, she told herself staunchly. *It's only that I'm busy. He doesn't intimidate me at all.* But she wasn't facing a mirror when she thought it.

Finally, almost two weeks after her arrival, she pulled off her apron and crossed the last item off her list. "Downstairs finished," she said with a weary sigh of satisfaction, blowing a curl off her forehead as she smiled at Mrs. McCavity, the housekeeper. "Now the upstairs. We'll start with the towers . . ." She broke off at the look on Mrs. McCavity's face. "Yes?"

"Well, milady, that is—"

"I bear no title, Mrs. McCavity. You may call me Delilah."

A horrified look crossed the woman's face. "Sure and the saints themselves strike me down afore I so disrespect me betters. What was your Da athinkin' to name ye after a heathen woman?" She blushed as her Irish brogue got the best of her.

Lil laughed. She was always tickled to find the clue to a person's humanity. In her servants. In her friends. Even, on occasion, in her enemies. Everyone had some mannerism or way of speaking that betrayed his strengths and weaknesses. The more emotional Jeremy was, the more colorfully he cursed. The more frightened Safira became, the more she retreated into her magic. When Mrs. McCavity was shocked or moved, she reverted to the brogue of her childhood.

And Ian Griffith? How vividly she could visualize that dark, enigmatic face. But she saw no weakness there. And little humanity.

Lil collected her scattered thoughts. The housekeeper looked puzzled, and she'd been so hardworking and kind that Lil felt she had to give the poor woman some explanation as to why her new mistress was so different from the former ladies of the Hall. "If you'd known my Pa, you'd understand that he challenged me from the time I was born to be better than a name, a title, an inheritance. 'Delilah,' he would say, 'a name has no more bearing on who we are than money defines what we are. Ye have three scourges to overcome—me trade, your name, and the filthy lucre that will be either the bane o' yer existence or yer deliverance. Take yer weaknesses and make them strengths.'" Lil's smile grew misty as she stared at Mrs. McCavity's attentive face. "I've always done my best to follow his advice. With the result that I fear I am not much welcomed in Denver drawing rooms, and doubtless will not be here, either."

"There you are wrong, mil—ma'am. Money in these parts hides an enormous quantity of sins." Mrs. McCavity ducked her head as if she was sorry she'd spoken so frankly, and she reached for the huge ring of keys at her waist. "Now, where do you want to start upstairs?"

"The towers." Lil led the way, but she turned back when she realized the housekeeper had not followed.

"We . . . are not supposed to go into the north tower. The south tower was set up as a governess's suite, but since we currently have no children in the house, it is vacant."

Frowning, Lil scarcely listened to the second half of the explanation. "You are telling me I own this estate and am not allowed to enter parts of my own ancestral home?"

" 'Tis an agreement made many years ago with the Griffith family by the first mistress. So long as a Griffith runs this estate, he may live where he pleases in the house, with no interference from the owners. The Griffiths have lived unmolested in that tower for almost a hundred years."

Lil was appalled. "Such an agreement could not possibly be legally binding. Why, if the house were sold—"

"And morally?"

Lil clamped her mouth shut. No wonder Ian Griffith strode around as if he owned the place! In a way, he did.

Without another word, she turned on her heel and led the way upstairs—to the south tower. But as they traversed the connecting hallway, she couldn't help looking in the opposite direction and wondering. Her steps slowed.

Each tower had its own entrance and exit. What guests did Ian Griffith invite inside? How many women had succumbed to his animal magnetism? What did his bed look like? Were his arms and long legs as muscular as they looked? She didn't have to close her eyes to visualize him sprawled on white sheets, all wild dark power and wild dark urges that made a woman—

She caught Mrs. McCavity's gaze. Blushing, she turned sharply in the opposite direction. Would she could turn her thoughts so easily.

That night, even after a soothing soak in the hip-deep copper tub, Lil was still restless. She tossed aside the weighty tome she was trying to read on the biology of Bodmin Moor, which lapped at the very foundation of this house. But improving her mind would have to wait for a less stressful day.

She'd worked herself to the point of exhaustion, and had had two glasses of sherry that night instead of one, but still she couldn't quiet her overactive imagination. She simply would not be able to sleep until she saw the north tower for herself. Ian Griffith had left word with the butler that he had gone into Bodmin for supplies and would not return until the next day, so she was safe invading his abode.

Wrapping the tie of her sweeping cashmere negligee tightly about her trim waist, shaking back the deep ruffles at her sleeves, she collected the enormous ring of keys the housekeeper had given her. Most were marked, but two, larger and more ornate than the others, were not. One of them had to open the north tower.

She had the right, she told herself, to be sure that illegal activities were not being conducted in her home. If she found an opium pipe, or smuggled goods, or . . . or scandalous pictures or novels . . . well, she'd have every reason to fire the arrogant blackguard.

On the long trek to the opposite wing of the house, her slippers made little sound on the thick carpets, but the lantern she carried threw her shadow upon the wall. Strange the way she danced, in a joyous way quite opposite to the sick, anticipatory queasiness in her stomach.

She looked down. Her hand was shaking.

She stopped. What was wrong with her? She was a woman grown, an experienced woman in every way since she'd made the mistake of letting her former fiancé talk her into his bed. She'd broken off the engagement when she found out that he, despite his greater guile than the others, also only wanted her money. He had not been a kind lover, and she'd had no interest in the act, illicit or sanctified, since.

Which was why her current obsession troubled her so. She took a deep breath, closed her eyes, and visualized her father's bright green eyes smiling at her. "Face yer fears, me darlin', and ye'll be the stronger for it."

"Yes, Pa." Hitching her skirts above her ankles so she could walk faster, she quelled her own foolish fears and hurried into the north wing. Sure enough, the stout oak door that met her, banded with steel like a Norman baron's of old, yielded to one of the ornate keys. She shoved the door inward and listened.

The round stairwell was pitch black, and she heard no sounds above. The entire household was asleep, as she should be at this ungodly hour, so she entered the gloom and shut the door quietly behind her, but left it unlocked.

In the feeble lantern light, the curving stairs and stone tower seemed to stretch to infinity. Finally she reached another door, this one glossy black and even heavier than the other. She tried the door handle, but it didn't open. She fumbled with the key chain again, and to her relief, the same key that opened the lower door also unlocked this one.

Taking a deep breath, she shoved the heavy portal open. The octagonal space inside was very dark. She quickly lit the gas sconces beside the door, and then the lamp next to the sofa before the fireplace.

She looked around, and some of her suspicions about her manager began to fade. No den of iniquity here. Only a tiny kitchen and dining area in one corner, and a living area across, plus a long table set up before shelves packed with books to make a rudimentary library.

A small but comfortable suite of rooms, a gentleman's retreat, all dark paneling and lush green velvet. Tasteful but spare. None of the heavy Empire and rococo styles so in vogue in this era when Queen Victoria ruled with a small but indomitable hand. Simple Sheraton writing armoire, marble-topped tables, monkish straight-backed chairs. The only nod to decadence was a plush emerald green silk divan that looked as if it should have a Turkish pasha reclining upon it.

Or an houri.

Wishing she could rid her head of such sensual images, Lil carried the lantern to illuminate the painting above the fireplace mantel. It was a picture of the moors. Because the walls of the tower curved slightly as the angles of the octagon met, it did not rest flat. Perhaps that accounted for the picture's odd depth and radiance.

The moors she'd seen on the train coming here had never looked like this. Yes, they stretched beyond sight as this one did, and yes, they were filled with intriguing patches of green, where moss or plants relieved the unrelenting brown. And yes, when the sun went down and night ruled, she'd even seen the same luminous, low-lying mist. But that moor had been intimidating, bleak, offering more peril than pleasure.

The same moor depicted in this painting was sensual, glowing with jewel tones of green and sapphire, where lichen-covered rocks dotted the muddy wastes, and pools of blue water reflected back the cloudless sky above. Even the mountains, hazy in the distance, had been added with bold, loving strokes. Here, they were not jagged teeth consuming the sky as they'd seemed to Lil, but hands offering a bounty of life and joy found nowhere else on earth.

Lil stumbled back a step. She wasn't sure why the image was so disquieting and riveting at the same time. Whoever had painted this loved the moors. Loved them as a man loved a woman, or a mother a son.

But there was something else . . . something troubling. She couldn't quite put her finger upon it, but the brushstrokes were deep, the dollops of paint standing up from the canvas in a style she'd never seen before. As if the painter used violent, passionate strokes to exorcise demons along with his emotions.

Had *he* painted it?

She visualized that primal male face, tried to picture him wearing a beret, daubing paint upon this canvas . . . Her mind balked. No, a man who looked as he did doubtless sported with guns, or horses, or women. He had the soul of a conqueror, not an artist.

Rubbing at her tingling nape, Lil forced herself to turn away. She looked at the armoire. She should search it, set her mind at ease once and for all that her manager had none of the strange tastes or motivations she suspected. But she couldn't. She already felt interloper enough.

Blowing out the lamps she'd lit, she walked toward the door. But something drew her gaze upward. A small circular stair led to another level of the tower, and she knew that must be the bedroom. She blew out the last lantern, but even when the lamp she held was all the light remaining and the spiral stairs were but an impression upon her unconscious, she still found herself walking toward them.

She had to see where he slept. Only then could she get these visions out of her head.

She had set one foot upon the first rung when the voice came, rough and low, right over her shoulder.

"If you wanted a tour, all you had to do was ask. And by all means, I agree with your priorities—bedroom first."

Gasping with fright at the sound of that deep, melodious voice, Lil whirled. Her slipper caught, and she would have fallen if Ian hadn't reached out and grabbed her. For an instant, every nerve in her body came alive to the touch of his hard warmth pressed so scandalously close. Through the thin layers of her lawn nightgown and fine cashmere robe, she could feel every expansion and contraction of that powerful rib cage.

His breathing had quickened, too. Despite the hard, even stare of those impenetrable amber eyes, he was affected by her as well.

Lil stumbled back and fell to her rump upon the third step. The lantern slipped in her nerveless hand, and she would have dropped it if he hadn't taken it and set it on an adjacent table.

The light from below threw his strong face into sharp relief as he drawled, "Would you care to bounce on my bed?"

Cursing her fair skin, hoping he couldn't see

her blush in the half light, Lil retorted, "You mean my bed?"

"Oh, you may own the mortar and stone, mistress, but I own the furnishings." His gaze raked over her, lighting upon her bosom like a touch. He might as well have said it: *With time, I will own you, too.*

Hoping her throbbing pulse wasn't visible beneath her thin robe, Lil stood and waved him back so she could exit the narrow spiral stair that had her imprisoned. He stood so close that his long legs almost brushed her feet, and . . .

. . . He didn't move. "I am not a dog to obey hand signals. I suggest you put your tongue to good use, or I will give it a better one." And for the first time, a smile stretched that dark face. His white teeth gleamed and he actually leaned closer, running his own tongue against the edge of his teeth in a way that made her mouth tingle.

Strange how his canines were slightly more prominent than his incisors. . . .

And then she was dumbfounded at his insolence, torn equally between outrage and temptation. She turned away in the only direction open to her—up. If, deep inside, she wasn't quite sure whether she wished to escape him or herself, well, of that, no one had to know. Least of all Ian Griffith.

Her former manager. She'd give him his walking papers first thing in the morning.

When she was halfway up the stairs, she stopped and scowled down at him, feeling secure in the distance between them. "I will examine your room for myself. And if I find nothing untoward, I may reconsider my decision to discharge you." She expected him to explode in wrath, or maybe even show a bit of remorse.

His smile only deepened as he nodded that arrogant dark head. "Be my guest. I guarantee you'll be surprised at what you find. But we might as well have truth between us, even from the beginning."

Lil almost ran up the rest of the stairs, holding her skirts high enough so that she didn't trip, but still careful to leave her ankles covered.

The room that came to life in the flare of the gas lamps she lit was unlike any she'd ever seen. Round, simple, whitewashed stone. Again, spare, but the velvet hangings on the vast four-poster bed were burgundy, tied back with gold ropes. At the foot of the bed was a bench, and upon the bench was a man's silk dressing gown. It was fiery red, and it had something embroidered on the back, something she couldn't quite make out. Her hands itched with the need to pick it up, but instinctively she knew not to.

Touching his things would lead to touching his person.

So she turned away, and it was then she noticed the easel and canvas set up beneath the enormous curving window. Next to it was a table and a sketchpad. Feeling as if she was finally finding some clue to his secretive personality, she walked toward the table. She was reaching out to pick up the pad when that voice spoke again, right over her shoulder this time.

"Go ahead. Discharge me if you wish."

She started and whirled. How did he walk so silently?

No smile upon that enigmatic face now as he said softly, "But you will still not be rid of me. Any more than I will be rid of you. The Haskell women and the Griffith men have been linked for centuries, Delilah. Your blood is as hot with the bond between us as my own."

Still holding her gaze, he reached around her for the sketchbook. He flipped it open and showed her the top picture, the next, and the next.

Heat started at the top of her head and ran like magma to her toes. The images got progressively more sensual.

And progressively more shocking.

They were all of her. Face only, then bust, then from the waist up. Dressed lightly at first, then only in chemise and stockings. Finally . . . as he flipped through the sketchbook, he ended on a full-length nude.

Of herself. Her arms lifted wantonly toward her lover, her lips ripe with a sensual smile as she lay upon the very bed in this room. Wanting him.

For she knew now, beyond doubt, that he had sketched them. And he had painted the landscape over the mantel. This driven, powerful man was an equally driven, powerful artist, able to appease his own hunger with these wanton images. How had he been able to draw her so accurately? Even the shape of her breasts, the size of her nipples, the triangle between her legs.

All the conflicting feelings troubling her for the past two weeks seemed to coalesce in her mind. Her senses narrowed to a minute speck, and then exploded outward in one glorious emotion.

Fury. Before she put thought to action, her hand lashed out and slapped that arrogant face hard enough to jerk his head to the side.

"You bounder! You have no right to even think of me so, much less—" She broke off with a gasp as he caught the back of her skull in both his powerful hands and tipped her head back. His touch swept through her like a tidal wave.

For a moment she was pristine, like a beach never stepped upon by human foot. And then he shoved her against the wall, pressing into her with his masculine frame that so strangely seemed to fit her own.

And she was marked.

Marked forever after, no matter what came of this night when it seemed only the two of them were awake in all the world. She felt the imprint of him, indelibly stamped through the shivering sands of pride and propriety straight to the bedrock of her soul.

When he kissed her, she tipped her head back to meet him.

And finally, she saw emotion in those strange amber eyes. . . .

Chapter Two

Lil had been kissed before, many times. Awkward kisses, earnest kisses, even a few experienced kisses. But this dark invader of her home, her mind, and ultimately, she knew, of her body, created his own lexicon. One her body interpreted even as her mind resisted.

Those lips were as warm and unyielding as the rest of him. But the way they moved—his exploration was unhurried, as if he'd always known her.

Kiss? How banal.

Invasion. Intimacy. Consummation. He'd barely touched her, yet already he'd filled her with his wild strength as surely as if he held her spread-eagled to the bed.

And Lil, stubborn as only one of Scots ancestry can be, tilted her head back to welcome the thrust of his tongue. He dipped, and danced, and tasted the rim of her teeth, lips suckling gently all the while. And she didn't just allow him intimacies she'd allowed no other.

She welcomed them.

She curled her tongue shyly around his, wondering why the moist heat didn't disgust her as it had with the others. When she answered the sexual foreplay so explicitly, the tenor of his embrace changed. During that first kiss, his hands had touched only the back of her skull, cradling it not with tenderness but with surety. As if he knew she knew he had strength enough to crush it—but no need.

He was already in her head.

But when she kissed him back, inexperience made eloquent by passion as great as his own, a shudder ran through that strong frame.

And Lil rejoiced. With a fierceness that almost frightened her. He was not so indomitable after all. He, too, had weaknesses. And he could not exploit hers without exposing his own.

The primitive symmetry was so seductive that Lil pulled her hands free from the heated trap between their bodies. He broke the kiss, looking down at her curiously. He was so much taller that her hands had to trail up from his waist, past his strong chest, over his sturdy collarbones before she could finally clasp the back of his neck.

His hands went slack upon her head and his

eyes went strangely unfocused. As if he needed the touch of her hands upon his flesh like he needed breath and water. And when she tugged his head down, tilting it to the side so *she* could kiss *him*, a stronger shudder wracked him.

The next thing she knew, her robe and night-gown were open, and his rough palm was learning the generous heft of her breast. Lil gasped into his consuming lips, but then his tongue thrust again, and the dark urges went wild within her. She thrust her breast into his hand. He sensed her need and circled her nipple gently with his thumb. She was already hard, and the grazing of that callused thumb made her long for the feel of his mouth there.

He took her in, suckling her nipple with nothing of the infant about him. He was all primitive male, tasting her, knowing her, completely.

Almost. . . . as if he took his birthright from the tip of her most vulnerable femininity.

Reject him? Slap him? The thought never crossed what little mind she had left. She could only slump, weak over the strong support of his arm at her back, and feel her heart fly to meet the gentle suction.

And then something curious happened. He rested his cheek against her left breast, eyes closed, long dark lashes like shadows upon his face. As if he didn't just listen to her heartbeat.

He felt it.

He hungered for it.

He wanted to hold it in his hands and feel its vibrant life.

His mouth opened. His tongue circled the rim of his teeth. Lil stared down at him, her own eyes dark with a desperate passion she could not control. For an instant, it seemed his canines grew to fangs. Still she could not move. She could only wait, helpless in his grip.

But if she was a victim, so was he.

A moan escaped him, high pitched, eerie, the sound of a wolf in pain. But when he turned his head to nuzzle between her clothes, the wool and silk dropped to her waist. Both her breasts were bare to him, high, round, firm, and white. Capped by thrusting, blushing nipples pouting for his kiss.

They were so much the essence of woman vulnerable to him that he drew a deep, shuddering breath. The wildness that had almost overtaken him was buried under the needs of a man for a woman. His expression grew tender. Gently kneading her flesh, he buried his face in her, drawing life, and strength and purity. And Lil was fed, too, from the bounty of the exchange.

Unbearable hunger in one breath, satiated in the next. The need only became more acute when she lost the feel of his mouth upon her flesh as he switched from one breast to the other.

The burning ache didn't stop at her breast. It went from her torso, down her legs, to her very toes. And it was so shocking, so atavistically beyond her control, that sanity returned for a split second as that mesmerizing mouth drew away.

For one sobering instant, Delilah, miner's

daughter, doughty Scots heiress, looked down upon that wild black head so intimately placed at her bosom.

With a cry of despair, she caught his thick hair in her hands and pulled his head away, squirming free. Pulling her clothes over her shamed flesh, she ran.

Ran as she should have the minute he appeared.

Down the spiral stairs, through the tower, all the long way from one wing to the next. Faster, faster—but far too slowly. No matter how fleet her feet, her heart almost burst with the knowledge her mind refused to heed.

Too late.

He had possessed her this night, in every way a man could. The intimate thrust of his manhood into her would be no more invasive or consuming than the feelings rioting through her from the wild tangle of blond hair to the tips of her tingling toes.

The second she reached her room, Lil threw every bolt and lock on the door. A long cheval mirror mocked her, but she turned away, stripped off her clothing, and threw the garments in the fire. Never again could she look at them.

For thirty minutes she scrubbed her torso, using strong lye soap, not the gentle French perfumed bar, until her skin was red and almost raw. If a hair shirt had been at hand, she would have slept in it.

Finally, the sky pink with dawn's first blush, she pulled on her primmest night rail and climbed into her bed. Even then, she tossed and turned, chaotic images whirling through her confused mind.

Ian painting upon the moors.

Ian, his lips curled back in a snarl as he listened to her beating heart.

Ian holding her with a tenderness no man had ever shown her, not even her own father.

And it was that last image that brought tears to her eyes and made the burning ache he'd left in his wake all the more difficult to quell. He gave tenderness so awkwardly, so shyly.

Like a man who'd known little of it in his own life.

Lil had been attracted to men before—heavens, she'd even slept with one she'd thought herself in love with. But nothing—no sane counsel her father had ever given her, none of the manners that snooty Eastern finishing school had taught her, not even Jeremy's salty oaths or Safira's mysterious philosophies—could quiet the torment in her mind and body.

Ian Griffith frightened her.

He thrilled her.

He mystified her.

And as certainly as she breathed, the next time he crooked a finger at her, she'd come running.

With a frustrated groan, she pulled the feather pillow over her foolish head.

But still he lurked there, even at the edge of sleep.

And doom . . .

Mr. Hyde's Assets

Sheridon Smythe

Get Ready . . . For the Time of Your Life!

Rugged Austin Hyde's mad-scientist brother has gone and appropriated Austin's "assets" to impregnate a tycoon's widow at his fertility clinic. Worse, rumor has it that the elegant Candice Vanausdale might be making a baby simply to inherit big bucks! Mr. Hyde is fit to be tied—but not tied down by a web of lies. Yet how to untangle "Dr. Jekyll's" deception?

Clearly, Austin has to go undercover. Get close enough to the breathtaking blonde to see for himself what the woman is made of. Hiring on as her handyman seems the perfect solution. Trouble is, the bashful, beleaguered beauty unleashes Austin's every possessive male instinct. Blast! How dare "Dr. Jekyll" domesticate Mr. Hyde?

___52356-6 $5.99 US/$6.99 CAN

AGAINST HIS WILL

TRISH JENSEN

Get Ready For . . . The Time of Your Life!

FBI agent Jake Donnelly is not a happy camper. His favorite aunt is gone and he's gained . . . not the childhood retreat he loves, but custody of a bulldog. Worse still, the terms of the will require him and Muffin to spend two weeks at a dog spa owned by a quack canine shrink named LeAnne.

But after one look at the luscious LeAnne, Jake knows the dogs aren't going to be the only ones drooling at the Hound Dog Hotel. At a place where doggie astrologists talk about the Puppy Love dating service and breakfast is eaten at the Chow Chow diner, it is easy for desires to be unleashed. Private therapy sessions with the lovely doctor soon have Jake eating out of her hand and deciding maybe Muffin *is* man's best friend if he can bring his owner and his trainer together for good.

___52377-9 $5.99 US/$6.99 CAN

Midnight Kisses

Kimberly Raye

Get Ready for ... The Time of Your Life!

Smooth, sensual, fantastic skin that begs to be tasted—Josephine Farrington just re-invented it. The new plastic is great for making lifelike toys, but she has a better idea: making a man. Tired of the pushy jerks that court her, Josie can now design the bronze-skinned, hard-muscled exterior of a robo-hunk that can fulfill all her deepest fantasies. And she knows just the man to build the body.

Matthew Taylor never had trouble erecting anything, and the handsome scientist knows that Josie's robot is something he can create. But the beautiful biochemist deserves better than the cold devotion of a machine; she needs the fiery embrace of a real man. In an instant, Matt knows his course: by day he vows to build her model of masculine perfection—by night he swears to be it.

___52361-2 $5.99 US/$6.99 CAN

Dorchester Publishing Co., Inc.
P.O. Box 6640
Wayne, PA 19087-8640

Please add $1.75 for shipping and handling for the first book and $.50 for each book thereafter. NY, NYC, and PA residents, please add appropriate sales tax. No cash, stamps, or C.O.D.s. All orders shipped within 6 weeks via postal service book rate. Canadian orders require $2.00 extra postage and must be paid in U.S. dollars through a U.S. banking facility.

Name_____
Address_____
City_____State_____Zip_____
I have enclosed $ _____ in payment for the checked book(s).
Payment <u>must</u> accompany all orders. ❑ Please send a free catalog.

THE LOVE POTION
SANDRA HILL

Get Ready . . . For the Time of Your Life!

A love potion in a jelly bean? Fame and fortune are surely only a swallow away when Dr. Sylvie Fontaine discovers a chemical formula guaranteed to attract the opposite sex. Though her own love life is purely hypothetical, the shy chemist's professional future is assured . . . as soon as she can find a human guinea pig. The only problem is the wrong man has swallowed Sylvie's love potion. Bad boy Lucien LeDeux is more than she can handle even before he's dosed with the Jelly Bean Fix. The wildly virile lawyer is the last person she'd choose to subject to the scientific method. When the dust settles, Sylvie and Luc have the answers to some burning questions—Can a man die of testosterone overload? Can a straight-laced female lose every single one of her inhibitions?—and they learn that old-fashioned romance is still the best catalyst for love.

___52349-3 $5.99 US/$6.99 CAN

AN ORIGINAL SIN
NINA BANGS

Fortune MacDonald listens to women's fantasies on a daily basis as she takes their orders for customized men. In a time when the male species is extinct, she is a valued man-maker. So when she awakes to find herself sharing a bed with the most lifelike, virile man she has ever laid eyes or hands on, she lets her gaze inventory his assets. From his long dark hair, to his knife-edged cheekbones, to his broad shoulders, to his jutting—well, all in the name of research, right?—it doesn't take an expert any time at all to realize that he is the genuine article, a bona fide man. And when Leith Campbell takes her in his arms, she knows real passion for the first time . . . but has she found true love?

____52324-8 $5.99 US/$6.99 CAN

Romeo & Julia

Annie Kimberlin

Liz Hadley is a cat person, and since she doesn't currently own a kitten, there is nothing that she wants more. The stray that was found in the snowy library parking lot is perfect; she can't wait to go home and cuddle. Still, the arms that hold the cat aren't so bad, either. The man her co-workers call Romeo apparently also has a soft spot for all things furry, though it appears to be the only soft spot on his entire body. The man has the build of a Greek god and his eyes are something altogether more heavenly. And in the poetry of his kisses, the lovely librarian finds something more profound than she's ever read and something sweeter than she's ever known.

___52341-8 $5.50 US/$6.50 CAN

Dorchester Publishing Co., Inc.
P.O. Box 6640
Wayne, PA 19087-8640

Lovers and Other Lunatics — Eugenia Riley

Get Ready for ... The Time of Your Life!

Teresa Phelps has heard of being crazy in love. But Charles Everett seems just plain mad. Her handsome kidnapper unnerves her with his charm and flabbergasts her with his accusations. He acts under the misguided belief that she holds the key to finding buried treasure. But all Tess feels she can unearth is one oddball after another.

While Charles' actions resemble those of a lunatic, his body arouses thoughts of a lover. And while Charles helps to fend off her dastardly and dangerous pursuers, Tess wonders if he has her best interests at heart—or is she just a pawn in his quest for riches? As the madcap misadventures ensue, Tess strives to dig up the truth. Who is the enigmatic Englishman? What is he after? And most important, in the hunt for hidden riches is the ultimate prize true love?

____52371-X $5.99 US/$6.99 CAN

Dorchester Publishing Co., Inc.
P.O. Box 6640
Wayne, PA 19087-8640

Please add $1.75 for shipping and handling for the first book and $.50 for each book thereafter. NY, NYC, and PA residents, please add appropriate sales tax. No cash, stamps, or C.O.D.s. All orders shipped within 6 weeks via postal service book rate. Canadian orders require $2.00 extra postage and must be paid in U.S. dollars through a U.S. banking facility.

Name_____
Address_____
City_____ State_____ Zip_____
I have enclosed $ _____ in payment for the checked book(s).
Payment <u>must</u> accompany all orders. ❑ Please send a free catalog.

TRULY, MADLY VIKING

SANDRA HILL

His boat off-course, somehow thrust into the twenty-first century, Jorund Ericsson has cause to question his surroundings. And though the befuddled Viking thinks he's found heaven when he spies the lovely doctor, she simply thinks him crazy. Jorund realizes what has truly driven him to the edge is her enticing figure.

He sails into Maggie's life, claiming to be a Viking from the tenth century, which makes her smile. But it isn't laughter that causes her stomach to flutter when the Hercules look-alike claims her lips. And soon he has her believing his story, though questioning her own sanity. Then the psychologist realizes there is another possibility: Neither of them is truly mad—but both are truly, madly in love.

___52387-6 $5.99 US/$6.99 CAN

Dorchester Publishing Co., Inc.
P.O. Box 6640
Wayne, PA 19087-8640

Please add $1.75 for shipping and handling for the first book and $.50 for each book thereafter. NY, NYC, and PA residents, please add appropriate sales tax. No cash, stamps, or C.O.D.s. All orders shipped within 6 weeks via postal service book rate. Canadian orders require $2.00 extra postage and must be paid in U.S. dollars through a U.S. banking facility.

Name_____
Address_____
City_____ State_____ Zip_____
I have enclosed $ _____ in payment for the checked book(s).
Payment <u>must</u> accompany all orders. ❑ Please send a free catalog.
CHECK OUT OUR WEBSITE! www.dorchesterpub.com